MW00720848

What Readers Say About
When Cobras Laugh...

"Are you ready for this? No more Christian fantasy land. No more missionary superheroes of mythical proportions. This is faith stripped of its hypocritical facades. Spiritual warfare gets messy. The battle is not where you expect it. From the experiences and observations of two real-life missionary warriors comes this tale that will slice open the world of reality and lay bare your own faith."
　　LINDA STOVER, youth pastor

"God always amazes by using flawed people to accomplish His purposes in the world. Shocking as this book is in places, it gives great hope to see Divine grace at work. It should act as a call to reality for mission leaders and all those who labor for the benefit of mankind."
　　PHIL DEMPSTER, chairman emeritus, Partners International

"Mesmerizes like the sway of a cobra."
　　DAVID LOUNSBURY, recent medical graduate

"A disturbing and enlightening read. The attitudes of the mission leaders made me so angry I could not put it down—I wanted to hit them with the book."
　　TENA BAKER, former teacher and children's ministries director

"It would make excellent movie material. There is so much angst."
　　DON R. GIBSON, literary critic
　　former Overseas Correspondent with the BBC

"I lived through the times so accurately portrayed in this book—I can only wish someone had written it years ago."
PHUTHUMILE BHENGU, Johannesburg, South Africa
national Christian worker and former radio programmer

"It has the perfume of a great best seller!"
DR. JOHN BASMAJIAN, Order of Canada, author of 52 books

When Cobras Laugh

Don Ranney
Ray Wiseman

CAPSTONE
FICTION

WATERFORD, VIRGINIA

When Cobras Laugh

Published in the U.S. by:
Capstone Publishing Group LLC
P.O. Box 8
Waterford, VA 20197

Visit Capstone Fiction at
www.capstonefiction.com

Cover design and images © 2008 by Alan Ranney
Photo of Don Ranney © 2007 by Danièlle Langlois
Photo of Ray Wiseman © 2007 by J.H. Fishback

Copyright © 2008 by Don Ranney and Ray Wiseman. All rights reserved.

Scripture taken from the New King James Version®. Copyright © 1982 by Thomas Nelson, Inc. Used by permission. All rights reserved.

ISBN: 978-1-60290-143-8

When Cobras Laugh is a work of fiction. Names, characters, places, and incidents either are the product of the authors' imaginations or are used fictitiously. Any resemblance to actual events (other than historical connections), locales, organizations, or persons, living or dead, is entirely coincidental and beyond the intent of either the author or the publisher.

✝

*To all those
who invest their lives or finances
in the service of God
and humanity.*

Acknowledgments

No book emerges from an author's keyboard fully mature and ready for the printing press. In this case, years of revisions and rewrites passed through the hands of many people before the authors thought it worthy of presentation to a publisher. We owe special thanks to the following:

- Brian Henry, Professor at Humber College, Don Ranney's mentor for several years and the one who first critiqued this manuscript.
- Anna Wiseman, who contributed her own memories of Africa and who proofread and critiqued every paragraph.
- Mary Lou Cornish, journalist and poet who offered encouragement and expert critique.
- Members of the Waterloo-Wellington editing circle of the Canadian Authors Association.
- Members of The Word Guild, who backed us with words of support and wise critique.

In addition, we acknowledge the editing expertise of Capstone Fiction's editorial director, Ramona Tucker, whose work gave this book its final shape.

Cast of Characters

AIYAPANDIAN, DR.—a brilliant scientist, epidemiologist, general manager, and superintendent of the Mission to the Outcast Leprosy Research and Training Center in Janglepit, Tamilnadu

AIYAPANDIAN, DR. (MRS.)—wife of (hence the coveted title "Mrs.") Dr. Aiyapandian and also Chief of Surgery at the Janglepit center

ALI KHAN, YASMINA—Steve's exotically beautiful Indian secretary

ALI KHAN, SALIM—Muslim father of Yasmina

ATKINSON, DR. GEORGE—British orthopedic surgeon sent to India

ATKINSON, YOLANDA—wife of George, a former fashion model

BAMBISA, LUCY—a beautiful African woman who turns men's heads

DORAISWAMI, SUBRAMANI—appointed General Manager at Janglepit by Rajalingam

DOW, LAO PANG (AKA LOU)—a friendly Buddhist with a Ph.D. in English from Oxford University

ELIZABETH—an effervescent girl Friday who has trouble buttoning her lip

FERGUSON, JACK—Cockney missionary

FERGUSON, LILA—American wife of Jack Ferguson

FOWLER, PETER—mission field director who leads from the other side of the field

HAMILTON-JONES, REV. DR. NICHOLAS—stuffy leader of God's Word Mission in Canada

HEATH, ANDREW—commercial artist and newly appointed missionary

HEATH, EDWARD—preteen son of Andrew and Nancy Heath

HEATH, JOHN—teenage son of Andrew and Nancy Heath

HEATH, NANCY—stunningly beautiful wife of Andrew Heath

JAMIESON, FRAN—a missionary curmudgeon stuck in the 19th century

JENNIFER—a Canadian operating room nurse, Steve's intended bride

MAKUNYANE, MUMSA—a wise woman and a proud Zulu

MAKUNYANE, THOMAS—husband of Mumsa and powerful African preacher

MANLEY, DR. STEVE—a young American orthopedic surgeon who has just completed his training and feels called to serve God in India with the Mission to the Outcast

MUIR, GORDON—manager of Mission Press and Andrew's superior.

RAJALINGAM, DR.—an ex-Indian Army stretcher-bearer who has become Field Secretary for South Asia of the Mission to the Outcast, a medical missionary organization with headquarters in London

SAKUNDRA—Steve's housekeeper in Janglepit

SANGRIA—Steve's housekeeper in Landour, Mussoorie

SMITHERS, REV. ARCHIBALD—an aging Anglican minister, superintendent of the Mission to the Outcast's Dhanbad Mission Station in West Bengal

SOMMERS, DR. RALPH—mission leader

SRINIVASAN, PROFESSOR—Professor of orthopedic surgery at the nearby Madras Medical School

THOMAS, PROFESSOR V.J.—Pathologist at Madras Medical School

TSATSI, BONGA—Edward Heath's African friend

YESUDASAN, BROTHER—the registered nurse in charge of the operating room at Janglepit. Male nurses in India are called "Brother" to distinguish them from their female counterparts, called "Sister."

Glossary

Afrikaaners—descendants of immigrants to South Africa from The Netherlands
Amara nom Sangria—Hindi for "My name is Sangria"

Baas—Afrikaans word for "master" or "boss," typically used by Africans when speaking to a white man
Baba—Zulu title for men, meaning "father" or "mister"
Biryani—Urdu word for north Indian dish in which rice and other ingredients are cooked together with spices
Boerewors—Afrikaans word for "farmer's sausage "
Bonga—Zulu for "thanks" or "praise"
Braaivleis—Afrikkaans word for a roast meat or barbeque
Bungla basha jano—Bengali, literally meaning "Bengali language I know"

Chai—Hindi word used in most, if not all of India, to mean tea

Deodars—very thin tall evergreen trees in north India, so named because they are trees of the gods

Ekhaya—a Zulu word used for the servant's room situated behind the house

Hai—Hindi for "there is" or, when used in a question means "is there"

Jao—Bengali for go

Kombi—a South African name for a VW minibus

Mama—Zulu title for women, meaning "mother," "Miss," or "Mrs."
Me—SeSotho title for women, meaning "mother," "Miss," or "Mrs."
Mealie pap—Afrikaans word for corn porridge

Puja—worship performed to a Hindu god in the presence of the idol

Sa'bona—Zulu greeting, used as English would use "hello"
Siyabonga—Zulu for "we thank you"

Vonacum—Tamil word for "hello"
Vonacumaiya—Tamil for "hello, sir"

Yebo—Zulu word for yes

Places

ASSINSOLE—a large railway center inland from Calcutta

BOMBAY—currently called Mumbai, one of four large urban areas referred to as cities, on about the midpoint of India's west coast

CALCUTTA—far north on the east coast of India, at the level of Tropic of Cancer; capital of West Bengal

DELHI—capital city of India, situated inland in northwest India

DHANBAD—a real village in Calcutta but not the site of the mission post described

DURBAN—key coastal city in Natal, South Africa

JANGLEPIT—a fictitious place in Tamilnadu where most of the Indian segment of the story takes place

JAN SMUTS AIRPORT—international airport east of Johannesburg

JO'BURG—Johannesburg, key city in Transvaal in South Africa

LANDOUR —a village in North India at an elevation of 6500 feet above sea level; considered a segment of another village in the foothills of the Himalayas north of Delhi, Mussoorie

MADRAS—smallest of the four cities, situated midway on the east coast of India

ORISSA—the state on India's west coast just south of West Bengal

ROODEPOORT—municipal area adjoining Johannesburg on the west

PIETERMARITZBURG—city in Natal, South Africa, 80 km (50 miles) northeast of Durban

SOWETO—huge African "township" south of Johannesburg

TAMILNADU—a large state in South India, formerly Madras state; Tamil word meaning the place of those who speak Tamil

WEST BENGAL—a most northerly state on the east coast of India, occupied by Hindus, where the Ganges River enters the Bay of Bengal. The land mass continues eastward into Bangladesh, a Bengali-speaking Muslim state, formerly known as East Bengal.

WEST RAND—ridge of gold-bearing rock running west from Johannesburg (Roodepoort is on the West Rand)

Prologue

S outh India has three seasons: the rainy season, the hot season, and the very hot season. In April, fans whirling at top-speed make paperweights essential office equipment. Work begins at 7 a.m., an hour earlier than usual, allowing a two-hour break from the midday heat that penetrates even to the bone.

The old mahogany chair creaked as Dr. Rajalingam swiveled round to look at the large bronze clock on the wall. His right hand shielded his eyes from the bright sunshine streaming horizontally from the split bamboo curtain on his office window.

"Five after seven. Where is that opinionated missionary troublemaker?"

He picked a cigarette stub out of the ashtray for one last puff, placed it delicately between his lips, and sucked on it like it was the last cigarette in the world. Reaching for another, he found his shirt pocket empty.

Wearily he raised his large frame from the chair and shuffled across the room toward the cabinet, where he knew he could always find a few cartons of cigarettes. Though they came from the U.S. with the name *Camel,* he liked to imagine they could be of Indian origin, or at least Arabic.

Halfway across the room he paused to gaze, as he so often did, at the picture of Col. Ramaswati awarding him a Doctor of Medicine diploma though he was only a young stretcher-bearer. This proud moment always brought back happy memories and guaranteed relief of any stress that might result from his busy life.

He had joined the Indian army just after Independence in 1947. War broke out with Pakistan the following year, and an acute shortage of medical officers meant stretcher-bearers had to do far more than carry the wounded. After a short course in trauma management, he worked as a medical assistant in the officer's infirmary where buttering up the right people won him favor in high places. To celebrate victory in that war, while many others received medals for bravery in battle, he was one of several given an honorary medical diploma.

This Government of India medical qualification secured for him his first civilian job, working in a foreign missionary hospital in the Punjab. All he had to do after that was bow low to the right people, lick boots when necessary, and in less than two decades he had become the south Asia Field Secretary of the Mission to the Outcast. Now he had everyone bowing to him—everyone but this bull-headed American surgeon.

Continuing his reverie, he strolled over to the tan-colored enamel cabinet, spun the dial on the combination lock three times, opened the door, and pulled out a packet of Camels. His hand trembled as he slipped a cigarette between his lips and lit it.

Few people knew his medical degree was just an honorary title. It brought him the respect he felt he deserved. People obeyed his commands. After all, he was in charge. But this Yankee, Steve Manley, seemed to have his own agenda, wanted to make India look like America, keep flies out of the surgical wards and make nurses clean the operating room when it had always been the sweeper's job.

As Steve had a gold medal from Harvard and was trained in surgery at the Mayo Clinic, Rajalingam knew Steve must be accustomed to groveling to the authorities in the United States. But in India, Steve was going around issuing directives as though he were an American Raj. Just thinking about Steve and his qualifications made Rajalingam want to spit.

And now Steve was stirring up anger by telling Muslims and Hindus that if they didn't love Jesus they were on their way to hell. Such arrogance and stupidity! Thought he was too good for India, too good to grovel to anyone but Americans. Well, Rajalingam would teach him otherwise.

At the approaching footsteps, he anxiously sucked the last few micrograms of nicotine from his cigarette and turned to face the door. A blond-haired, bearded Caucasian stopped and stood in the open doorway. Steve Manley, dressed in a rumpled green surgical jumpsuit, was five foot ten, had a slim waist, and broad shoulders. With tousled hair hanging down over droopy eyelids, he looked like he had just gotten out of bed and was still half-asleep.

"Come in, Steve. You've kept me waiting nearly fifteen minutes."

"I hope you don't mind me coming here in my scrub suit, sir. Been up since 3 a.m. I just finished a complicated three-hour emergency operation and didn't want to keep you waiting any longer. This elderly woman was hit by a bus and—"

"We are a nation of patient people," Rajalingam said, forcing a smile, "unlike you Westerners who are always in a hurry. No doubt you've heard the expression 'They buried the man who hurried the East.'"

"Yes. Reverend Archibald Smithers told me that in my orientation program in West Bengal, when I first arrived in India four years ago."

"Well, your arrival in India is a good place to start, and orientation is one of my favorite words. It means facing the East. I want to talk to you about your particular orientation."

Steve dragged a chair to a spot directly under the ceiling fan and sat down. The breeze blew down the opening in his suit to ruffle the hair on his chest. Rajalingam moved back to his chair behind the desk and tried to look fatherly as he lit another cigarette.

"When Dr. and Mrs. Aiyapandian were expelled from here," he began, "and I asked you to take over Mrs. Aiyapandian's post as chief surgeon, I had great hopes for you, Steve. I hoped that you were young enough to be molded into the kind of person who does well in this country. Yes, you were young and enthusiastic—perhaps too enthusiastic. I thought that in time you would learn a little self-control. But you're like a wild horse! It's always your way or no way. You can't accept that certain things just have to be, and that's the end of it."

"Can you be more specific, sir?" Steve ran the fingers of his right hand through his hair.

"Alright, let's start with chain of command. A few weeks ago you ordered some expensive operating tools without the permission of Doraiswami, the hospital manager. We can't afford it."

Steve frowned. "But this was a gift donated by American Aid to Overseas Missions. It didn't need to go through the hospital books because it wouldn't cost anything."

Rajalingam stood and glared down at him. "You begged America for help! India is a nation of beggars, and we don't need American aid to teach us how to beg."

"You mean you're too proud to beg." Steve threw his hands in the air. "Why be so proud of a second-class civilization—"

"Dr. Manley, you go too far! Did they teach you to insult entire civilizations at that fancy medical school of yours? Perhaps you took a special course: American Superiority 101."

Steve flushed at Rajalingam's words.

Rajalingam had always suspected Steve's conflict with authority grew out of his pride. He was very good at what he did—but seemed to want the whole world to acknowledge this.

"Oh," Rajalingam sneered, "and I suppose you came to India to bring us the best surgeon in the world." He sat in his chair and with a smirk on his face continued, "But I say you can't be a good surgeon. You're not even a good human being."

Steve rose to his feet, eyes blazing. Rajalingam rose to face him. Both the same height, they stood nose to nose.

"Steve, you're not the least bit humble. You never listen to what other people have to say. You have so much to learn. So sit down now, and listen to what I have to say. I'm going to tell you a little parable."

Steve fell back into his chair and let his hands drop to his sides.

"Long ago," Rajalingam began, "there was a palm tree and an oak tree, living side by side in the forest. A great wind blew. The palm tree knew it could never stand up to such a strong force."

Steve looked up at the ceiling, tilted his head, and sighed. "So the palm tree allowed itself to be bent by the wind, I suppose."

"Yes," Rajalingam replied, "but the mighty oak stood up straight and tall, proudly resisting the wind. One day a gust of wind came along so strong that the oak tree was blown away."

"I understand your point completely," Steve replied, leaping back to his feet. "You want me to compromise my principles in order to save my own skin. Well, I won't do it! We must stand up for what we know is right. Here's an example.

"Yesterday I preached in the chapel, taking my turn as usual. I used the Scripture assigned for the day, about the time when Jesus said He was the only way to God. Many Hindus and Muslims took offense. So what if they did? We must speak the truth."

"No, No, No!" shouted Rajalingam. "You can believe the truth, but do not speak it if it will harm our work."

Steve leaped to his feet. "And what is our work? Our mandate is to preach the gospel."

"Steve, Steve, you are so stubborn! Well, your term is up in, let's see..." He counted on his fingers. "I make it one year and four months."

Looking at Steve through half-closed eyes, he added, "I wonder if you'll last that long."

S

Book One

One

May 1970 was a tranquil month, the storms of March and April a distant memory. Large cumulus clouds rolled across the Toronto skyline interspersed with broad beams of brilliant sunshine. Doves cooed. Robins chirped. The scent of lilac and apple blossoms filled the air. Young lovers' thoughts turned to marriage.

A muscular, broad-shouldered man in his late twenties strode confidently up the stone steps of a Gothic cathedral near the city center. Steve Manley was the kind of person who would recognize no obstacles. He had a reputation for thriving in any crisis. So much so, his best friend had told him that if there weren't a crisis he would create one, and conquer it. But there would be no crisis today; for in one week he would marry the most wonderful woman in the world.

Steve brushed aside a lock of curly blond hair to reveal a firm jaw and a boyish grin. With the love of his life now in clear view he bounded up the last six steps and flung his arms around a slim dark-haired woman, five years younger. Faded blue jeans hugged her buttocks. Her white cotton sweater looked ready to burst.

"Jennifer," he said, "you are gorgeous, as always."

She chastely offered her cheek as Steve stepped forward for a kiss. But he hugged her close and whispered in her ear, "I can't wait to see you in your wedding gown."

Pulling back a little, she took hold of each hand and looked at him intently. Steve had never seen such beautiful eyes. Surrounded by a cascade of rust-tinged dark brown curls they sparkled like the shimmering emerald pools he'd once seen in the Rocky Mountains. A man could drown in those eyes.

Six months ago they had first transfixed him across an operating room table at the Hospital for Sick Children when he visited Toronto on an Orthopedic Traveling Fellowship. Always those eyes had sparkled with inner joy—but not today.

"Steve, my darling, the wedding is just what I want to discuss with you."

"No better time than at the rehearsal. Come! I want you to meet my best man. Andrew, where are you?"

"If you mean the man in the tweed jacket, he must have gone inside."

With a gentle tug, Steve drew Jennifer into the cathedral and propelled her to the front of the sanctuary where a round little man with an unremarkable face seemed lost in the beauty of a stained glass window.

"Andrew," said Steve, "here she is, the world's most beautiful woman."

Andrew grinned in response as Jennifer held out her delicate white hand.

"It's a pleasure to meet you," she said. "Steve tells me you're leaving for a mission in South Africa about the same time Steve plans to go to India."

"Yes," agreed Andrew, "I and my wife and our two boys."

Jennifer cocked her head quizzically. "Steve tells me you're an artist. Why would an artist want to be a missionary? I mean, what would you do on a mission field in Africa? I can see the point of going as surgeon and operating room nurse as Steve and I had intended—"

"Had intended?" Steve gasped. "What do you mean?"

Jennifer turned back to Steve, held both his hands once more, and seemed to study his face for a moment. Gently she led him out of the sanctuary into the foyer of the church, where they could speak more privately.

"My dear, sweet darling," she began. "Ever since we first met, you've talked about how God had called you to be a missionary, and about your need to follow that call. It was that dedication to serve God and to help the poor suffering people of India that first attracted me to you. I felt I could help you reach that goal and at the same time have such a kind and wonderful man as my husband. But I never felt the call of God and I'm not strong like you. I couldn't bear to look at all that suffering and poverty. I just couldn't take it. That's why I can't go with

4

you."

"Do you mean we're not getting married? You, you can't mean that. Is this your voice I hear—or your father's?"

Her green eyes glistened in response.

"Jennifer, my darling, I delayed my trip to India six months just to get to know you in the hope that we could spend our lives there together. I thought you shared my dream. Don't you love me anymore?"

"I love you more than you can ever know. And that is exactly why I can't marry you. I love you too much to be a burden around your neck. That's what I'd be if I went with you to India. I also care about the people of India who need you, so I won't hold you back." Jennifer averted her eyes. "Daddy thinks I should go away for a while. He's sending me to Paris. I couldn't leave without explaining."

She squeezed his hands gently and dropped them. Tears welled up in her eyes, flowed through long dark eyelashes, and poured down across her soft, pink-tinged cheeks.

Steve stood there for a minute, open-mouthed. His face turned pale, then flushed with anger. He turned to follow her as she walked back to the head of the stairs, but his legs refused to carry him. Andrew rushed forward to catch him as Steve's knees began to buckle.

Leaning heavily on the banister, Jennifer made her way down the staircase and into a waiting taxi.

Until now, Steve's life had been too easy. He loved a challenge, but learning the art of surgery had proved to be no problem for him. He was always at the top of his class. Now he wanted to use that knowledge to help others. So he'd decided to go as a medical missionary to India. That would be a real challenge.

He'd expected to find happiness along the way. When Jennifer came into his life she seemed to be just the one he needed. She shared his interests and had a strong faith in God. He had thought of her as loving and compassionate. Had her beauty blinded him?

Steve needed beauty in his life. He loved the challenge of working with people with deformities, correcting the problems they faced. But at the end of the day he needed music, art, and a beautiful woman to restore his sense of balance. He thought Jennifer could do all that for him.

But now his dream had come crashing down around him. It was just too much.

"Come," Andrew said. "I'll drive you back to the hostel. We'll talk about it there."

Andrew helped Steve into his light-brown Morris Oxford and together they drove off. It was a car rarely seen in America, and he liked it for that reason.

Andrew considered himself rather unique. He regretted he hadn't had a chance to explain to Jennifer what a vital role he could play as a missionary in Africa, or how she could complement Steve's life in India.

Steve remained silent as they drove along. Andrew began to reflect on how they had met just a few weeks earlier and quickly become close friends.

Two

A ndrew first met Steve a few weeks earlier in a gray-stone Victorian mansion on Spadina Avenue, the Canadian headquarters of God's Word Mission. For more than 100 years, this organization had distributed Bibles and Christian literature around the world. By 1970, more than 500 expatriate missionaries worked at various tasks in 15 countries. Some labored as translators, producing written materials in the vernacular. Others, highly trained artisans, prepared and printed magazines, gospel tracts, and Bible courses. Some, known as colporteurs, distributed Bibles and literature in rural areas or operated bookshops in urban districts. Evangelists did the same, along with traditional missionary work.

All of the 117 Canadians currently with this international organization had passed through this building. They came here to file application papers and undergo rigorous examinations by the official board and the Secretary General, the Reverend Dr. Nicholas Hamilton-Jones. They used the guest rooms when passing through Toronto, coming or going to their foreign assignments. Some stayed here for orientation programs or other courses.

Andrew Heath, commercial artist and missionary appointee, would share a bedroom on the third floor, and use the kitchen and common room on the second. He parked his battered, aging Morris Oxford behind the building and walked around to the front door. There was also a rear door leading into the office area, but Andrew felt a trifle uneasy entering that way—possibly when he got to know Hamilton-Jones and the others better...

The front door led into a large waiting room that fully encircled a massive central staircase to the second floor. A small booth-like room protruded unnaturally from the back wall beside the stairway—an obvious and somewhat crude addition of recent years. Andrew peered through a window into the booth and smiled at the pretty receptionist with blond ringlets down to her shoulders. She beamed back and handed him a note.

The smile remained on Andrew's face as he propelled his five-foot six-inch frame up the stairs two at a time. His brain raced along at an equally fast pace.

Andrew was short, bald, ten pounds overweight, and a tad ugly, but women seemed to like him—he never knew why.

His pace slowed and his smile widened as he thought of the woman in his life, Nancy. She had long auburn hair, stood five-feet, ten-inches and at age 40 could still pass for a movie queen.

He never understood how he won her, and on the other hand, why he still noticed other woman the way he did.

As Andrew entered his room, he remembered to read the note from Dr. Hamilton-Jones' assistant. "Oh cripes, an American for a roommate," he muttered under his breath. "And he's not even with our mission."

Andrew shrugged, thinking, *If I'm going overseas with a mission board, I'd better get rid of my biases. And I'd better forget words like cripes.*

He remembered his old theology professor used to say, "Cripes is nothing but a euphemism for Christ!"

Andrew entered the room that would house him during his four-week stay at the Toronto Institute of Linguistics, commonly called T.I.L. He liked the room; its big window faced out from the third floor onto Spadina Avenue. Pressing his nose to the window, he could look southward on Spadina toward part of the University of Toronto. But its affiliate, Victoria College, the venue of the linguistics school, was out of sight further to the east.

Andrew dropped his suitcase on the lower bunk. The American would have to take the upper one.

Andrew didn't like separation from his wife, Nancy, and the kids. But he'd handle it. As a 40-year-old, he also felt a little tension about returning to school, especially to study something as daunting as linguistics and anthropology. But then he'd made it successfully though Bible college.

As a commercial artist, recruited to work at a mission press, he had difficulty grasping why he needed to worry about learning another language, especially for an assignment in South Africa, where everyone speaks English.

A voice cut into his thoughts. "Hi, I'm Steve."

Andrew sprang to his feet and extended his hand. "Good to meet you. I'm Andrew."

Steve looked about 10 years younger than Andrew, but a little taller, with blond hair and, Andrew thought, a gleam of determination in his eye.

Andrew motioned to the upper bunk, grinning as he said, "Up there. Beat you here and got first choice."

"Oh, bugger," said Steve, tossing a small bag onto the bed. "I didn't bring much. I've been staying with my cousin in the east end of town, but this is closer to the school. I left most of my stuff with her."

"Canadians consider *bugger* a swear word," Andrew snapped, then wished he hadn't.

"Sorry! I'll watch that. Been here long enough to know better."

Andrew felt a touch of guilt, remembering he too needed to watch his own language. "So you live in Toronto?"

"Only temporarily. I'm an orthopedic surgeon, just completed a traveling fellowship with Toronto my last stop on a one-year tour of the top English-speaking hospitals outside the United States. After linguistics school, I'm going to marry Jennifer, a wonderful woman I met right here in Toronto. Then we'll go off to India with the Mission to the Outcast. Are you married?"

"Wife and two boys. I left them at the Bible college in Saskatchewan. They'll join me after T.I.L. so we can do more deputation work in Ontario. We still need to raise a lot of support before we can go to the field."

Steve frowned, "You have to raise your own support? The Mission to the Outcast pays us from a central fund. Jennifer and I won't need to worry about that."

"Yeah, well, we're with a so-called faith mission. But I'm beginning to believe it's not the mission but the *missionary* who has to exercise all the faith."

"Andrew, I'm hungry. Let's go out and get some pizza. We can talk while we eat and get to know each other better—and I'll try not to swear."

Andrew nodded. He'd never eaten pizza but heard it had just been introduced into Canada. Maybe he could learn something from this American.

During the next few days, Andrew and Steve did everything together. They ate, slept, walked, studied, and debated missions, linguistics, and cross-cultural communications. To Andrew's amazement, a solid bond developed.

But an assignment during the second week came close to breaking up the new friendship. Steve and Andrew had dropped heavily into chairs in a student lounge following a late-afternoon missiology lecture.

As Steve opened a three-ring binder, his brow furrowed. "Dr. Croker pushes things a little too far. He seems to bend the Bible to fit his theories on cultural issues. I'd just as soon spend my time on linguistics—that's why I came here."

Andrew took a first swallow from his Coke can. "I'd rather study missiology myself. And I found Croker's thoughts on interpreting the Bible in the light of culture very helpful."

"That's just it!" Steve said, his body tensing, and his hands gesturing to emphasize each word. "You can't bend the Bible to fit some primitive tribe's warped cultural pattern. The Bible is immutable; it's the Canon, the measuring rod, against which we must measure every human act."

"Maybe that's the problem; we expect to do the measuring instead of letting God do it."

Steve frowned at Andrew. "God has given us the Bible so we can use it to determine His will."

Three other students, attracted by the raised voices, joined them. Andrew slid along the settee to make room for Melissa, a pretty brunette with huge brown eyes.

"Let's put this in practical terms," Andrew said with a lingering smile prompted by Melissa's presence. "Friends of ours work as missionaries among a primitive tribe where many have turned to the Lord. When a chief and his numerous wives became Christians, they faced a problem. Could the chief and his wives all join the church, or must he give up all but one of his wives before joining the church?"

Steve shook his head. "No question. The Bible is clear. He has to give up his extra wives."

Andrew waited before responding, as though giving Steve an opportunity to change his mind.

"No. They allowed them all to join. Otherwise it would have broken up the family and the discarded wives would have become prostitutes in order to survive."

Steve took a Bible out of his briefcase and waved it at Andrew. "But the book says 'the husband of one wife—'"

Andrew cut in, "Wrong again. The Bible says to become a church leader a man must have one wife. Nowhere does it deny a person involved in a plural marriage the right to become part of a local assembly."

"I agree," said Melissa, standing up to leave. "This is a good example of our male-dominated culture distorting the biblical message."

The other students followed her out, leaving Andrew and Steve staring at each other.

Steve spoke first. "Truce? We can think about this and discuss it again. But I did notice your body language when Melissa arrived. Not thinking of adding another wife yourself, are you?"

Andrew drained his Coke can, crunched it flat, and tossed it into a waiting garbage container. "Let's go find some pizza."

In the final week of T.I.L., strange words like *fricative* and *glottal stop* filled their minds and notebooks. Their throats and mouths ached from the many strange sounds they had learned. Yet they still had energy to argue over areas that reflected major differences.

"Andrew, telephone!" a voice called from the mission home's common area.

Andrew jumped up and hurried from the room. He returned in five minutes with a broad smile on his face.

"That was Pastor Corbett from Northview People's Church. They want me to come back and make another presentation. But he says it's pretty sure they will take on $100 a month support. I'm more than halfway."

"Halfway to where?" asked Steve closing his books.

"To $600 per-month support. We need that much to pay our living expenses, housing, transportation, station expenses, and so on. They won't let us go to the field until we have 80 percent of that."

"And you get all that by begging from friends and churches?"

"Look Steve, it isn't begging. Not exactly. People and churches covenant, that is, guarantee to send a certain amount to the mission office every month. In addition to the monthly support, I need to raise three or four thousand for a car and about half that for air transportation to the field. I have about half of that as well."

Steve frowned. "What does your mission office do for you? How much do they provide?"

"They give me leads. But the rest is up to me. In fact, they hold back about 20 percent from the support I raise to run the home office."

"And they call that a faith mission? My mission pays everything. The home office people raise all the funds and assume full responsibility for me."

Andrew couldn't answer. He began to wonder if he'd done the right thing when he joined God's Word Mission. But he hadn't just "joined" the way one would with a secular job. After all, God had called him and Nancy to this ministry, hadn't He?

Andrew and Nancy sat in the boardroom of Kitchener's prestigious Market Lane Baptist Church, waiting for the pastor and members of the church's mission's committee. They could hear the rumble of the pastor's voice in the next room.

Andrew squeezed Nancy's hand and spoke softly. "I'm glad you and the boys are back, Nancy."

"So I could attend this meeting with you?"

"No. Because I missed you."

"It was difficult, Andrew—those three days on the bus from Saskatchewan."

Andrew released her hand and squirmed in his chair. "I'm sorry, but we didn't have the money for airfare. The funds just aren't coming in fast enough—maybe I should have taken a job for a few months."

Nancy didn't offer an opinion and the two of them fell silent, but Andrew mentally reviewed the circumstances that had brought them to this point.

Ten years back they had joined Market Lane Baptist Church and had got so excited about it they threw themselves into almost every ministry and outreach program that the church had: the men's fellowship, the Women's Missionary Fellowship, Christian Service Brigade, and Pioneer Girls. Then four years ago during the annual missionary conference, they felt God calling them to attend Bible college and apply for service with an overseas mission organization. At least Andrew felt called. Nancy had simply looked at him and quoted the words from the book of Ruth, " 'Where you go I will go, and where you stay, I will stay.'"

Andrew looked at his wife. She had closed her eyes and looked tired.

I'm wearing her out. She went with me to Bible college and soon, when we get all our support, she'll go with me to South Africa.

Almost as if she had heard Andrew's thoughts, Nancy whispered, "The Church has given the last three church members to go to the mission field $150 a month. Because both of us have membership here, does that mean they'll give us $300?"

"They should. We're both members, so we don't have two churches to appeal to like the other couples who met during their college years." Andrew also spoke quietly, not in deference to a hallowed place, but so that the committee members in the next room couldn't overhear.

"Wow, if we get $300, that'll put us over the top."

The door opened. Dr. Sloan entered with the committee in his wake.

"We're all off to lunch," he said in his usual pompous fashion, "so we'll give you the news and get on our way. We have agreed to give you the same as the other couples who have gone out recently—$150. You are a deserving couple and we wish you Godspeed."

They left the room in the same fashion as they arrived, with Dr. Sloan sailing in the lead like an admiral's flagship.

"They could have taken us to lunch," Nancy said sharply.

"Don't be ungrateful. At least they found us worthy."

Nancy shook her head angrily, jumped to her feet, and spat out, "They found one of us worthy."

Andrew rose more slowly. "Still more than $100 to go."

Three

Andrew had told Steve his depression would clear in a few days. But the "few days" had stretched into weeks as his despondency deepened. By the end of the first week they had moved out of the hostel to make room for others. Andrew had driven him back to his cousin's house in East Toronto. While Andrew and Nancy prepared to leave for Africa via England, someone else would have to look after him.

Steve refused to leave his bed or even talk to anyone. For most of the time he lay on his side with his knees drawn up to his chin, like a fetus wishing not to be born.

His mind raced. *Am I too impetuous, too quick to fall in love? Did Jennifer ever love me? Does even God love me?*

In his tortured sleep he began to mutter aloud, "The sun will never shine again. The birds will never sing. God, where are you?"

He lay in bed or on the bed for more than a month, refusing all but the least amount of food needed to stay alive. His cousin's doctor offered antidepressant medication but he refused that also.

The days became warmer and green leaves covered the trees as summer approached. But Steve noticed none of this.

One day a robin perched on the open windowsill of his small bedroom, and sang to him. Looking straight at the bird he said, "God, where are you?"

A small voice inside his head replied, "Right where I have always been, beside you. But where are you? You're supposed to be getting ready to go to India! I called you to serve me—not Jennifer."

Steve shot out of bed, stood on his feet, and collapsed in a heap. It would take quite a few days to regain his strength.

And there was much to do. He wanted to visit his parents in Minneapolis before leaving for India. There he would renew his passport. He had to get a visa for India, and he had not yet told the mission board he would be going alone. He had to buy tickets and pack his bags. His life had turned upside down, but he would go where God wanted him to go—somehow.

There'd been no word from Jennifer, not even a postcard from Paris. Steve wondered if she even knew where he was.

September was a good month to go to north India. The monsoon rains had moistened the arid soil, and cooled the air to bearable temperatures. Steve had traveled so much in the past 18 months that for him the trip was unspectacular. Only the stopover in London stood out in his mind.

All his previous negotiations with the Mission to the Outcast had been by correspondence except for one personal interview. Now in London he met the Members of the Board for the first time. Head Office was in the shadow of Buckingham Palace and, had he not known otherwise, he might have thought this was a meeting with members of the House of Lords. All but a few, the ones who seemed to do the work, were over 65, and they talked about India as though it were still a colony. They seemed happy to have an American "on board" and wondered if Steve would be adaptable to their way of doing things. Steve wasn't quite sure what that meant. The meeting ended with general well-wishing, but not much enthusiasm. Steve was reflecting on this meeting when his eyes caught sight of palm trees. They were about to land at Dum-Dum Airport in Calcutta, West Bengal.

Water from a late shower covered the runway. The plane skidded and bumped, but with engines in full reverse managed to stop just short of disaster. The pilot announced the temperature was 94 degrees and humidity 85 percent.

"Enjoy your stay," he added.

Steve smiled. He reflected on the cold reception he'd had in London that had engendered some foreboding thoughts. His hand drummed impatiently on the arm rests at his sides as he realized he would soon be where God wanted him to be. He would spend the rest of his life making crippled hands work again, helping the lame walk— and who knows what else God had in store for him. With this came the excitement of visiting a whole new world, one in which he might raise the standards of medical care.

Getting off was the usual airport hassle. He stood in line in a stuffy plane with sweat dripping from his forehead and clothes sticking to his body, waiting for people ahead to move. Then there was the noise and bustle of an overcrowded airport. But he was pleasantly surprised to find none of his luggage missing.

Getting through customs was another matter. He found he had two problems. One, he was American. Nobody liked Americans. They loved American money, not the people who made it. He was also a missionary. He soon discovered that all missionaries were suspected felons until proved otherwise. His task was to prove he was not smuggling anything into the country. He began to sense this when he had to wait in a special line labeled "Immigrating Aliens," fill out similarly named forms, and wait 20 minutes for an interview. He'd assumed that having a visa would be enough. But the customs officer's plan seemed to be to establish him as a smuggler and block his entry.

"Aha, vat is dis?" the man with the black cap asked him. "Film, film, film," he screamed, as he unwound reel after reel of audiotape on the floor. "You cannot bring movie film into this country. We have our own film. You buy here!"

"But it's not film!" Steve said. "That's audiotape, so I can learn Bengali."

"And why learn Bengali? So you can corrupt the minds of the people?"

Steve began to wish he were back in Toronto with Jennifer, talking about India, rather than in Calcutta experiencing it. Another member of Steve's flight, waiting in line behind him, began talking to the customs officer in some unknown language.

The passenger turned to Steve and said, "Give him a few American dollars and he'll let you through. In Bengali the word used for bribe is also translated to mean 'the usual thing.'"

Steve grudgingly handed over a five-dollar bill. Both the other men smiled. The bags were stamped and he was on his way.

What joy to meet, as he walked down the long hallway, a blond, curly-headed young woman carrying a sign with his name on it. She looked English. She was pretty too, but no match for Jennifer.

"Hello, I'm Bonnie Stubbings. I'll take you to the train. Quick. We must hurry! Your plane was an hour late and travel through town will be slow. There's a big crowd in Calcutta today, celebrating a festival. Taxis can't make it through crowds like this. We'll each have to go in separate rickshaws."

They managed to find two hand-drawn rickshaws, loaded half the luggage on each, and, with Bonnie in one and him in the other, they took off for the railway station. He soon lost sight of Bonnie. Steve found himself all alone in a sea of humanity with only half his luggage. He didn't really know where he was going and couldn't tell anyone if he did.

But the surgeon's keen eye took note of everything. Filth was everywhere. You could smell it. Cow dung and garbage mixed together by a recent downpour of rain flooded the streets. Yet people didn't seem to care. Their lithe semi-naked bodies pushed, pulled, twisted, and struggled in an endless battle to survive.

He passed close by a woman in a dirty, tattered sari, sitting in a pile of garbage. The stench of rotting cabbage filled Steve's nostrils as she hacked one of them to pieces with a large machete. After throwing away the very decayed parts she put the remainder in a brown sack at her feet. Just beyond her, an old woman stuffed a banana into her mouth. It had just been run over by a bullock cart.

These two-wheeled bullock carts where grossly overloaded. Animals with little more than their bones to hold them together struggled to move them. One foamed at the mouth as it was fiercely whipped with a bamboo cane.

Clearly, the worship of cattle only applied to the female of the species. India was not for the sensitive heart. Jennifer was right to stay home.

At last he could say it. "Good-bye, Jennifer."

They crossed a wide, turbulent, storm-swollen river on an iron bridge 300 feet long. It was built to take four lanes of traffic, but three were going one way and three the other. A truck abandoned near the center didn't help the situation. Somehow they got across and Steve found Bonnie waiting for him at the station.

"Hurry," she said. "The train is starting to move. We had to buy the tickets two weeks ago to make sure we got sleeping quarters. And there are no exchanges. You get in here. I have to get in the women's section. I'll see you in the morning."

"But where are we getting off?"

"Assinsole," she replied.

The steam engine chugged slower and slower. Brakes screeched, metal on metal, as the train skidded toward a wooden platform crowded with people. The morning sun shone brightly into Steve's eyes. It was 6 a.m., and for everyone but Steve the day was already well underway.

"*Chai, Chai*," a boy shouted through the open window of Steve's railway carriage. A small brown hand reached between the bars that covered them.

"*Chai?* I'd hoped we were in Assinsole."

"We are." Bonnie's head appeared next to the boy's. "He's asking you to buy tea. *Chai* means tea. Get your things and we'll have some tea before leaving the station."

Steve opened the door, passed out his suitcases, and stepped onto the platform. Instinctively he drew his shoulders together to avoid being contaminated by typhoid bacteria or whatever else might be out there.

Bonnie handed him a cup of *chai*.

"Can we drink this? Is it clean?"

"Freshly boiled and served in cups that have never before touched human lips and never will again."

Steve stared in amazement at the terracotta cup in his hand as Bonnie explained. "Hundreds of years ago the Brahmins invented disposable cups of unglazed pottery to avoid ritual defilement. They must never drink from a vessel that has touched the lips of a lower caste person. So when you're finished you throw it on the ground and it returns to the soil. Then a Brahmin won't face the risk of drinking from your cup. Their idea of impurity is far removed from ours, but serves us well."

"So does the tea. I'm so thirsty," Steve said, as the train chugged its way out of the station.

The boy came over and refilled his cup without being asked. "*Eck rupee*," he said.

Steve wanted to show his appreciation and gave him a bill with number one on it.

"Did I tip him too much?"

"You gave him the exact price. That's about ten cents."

For the rest of the journey Steve and Bonnie rode nearly six hours in a taxi. It was a black and cream-colored, mid-sized car called an Ambassador. It reminded Steve of the Morris Oxford Andrew had driven in Toronto and made him wonder if Andrew had made it to South Africa. There were big round fenders front and back. A fifth hump, at the rear, formed the trunk lid, which was hinged at the top.

They piled luggage in the back seat. Bonnie and Steve crowded into the front seat beside the driver.

"Why isn't the luggage in the trunk?" Steve asked.

"Some of these taxis are so old they won't start on their own. The boy who carries the luggage pushes the car. When it is rolling he hops in the trunk and pulls the lid down. There's no room for luggage in the trunk".

The taxi rumbled along at 20 miles an hour on an eight-foot wide ribbon of asphalt toward the village of Dhanbad. This "highway" was a public road, and the public made good use of it. People and cattle wandered aimlessly. Others laid saris and blankets on the black asphalt to dry in the sun. The taxi was as much off the road as on. The driver blasted the horn repeatedly to declare his right to a part of the highway—any part.

The noise and confusion of the road stood in stark contrast to the tranquility of the lush green countryside on each side. A row of toddy palms bordered the road, some standing erect, most of them leaning to one side or the other. Between them Steve rested his eyes on lime-green rice fields interspersed with patches of taller mauve-topped sugar cane.

It was a long drive, but an interesting one, a picturesque introduction to the culture of India. Eventually the taxi entered the large village of Dhanbad, and minutes later, the hospital compound. It circled around to the right and stopped in front of a small sand-colored stucco building. A wooden sign over the doorway declared it to be the Guest Quarters.

"Here's where you'll stay for now," Bonnie announced, "till the Hospital superintendent, Reverend Archibald Smithers, decides what to do with you."

"What to do with me? I thought he'd been waiting for a surgeon for more than a year. Surely he must have everything planned."

"You're to meet him in his office at four this afternoon to talk about that. Meanwhile, get some rest. I'll send some food over."

While they were talking, the boy from the trunk of the car had carried Steve's suitcases into the room, two at a time on the top of his head. A few minutes later the taxi drove off under a dazzling noonday sun, leaving a swirling cloud of dust behind it.

Steve stood for a moment in the doorway, letting his eyes adjust to the relative darkness before entering. A small bed stood against the opposite wall. At one end of the room was a dresser and, at the other, a desk, chair and lamp. A two-inch long cockroach scurried across the floor to find refuge under the bed.

Steve walked slowly across the room and sat down on it. The bed felt firm enough to support an elephant. But he was tired and it would do.

As his gaze drifted up toward the open doorway, movement attracted him—a green, sinuous, undulating movement. What he feared most about India, a large king cobra, had come out from under the dresser and slithered toward the sunlight.

It had almost reached its goal when it stopped, raised its head 18 inches off the ground and turned in Steve's direction. Its tongue darted from right to left and back again while its beady eyes studied him intently.

Beads of perspiration formed on Steve's forehead and dripped onto the bare floor between his feet. *What goes through the mind of a cobra—just before it strikes?*

Footsteps outside the door approached, and abruptly halted. Steve heard the tapping of a stick—followed by, "*Jao! Jao! Jao!*"

The snake turned toward the sound and quickly slithered out the door.

"Food, sahr."

A bearded man wearing a dirty gray turban came in with a bowl of soup, a sandwich, and a large glass of fresh lime juice. He calmly set them down on the desk and turned to leave.

"Thank you, thank you, thank you," Steve said. "You saved my life."

"*Bungla basha jano.* No English."

Steve smiled and placed one palm against the other. The man did the same and left.

Steve thought, *If I believed in omens, that cobra might reflect badly on my future in India.* He had no appetite for food now. Neither could he rest.

Superintendent Smithers lived in a palatial-looking bungalow with 15-foot ceilings situated almost a hundred yards from the hospital. He apparently used one of the rooms as his office. The house looked as though it had been built in the previous century. There were holes in each of the walls through which a rope could pass, so that a servant outside could move a fan inside the house while the inhabitants slept. A veranda completely surrounded the house to prevent the sun shining directly into the windows.

Steve pulled the chain attached to the door and a bell rang inside. Through the screen door, he saw an elderly man approaching.

"Come in," the man said, pushing open the screen. "I'm Smithers. You must be the new Yankee doctor."

"Pleased to meet you, Reverend Smithers. I'm Steve Manley."

"Tush, tush, I know who you are. Come into the office. A parcel just arrived with your name on it. I opened it, of course, as I do with everything that comes from Headquarters. As superintendent I have the final word on everything that happens here. "It seems they have sent you a child's hand puppet. Now what would you want with that?"

"How wonderful! I can hardly wait to get my hands on it. You see, at Bible college a student told us what a great tool this is for preaching the gospel. I could also use it to teach public health—you know, put on a little skit that grabs their attention. I asked the Mission to get me one and said I would pay for it. But I was told it would be sent to me at no cost."

"But you don't speak their language. You would have to learn Bengali."

"Of course, and I will."

"But you didn't pay for it."

"No."

"Then it isn't yours. I'm going to give it to our public health nurse. She'll make better use of it."

"Please, can I hold it, just for a minute?"

"No. Now about language study. Next Friday you will leave for Darjeeling to study Bengali. You'll be in a class with others, much cheaper than private classes here. After Christmas break you go for a nine-month leprosy surgery course at Janglepit in South India, then another three months of language study. You won't be back here till a year this Christmas. So don't start putting roots down yet."

"A year Christmas?"

Smithers simply smiled at Steve's dismay, and Steve smothered the rest of his objection. He would be in India for a lifetime. Against this time frame, returning a year from Christmas was something he could tolerate.

"Well it's nice to feel welcome. I guess I'll be sleeping in the Guest Quarters till I leave. But what about when all my training is over?"

"This is the Surgeon's House. You'll live here. I'll find another place, when the time comes."

Over the next few days Steve spent his time visiting patients on the wards. The hospital was somewhat run down and no one seemed to care. But he suspected he could do a great deal to improve it once Smithers was out of the way.

In the meantime, he had to improve relationships—in reality, establish one.

A few days later, Steve found something he knew would interest the superintendent. It was an aerial photograph and newspaper account about the sighting of a large structure on Mount Ararat in Turkey. It was thought to be a remnant of Noah's Ark. Surely this would intrigue this Anglican minister and make for a more enjoyable conversation than they'd had about the puppet.

But Smithers' only comment was, "Perhaps some of those old Bible stories aren't really fables after all."

This shocked Steve to the core. *This man doesn't believe the Bible to be the Word of God!*

What have I gotten myself into? Are these missionaries really followers of Christ, or just a bunch of do-gooders who can't make a living back home?

Steve hoped Andrew was having a better experience in South Africa.

He hurried back to the Guest Quarters to pack his bags for Darjeeling.

The language course in Darjeeling was an exhilarating experience. It fascinated Steve to find Bengali similar in many respects to other languages he had learned. As in German, the Bengali verb usually came at the end of the sentence, to show the importance of action. There

24

were many other similarities.

"How can this be?" he asked his teacher.

"Linguists," Mr. Chatterji replied, "have traced a common ancestor to Germanic and Sanskrit languages like Bengali and Hindi. Be happy you can learn a language that has some resemblance to your own. Now if you had to learn a South Indian language, like Tamil, you would be finding it most difficult. It is so very difficult that even I, a teacher of Indian languages but born in the north—even I will never have the facility to speak it well."

Steve enjoyed also the cool, mountain air and hilly terrain. But it all came to an end as the December snow began to fall. The snow reminded him of his home in Minnesota. It was time to return to Dhanbad, and from there head south to the land where they spoke this mysterious language, Tamil.

Refreshed in mind and body, he was now ready to take on a new assignment, learning leprosy surgery in South India. But first he had to return to Dhanbad and report to Reverend Smithers. He didn't relish that prospect.

On arriving back at the hospital compound that was to be his home for many years, he felt a sense of disappointment, of sadness bordering on depression. In Darjeeling he had experienced a spiritual uplift. He wondered if it was just the mountain grandeur that enveloped him there, or whether it was the domineering attitude of Reverend Smithers that weighed so heavily on him here in Dhanbad.

A few days later his emotions changed and he began to whistle as he boarded the train to South India for a nine-month course in leprosy reconstructive surgery. Then with the skills he already possessed, and a remarkable command of Bengali, he would be ready to serve God in the place He had sent him.

Four

"*B ungla basha jano,*" Steve said as he stretched out to touch his feet on the end of the berth.

Climbing the hills that are everywhere in Darjeeling had made his legs stronger, and they ached pleasantly as he stretched. He always enjoyed sleeping on the train, and particularly this time, as the train was taking him away from Dhanbad.

He was well-rested and happy as he reflected on his three-month Bengali language course in Darjeeling. It had been such a wonderful experience. At 7,000 feet above sea level the air had been cool and fresh. Everyone was friendly, especially the Tibetans. It seemed they never stopped smiling.

"*Bungla basha jano,*" he said aloud. He liked the sound of it.

That's what the man who chased the snake away was saying, he reminisced. *Now I know what it means. He was telling me he knew Bengali. And now I do too.*

A smile spread across his face.

The Toronto Institute of Linguistics had given him an understanding of how languages are constructed. But the teachers had also emphasized the importance of learning all the idioms so that ideas would be better understood.

"You can reach their minds with broken speech," they had told him, "But you only get through to the hearts of the people if you speak their language exactly as they do."

With this in mind, he wondered at the wisdom of going to South India to learn leprosy surgery so soon. Perhaps he would be better to stay in West Bengal a while until really proficient in Bengali. Smithers seemed intent on keeping him away, probably until he retired, so he could avoid moving into another house before returning to England.

Thinking of Smithers and the run-down hospital in Dhanbad gave him a cold tingle on the back of his neck that spread up to his scalp.

Steve had been riding all night, down the east coast of India toward Madras. Unlike the second and third-class railway coaches, a first-class sleeper had no connecting corridor between the compartments. Entrance was through a lockable door on each side. The seats were wide, well-padded, vinyl benches, one facing the direction of travel and the opposite one facing backwards. Each would comfortably seat three people. Above these benches, the upper bunks folded into the walls. Four could sleep or six could sit.

"I can't believe these old trains can go so fast," he muttered to himself as palm trees passed quickly by the window.

The morning sun reflecting off water-covered rice fields dazzled his eyes. He pulled down the window shade and soon after heard a scratching. *What can it be? Something scratching on the shade?*

He raised it quickly, and jumped in fright. A man's head and shoulders pressed against the window of a train traveling 50 miles an hour. *Am I dreaming?*

"Shoeshine?" the man asked as he rattled the door handle next to the window.

Steve quickly opened the door, if only to save the man's life. It would also be a chance to practice Bengali. The "clickety-clack" made by the wheels grew louder as the door opened and a man with a wooden box slung over his shoulder came in.

"Good morning," Steve said in Bengali as he closed the door.

"Not Bengali, but Bengali speak. From Orissa, speaking four Indian languages. Very little English."

"Four out of 28 is pretty good," Steve said in Bengali. "I only know one. But tell me, how do you travel on the outside of a train?"

The shoeshine man put down his box and re-opened the door.

"Look." He pointed down to the three-inch wide ledge that ran the length of each coach. "This how I find my customers."

"Sorry, I don't have any shoes," Steve told him, "just these sandals."

"I do sandals, one rupee."

Steve, still bare-footed, handed him his sandals.

"But aren't you afraid of falling when you move about like that?"

"Lord Krishna protects. Perhaps I have been good in a past life. If

28

not, what can I do? My fate is my fate. I can only influence the next life in this one. So I work hard and do puja to Lord Krishna, take pilgrimage. And maybe I will be reborn as cow in next life. One rupee extra will help me save for pilgrimage next year."

"Take five." Steve chuckled as he recalled a jazz tune by that name. It seemed a lifetime ago that he'd heard it. Yet it had been only a few months. He was in another world now, living another life.

These people had such hard lives they had to believe in reincarnation. Certainly, it seemed to Steve, they deserved a chance at a better life.

A few hours later the train slowed and stopped at a station. Steve got out to buy breakfast at a nearby stall where a young man was calling, "Copee, copee, copee."

In each hand he held a tin cup. With one at hip level and the other high above his head, he poured coffee back and forth from one cup to the other. It was a great show that mixed milk and sweetened coffee together to produce a drink with a light brown froth on top. Steve bought a cup and found it delicious. He also bought two bananas and an orange.

He just made it back to his carriage when a shrill whistle indicated the train was leaving. A group of five Indians were sitting in his compartment, a man, a woman, and three children. There was room for one more, but the seat he'd occupied had been taken. He would have to travel facing backward.

He spoke a few words of Bengali. The man sitting opposite just stared at him.

After a few minutes the man said, "Vee arrr not from north, but vee speak English vedy vell."

Steve smiled and switched to English. "Will we soon be in Janglepit?"

"Trrrain not go Janglepit. Next shtop Madrash. Change train to narrrow gauge. Get off Chitoor. Then taxi. Ish long vay."

∽

The scent of jasmine greeted Steve as the taxi stopped in front of the leprosy training center in Janglepit, Tamilnadu. The dove-gray concrete-block buildings were impressive, approaching western standards. A two-story section stretched 200 feet to his right. Steve suspected it housed the inpatient wards and that behind the air-conditioner on the second floor lay the operating room.

What a great little hospital!

To his left, he saw workers adding an extension to a single-story structure labeled *Outpatient Pavilion.* It had ramps for wheelchair access. There were beds as well as chairs on an outside verandah, apparently for really sick patients who arrived before opening time.

A large blue bus was beginning to take on passengers, while many of the patients were finishing lunch. Steve was glad he had taken time to eat rice and curry at the train station. He didn't want to arrive looking as though he expected a meal.

Between these two clinical units he saw a small building with a sign over the door that said *Administration.* To its left, a path bore a sign that read *Chapel.* Trees and flowering shrubs gave shade and color to the scene, including a dozen six-foot-high poinsettias ablaze with large red flowers.

Steve left his four suitcases at the side of the dusty gravel road and made straight for the admin building to find the hospital superintendent. As the office door was open, he knocked on the doorframe. A small man on the other side of a huge desk looked up at him over a pair of horn-rimmed glasses. He had a long sharp nose and bushy eyebrows.

When he saw Steve he smiled. "You must be Steve Manley, from Minnesota. I'm Dr. Aiyapandian. We've been expecting you. Dr. Rajalingam said to expect you this afternoon. It is now 1 p.m.—after noon, and here you are. You see, I am a man of logic and science."

"You are indeed. But who is this Rajalingam?"

"He is the man at the top, the south Asia Field Secretary for the

Mission. It is he who tells us what to do. Comes and visits every six months. We have quite a chain of command here, just like in the army."

"So I gather."

Dhanbad, Janglepit—Steve was beginning to get a picture of life with the Mission to the Outcast, and he didn't like what he saw.

"Come. I'll show you around."

Next to the superintendent's office was the records department. "According to World Health Organization," Dr. Aiyapandian began, "we have best record system in Third World. Each patient has chart that goes out with epidemiological team when they hold village outpatient clinic near his home, basically once every four weeks. Medication taken and any change in health status are recorded meticulously. Everyone comes to clinic for more medicine and to be assessed by a doctor. Any that fail to appear are hunted down and assessed by paramedics in their homes. This way everything is monitored."

"Very thorough. But it must be very expensive."

"Planning, young man. Planning is the secret. You see, we not only treat patients and train people like yourself. We also do great deal of research. In one of our many projects, we are studying effectiveness of low dose DDS. That's dimethyl diphenyl sulphone, a very cheap drug we are using nearly 15 years. Most leprosy cases it can cure, and holds disease in check in the others. But in some, DDS seems to cause a reaction that destroys nerves. We are trying to see if we can give them much lower dose, control disease but not cause this terrible reaction."

Steve stopped and turned to face him.

"But that could be extremely dangerous. It could lead to DDS-resistant strains that would be impossible to control."

"Quite so." Aiyapandian smiled up at the tall foreigner. "They said you were bright and you have hit the nail squarely on its head. Quite right indeed! That is why we must follow every development quite closely."

He brought his hand down on the table. "Now it happens there is possible successor to DDS if such disaster should occur, and the manufacturer of this drug wants us to test its effectiveness. So they are putting more money into this hospital than is given by the Mission to the Outcast. Along with other research grants our budget is almost tripled. And I control it all."

Dr. Aiyapandian seemed to grow a little taller as he spoke. "That is how we can afford the elaborate system of record-keeping and village supervision we have. W.H.O. says is model for others to follow. Everyone is overlooking fact that I must run the hospital in order to make the system work. We have superior management. I am the secret ingredient."

Steve felt his eyes widen, not at the genius of this little man but at the boldness of his plan. *He's another Napoleon.*

"How expensive would this new drug be?" he asked.

"Oh, very. No one could afford it."

"Then if resistance developed, India and the world would be in deep trouble."

"Oh, yes. So we must not let it happen. We have a tiger by the tail. It is most exciting." Aiyapandian's face broke into a broad grin.

"It's too bad the leprosy bacillus cannot be grown in laboratory animals," Steve said. "Then you could use them to test DDS dosages safely, perhaps even develop and test new drugs."

Aiyapandian's eyes twinkled. "Whoever does that could win Nobel Prize. Now come and meet my wife. She is Chief Surgeon."

They left the administration block without visiting any of the other rooms. One of them was obviously the hospital laboratory and another, with a noisy air conditioner attached, housed a large colony of small animals. They crossed a small courtyard to enter the two-story inpatient block. Over the first door on the right, a sign read *Chief Surgeon.*

Mrs. Aiyapandian's door was open, but the room was empty. A tall, slim, dark-skinned Indian woman in a flowing, mauve-colored sari entered through a connecting door from the adjoining room.

"Good afternoon, sir," she said, nodding toward the diminutive superintendent. "If you are seeking your wife, she is presently in the operating room. Dr. (Mrs.) Aiyapandian has intimated that Dr. Manley could join her there. You are Dr. Manley?"

"Uh, uh, yes," Steve answered. "Does everyone speak English

here?"

"Of course. We learn it at school. Not everyone goes to school, but those who do are required by law to learn three languages: the state language, which here is Tamil, Hindi, and one other—"

"Steve," Dr. Aiyapandian interjected, "This is Victoria, Mrs. Aiyapandian's personal secretary. Later you will meet the two others who take dictation from the surgical trainees."

"In South India," Victoria continued, "that third language is usually English."

"What about the patients?"

"Most of them speak only Tamil."

"Does anyone speak Bengali?"

"No. But sometimes we have a patient sent here from West Bengal. It is now many years since they have had a surgeon there who can do leprosy reconstructive surgery. It can be very hard to communicate with Bengalis."

"I'm your man."

Steve grinned broadly to think he might be useful for something. His self-esteem had not fully recovered from his last encounter with Archibald Smithers, but it was on the way up. He was glad he had come to Tamilnadu.

"Thank you, sir," he said to Dr. Aiyapandian—and to Victoria, "Please take me to see Mrs. Dr. Aiyapandian."

"Dr. (Mrs.), not Mrs. Dr. That is the way we say it."

"I see I have much to learn."

"Please follow me, Dr. Manley."

Steve was fascinated by the way Victoria's hips swayed as she walked. Her hips were at eye level as they climbed the stairs to the second floor, their movement reminding Steve of the way movie stars walked in the '40s.

Victoria led him to the change room, showed him the lockers, and indicated the door to the scrub room. After she left, the scent of lilac remained. Steve wondered if she chose her perfume to match the color of her sari.

He slipped out of his street clothes and put on a green jumpsuit and white rubber boots. After a five-minute scrub he entered Operating

Room One.

"Welcome. You must be Steve. My name is Dr. (Mrs.) Aiyapandian. Suit up and you can come closer. We are just now doing an EF4T using ERCB extended with fascia lata graft."

"An EF4T?"

"Sorry. We are using far too many short forms in medicine, isn't it? EF4T means 'Extensor-Flexor Four Tailed.' Watch and I will show you. First we take a wrist extensor muscle, extensor carpi radialis brevis, and make it into a flexor."

She made a short incision on the back of the wrist, found a pearly white structure, put a small clamp on it and severed its connection to bone.

"Now when I pull on this tendon I can feel where is the belly of this muscle we call ECRB. That is the one we want to have its effect in a far different way than God intended. You see when there is paralysis on one side of the wrist we must make up for the loss on the weak side by taking from the strong side."

She made a second short incision where she had felt the muscle move, and after releasing the clamp on the tendon, pulled the muscle and its tendon out of the second incision. She flipped the hand over, quickly made a third incision three inches above the front of the wrist, inserted a long clamp and pushed on it till its mouth-like end protruded through the second incision. Into that mouth she fed the ECRB tendon. The mouth closed and she pulled this tendon right through to the "weak" side of the forearm.

"Now," she said, "we must make this tendon longer by adding strip of tissue from thigh. Then we pass this strip across the wrist through the carpal tunnel. After cutting its end into four tails we must tunnel each one into a finger and fix it to its extensor tendon. So when patient reaches for something, as the wrist extends, fingers straighten."

With her free hand she curled her fingers into her palm, then, flinging her wrist back quickly, straightened them.

"In India, hands are more flexible than in West. So we can't use same operations you may be used to, like the sublimus transfer."

"I must tell you," Steve said, " that I worked in a spinal injuries unit for just three months, as part of my training—and did just a few tendon transfers to replace paralyzed muscles. The things you do here I've only read about. I'm anxious to learn your techniques."

"We are getting quite expert at a few things now. Specialization is like a pyramid."

She held her hands together to form a triangle with two thumbs as the base and each index finger as a side. "Every day we are getting to know more and more about less and less. Is nearly 20 years now we are using some special techniques for special kinds of paralysis we find. When disease is no longer progressing, patients are left with certain patterns of nerve damage. Here in South India, we have learned how to adapt established operations and devise new ones, to restore the balance of forces in partially-paralyzed hands. For example we have many claw hands because the ulnar nerve at the elbow is commonly destroyed—"

"Oh, yes," Steve interjected. "I just saw a man at the Outpatient Pavilion whose fingers were curled up in his palm so much he could hardly eat."

Dr. (Mrs.) Aiyapandian scowled at him across the operating table. "Please, you must never interrupt. Now, where was I?"

Smiling once more she added, "Because of ulnar nerve damage we do lot of EF4Ts. We also correct thumb paralysis, wrist drop, foot drop, sunken noses, facial paralysis, eyebrow loss—the list goes on and on. People come here from many parts of the world to learn what we do. They call them miracles."

Steve spent many hours of many weeks in the operating room with "The Chief," as they called their teacher behind her back. Like her and the trainees in the program before him, Steve was becoming a miracle worker—making hands with curled-up fingers open and hold things, even making thumbs that lay flat beside the palm stand upright, then move across the palm to touch the fingers.

"You are such a brute of a man to look at," she said one day as she watched him at work. "Yet you hold the tissues so softly and gently in your forceps. It is really quite amazing."

"When I look at a tendon," he said, "I see the delicate film on its surface that will help it glide through the hand. I almost think I can see the cells that lie there, and I don't want to bruise even one of them."

"I think you must feel the same way about patients," she added, "because I am seeing how you take their hands in yours and gently touch them. Since they have little sensation, they may not feel how gentle you are. But, just as I can tell by watching you, they know that you care for them very deeply."

Steve stopped his work and looked at her across the operating table. "Stop that. You're making me blush."

They both laughed, and he quietly went on with the operation.

"It's a good thing this patient doesn't understand English," Steve said while stitching the skin. "I'd be too embarrassed for words."

Bees buzzed, birds flew, and a gentle early morning breeze fluttered the leaves of the palm trees as Steve walked from Guest Quarters to the hospital. It was early March, and the sun's heat grew stronger every day. A portly middle-aged English man stopped ahead of him on the path to wipe sweat from his forehead.

"Are you alright?" Steve asked as he stepped up alongside him.

The man cursed the hot weather with words that would shame even the most rebellious teenager.

Steve was speechless. Who was this guy with the filthy mouth? What was he doing on a mission station? He hoped none of the locals heard the way he talked.

Recovering his composure, he said, "You'll get used to it in time. What mission board are you with?"

"Oh, I'm not one of your bloody missionaries, thank God. I'm an epidemiological statistician from London. Dr. Aiyapandian asked me to analyze some of his research data and give him advice on future directions. He said some of my suggestions were impracticable, and that I had to come here to experience the environment in which he works. Well, I think I've had more than enough experience of that—and nothing works."

As the path joined the road at the entrance to the hospital Steve asked, "Are you coming to the chapel service?"

"No fear on that score. Haven't darkened the door of a church for as long as I can remember."

Steve was glad they had reached the point where he could politely say good-bye and hurried off to the chapel service before going on ward rounds.

By July it was even hotter, and also humid. In the Department of Pathology at Madras Medical School, the fan churned noisily above a desk covered with documents. A paperweight sat on each pile. Professor V. J. Thomas, a tall man, hunched over one pile and stroked his short black beard as he reviewed a paper submitted for publication in the *Indian Journal of Science.*

"Impossible," he said aloud. "The author claims to have grown leprosy bacilli in the footpads of mice, even transferred them to other mice, and done so three times. I couldn't do that, though I've tried for years."

Anxiously he read the methodology. "Aha! He removes the thymus gland at birth. That would prevent the T-lymphocytes from recognizing leprosy bacilli as foreign and they would not be destroyed. My goodness! What a most clever idea. Who is this genius?"

He turned to the covering letter and found the signature. "Aha! It's that old scoundrel Aiyapandian."

Thomas brought his fist down on the table so hard that one of the piles of paper cascaded onto the floor. The breeze from the overhead fan scattered pages across the room.

Thomas thought Aiyapandian a pompous braggart and scalawag. He wondered if he really did what he said and got the results he claimed. He couldn't possibly have a lab that could do this. He would need special staff, and a secure and carefully controlled bacteria-free environment. He would have to have air-conditioning to maintain a low enough temperature.

"Does he have an air conditioner?" Thomas said. "I wish I did. It's so beastly hot here."

He looked at his watch. It was 8.30 p.m. Dinner was waiting. But he knew that in this heat, the food would not get cold.

Carefully he considered all the political implications of this research. The hospital budget in the annual report had no mention of expenditure for an air conditioner. Rajalingam would have vetoed a request for such an expenditure if it had been proposed. So Aiyapandian had gone behind Rajalingam's back on this.

"What's this?" Thomas said as he read further. "He says Geigy, Switzerland, funded this work. So that could be how he got all this expensive equipment without getting Rajalingam's approval. But there was no mention of a donation from Geigy in the hospital report. So either he's lying about this research, or he's falsified the annual report. Either way, his goose will be cooked when I show this paper to Rajalingam."

Thomas picked up a pen and quickly wrote two notes to his secretary. The first said, "Write a polite letter to the publisher saying this paper lacks a convincing methodology. Rejected for publication. No re-submission to be allowed." The second told her to copy the paper for the file *Aiyapandian.*

He attached both notes to the document labeled *Confidential. Do not copy. Return within 48 hours.* He placed them neatly on her desk, and, with a sense of work well done, walked briskly out the door.

Five

S ummer held its breath. Silently. Nothing moved.

Normally the monsoon rains of June cooled the dry desert air—but not this year. Everyone said the weather had never been typical since atom bombs began exploding in the stratosphere. Good weather was "typical"…what they deserved. Bad weather must be blamed on the Americans disturbing nature with their atom bomb tests.

Unexpected news shattered the stillness.

"Dr. Rajalingam is coming," Dr. Aiyapandian announced in the morning chapel service. "He is planning an Extraordinary Meeting of the Board of Directors. What for, God only knows."

Professor V. J. Thomas smiled as he sensed a note of alarm in Aiyapandian's voice. As Consulting Pathologist to the hospital he visited every Thursday and always came early enough to attend morning devotions in the chapel. There were no chairs. Everyone sat cross-legged on the floor, patients in front and staff at the back, men on the left and women on the right.

"Today," Aiyapandian continued, "Professor Thomas will read to us from a Bible text he has chosen."

Thomas walked to the front. Speaking first in English and then in Tamil so that even the most uneducated could understand, he read the story about the faithful servant and the unfaithful servant.

At the end of the reading he added, "The Master had traveled to a far country, and on returning gave a reward to the one who had done well. He punished the one who had failed to do right. We must never forget that whatever we do, we must give an account both in this world and the next."

"Nothing new there," Steve whispered to another doctor next to him. "Why is he saying this now? Does it have anything to do with the visit of Dr. Rajalingam? Personally, I'm anxious to meet that guy."

"I want to thank you all for coming." Rajalingam smiled like a Halloween pumpkin as he looked around the room.

He sat at one end of a sixteen-foot mahogany table in the dining hall of Guest Quarters with Thomas to his right, his personal secretary on the left. Three other board members sat on each side of the table, leaving Aiyapandian alone at the far end. Methodically, with nicotine-stained fingers, Rajalingam squashed a small cigarette stub against two others on a very large ashtray in front of his secretary, took a deep breath, then looked around the room again.

"This meeting has been called on very short notice because of the urgent nature of the business we have to discuss. Urgent because it is so serious. We have never before called for an external audit of the financial records, but I would like to propose one now."

"I'll second that," said Thomas.

Rajalingam continued. "Dr. Aiyapandian has done a fine job of running this institution and achieved so much with the limited budget at his disposal that we, and here I speak on behalf of the Mission, have often wondered how he did so well. Furthermore, I believe there may have been some expenditures not recorded in the Annual Report."

"To what do you refer?" Aiyapandian asked, raising his chin in the air.

"The air-conditioner for one."

Then to those on each side of the table he added, "Can you believe he has a laboratory full of mice that live in the comfort of an air-conditioned room? It sounds preposterous. But in a few moments we shall all go over and see it—cool off in the presence of these humble four-legged creatures. "

Laughter filled the room.

"Just a minute," Aiyapandian said. "The air conditioner is an old one given by an anonymous donor. These past few years I'm doing research that requires a constant temperature. It must be kept below human body temperature because I'm trying to grow leprosy bacilli in

40

the feet of these mice."

"Then you haven't actually grown them yet," Thomas said. It was a statement, not a question.

"Yes, I have."

"Has anyone else verified your findings?"

"My lab assistant can confirm what I say. Also colored pictures there are, and I have sent the same as evidence in an article submitted to the *Indian Journal of Science*. It is now two weeks ago they were dispatched."

"Let's leave the lab issues for the visit," Rajalingam said. "Are we all in favor of an external audit?"

All hands were raised around the table except one. There were no objections. Rajalingam noted Aiyapandian did not vote.

"The vote is almost unanimous. As we speak, those records are already in the hands of an auditor. Let's reassemble in that delightfully cool laboratory."

"No. It is not allowed for you to go in there!" Aiyapandian said.

"Not allowed?" Rajalingam stood to his feet and glared down at him. "I am the Field Secretary for south Asia! I go where I please, when I please, and how I please."

"But you don't understand. To get leprosy bacilli growing in mice, I have had to destroy their immunity. Germs we all carry and breathe out of our noses would kill them."

"But you go in there."

"Perhaps they are used to me."

"Then let them get used to me too. I'll take in Thomas. He'll find out if this thing you are doing is worth all the time you must spend on it."

"He is right, sir," Thomas said to Rajalingam. "We can't all go in, but if you and I scrub up and wear a surgical gown and gloves like he does, it will practically eliminate any risk."

"How do you know what I do?" Aiyapandian asked.

"This may take a while, sir." Thomas said. "I suggest we get on with it and not keep the other board members waiting too long for the results of our lab visit.

S

The three men drove to the lab in Dr. Rajalingam's air-conditioned Mercedes-Benz. Once inside the administration building, Aiyapandian unlocked the door to the lab.

"Rosemary," he said. "We have some unexpected visitors, Drs. Rajalingam and Thomas. Gentlemen, meet Rosemary. She is paid directly from Head Office, London." This last comment was a volley aimed at Rajalingam.

In a few minutes they had changed, scrubbed, donned white gowns and gloves, and entered a room marked *No Unauthorized Entry.*

"Here in this cage is mouse number 847, my first one to be successfully infected. Please bring him out, Rosemary."

She put on a thick pair of leather gloves and held the mouse up to display a red swollen right forepaw.

"Now I will show you what has caused that swelling." Aiyapandian grinned at his visitors. They simply stared back at him.

Placing a slide under a microscope and focusing it briefly he said, "Have a look, Dr. Rajalingam."

Rajalingam squinted as he looked into the eyepiece while still wearing his glasses. "It's all a blur."

"Didn't you learn how to use a microscope in your army medical course?" Thomas asked. "Take off your glasses and adjust the focus with that knob on the right hand side."

Rajalingam did so, quickly turning the knob one way and then the other. "No difference. I can't see a thing. In the army this kind of thing was assigned to technicians. We doctors went about saving lives. Thomas, you have a look and tell me what you see."

Thomas swallowed hard and moved into position. His great moment had come. Looking down the microscope he saw gram negative rods typical of leprosy bacilli and realized Aiyapandian had successfully transferred them from humans to mice. This was a tricky situation. He had to think of a way to get some of the credit for himself.

"What about transfers to other mice?" Thomas asked. "I mean, how do we know these are living bacteria?"

"I've done that too. I can show you other mice, other slides. I have my records."

"Anyone can fabricate records. What about independent verification?"

"After my paper is published, many will be duplicating these results. I have described the methodology extremely precisely."

"Suppose, just suppose now I were to come into the lab and do a small study—quickly verify your findings in a short paper..."

"Us? Work together?" Aiyapandian scratched his head and looked at Thomas with raised eyebrows. "You mean bury the hatchet after all these years?"

"Quite so." *And I know exactly where I'll bury it.*

"We have a deal," Aiyapandian replied, smiling broadly. "I am above all a peacemaker, and I shall make peace with you—after I hear my paper has been accepted."

Two weeks later Steve woke to a knock on his door. Turning on the light, he looked at the clock. It was 1:25 a.m.

"Sahr, me Babu, night porter. Nurse Johnson say 'Come.' Patient high fever."

"Coming, Babu."

Steve quickly put on his white shirt, white trousers, and a pair of brown sandals. In barely two minutes he had cycled past the night porter, who was shuffling along on the dirt road that led to the hospital. In his hand, the porter held high a kerosene lantern to watch for snakes.

Minutes later Steve's bicycle light picked up the outline of a small brown thing, six inches tall, just ahead. He stopped to look. It was a tiny snake, challenging his right to pass. Steve figured it must have the ability to project a stream of strong poison. Otherwise it would not challenge so tall a creature as a man on a bicycle.

Bowing slightly at a respectful distance, he spoke in a quiet voice.

"After you, sir. I am your friend. Do as you wish."

The little snake hesitated a moment, as though considering what it heard. Then it slid silently into the dense dark grass at the roadside.

After taking care of the patient's needs, Steve started back to his room. This same path brought him around behind the lab. Movement in the bushes near one of the windows made him stop to investigate.

He heard a screeching noise like someone prying open a window with a crowbar. Steve turned his light in that direction. A shadowy figure dropped to the ground.

"Dr. Aiyapandian!" he said. "What are you *doing* here? Breaking into your own lab?"

"Oh, you are looking at the most miserable of creatures," Aiyapandian sobbed. "They have locked me out of my own lab. Thomas is the only one with a key for the padlock Rajalingam has put there. I have been given one month's salary and told to leave immediately. It is most unfair, illegal, improper, immoral, and flies in the face of all that is Christian. This is my own research. I am the one whose name is on three contracts with foreign drug companies who sponsor it. These are my mice. This is my equipment. They cannot do what in fact they are doing. My effort of past four years is falling into hands of unscrupulous people."

"But why are you here tonight?"

"See that truck. I have friend who will hide my mice until I can relocate. I have many friends, you know. They are good honest people. They will help me."

"So will I. I know from the lectures you gave us on leprosy that you are a great scientist. Your work must continue."

"No. No. Keep out of this matter. Go off to West Bengal and help the people there. Do not become entangled in this political intrigue. If you do, Rajalingam will destroy your life as he has mine."

Bang! It sounded like rifle shot. Brown fluid began pouring out of the air-conditioner.

Aiyapandian stood up and grinned. "Well, that is one piece of equipment he shall not have. I knew it would go sooner or later and I just received a letter saying the new one is in Delhi, waiting for me to collect it at customs."

He crawled into the lab through the open window as Steve watched from the outside.

"Hand me the cages as you bring them to the window," Steve said. "You can't really do all this by yourself."

In half an hour, the animals were in the truck. Next came the microscopes and other small equipment. Larger items, like the refrigerator, were too big to lift through and had to be left behind.

Steve went back to bed, but sleep eluded him.

Next morning, Rajalingam sat with his feet on Aiyapandian's desk, enjoying his situation, thinking, *This could be a nice place to spend the next six months, maybe much longer.*

Steve walked in. "You sent for me, sir?"

"Steve, I know you like a challenge. Here's one for you. Dr. and Mrs. Aiyapandian will be leaving here shortly. It is quite an unexpected move and I don't want to discuss the details. I've been up most of the night working out a plan for their replacement."

"You must be tired, sir." Steve said, stifling a yawn.

"Dr. Thomas has kindly offered to continue Dr. Aiyapandian's research and fill in as Chief of Medicine until a replacement is available."

"But he's a pathologist, and has another full-time job, I understand. Don't you need an epidemiologist?"

"He will visit two days per week instead of one as he did in the past, and interns from Madras University will rotate through every three months to cover the day-to-day needs on the medical wards. Today we are hiring someone for a new post, Hospital Manager. We have asked Headquarters to send out an epidemiologist from London if we cannot find one here."

Steve looked out the window and said, "Too bad you had to let Aiyapandian go. It seems you need three or four people to replace him."

Rajalingam cleared his voice loudly, frowned, and looked at Steve through half-closed eyes.

"We need a surgeon to replace Dr. (Mrs.) Aiyapandian. You're not the best choice, of course. You're a foreigner. Our government is highly suspicious of missionaries, especially Americans. They could ask you to leave the country at any time. But I think you could handle it, for a time at least."

"What about Dhanbad? That's where God called me to serve. They need a surgeon there."

"That backwater hasn't had a surgeon for so long I don't think they would know what to do with one if you went there. We need you here. We have a series of surgical trainees lined up to visit, the next one due in two months, and a large research project in surgical rehabilitation funded by the U.S. Government, your people."

"Is Mrs. Aiyapandian the one who signed the contract for that research?"

Rajalingam eyed him suspiciously. "No. I did, on behalf of the Mission. Because it was an American Government research contract it had to go through the Indian Council of Scientific Research, and I.C.S.R. insisted that it be agreed upon at a higher level. The contract belongs to this institution, not to any individual. But we have to have a surgeon here or we shall lose this 120,000 U.S. dollar contract."

"I am deeply honored by your offer, sir. I shall give it serious thought and pray about it."

"Pray about it? Why would you pray about it? Jesus commanded his disciples to 'go into all the world' and 'cleanse the lepers.' I'm giving you a chance to do just that, to be a specialist in leprosy reconstructive surgery rather than go back to Dhanbad and do general orthopedics. Why do you have to pray?"

"Well, can I let you know tomorrow? It's a big decision."

"Of course."

"Tonight I'm going to think about it," Steve said, adding as he turned to leave, "and ask God what He thinks about it."

As Steve walked out the door, a dark-skinned jovial-looking bald-

46

headed man with thick glasses walked in.

Placing one hand against the other he bowed slightly to Rajalingam and said, "My name is Subramani Doraiswami, sir. I have been informed that you would be looking for one qualified to be hospital superintendent."

"We are indeed. Please sit down and tell me about yourself."

"I am fully qualified in Business Administration, having degree from Pondicherry. See, I have transcripts and letters of reference."

He handed over a thin file of documents.

"What languages do you speak?"

"In addition to English—Tamil, Hindi, and a little Malayalum."

"Religion?"

"Hindu. Non-smoker, never touched alcohol."

"Experience?"

"Seven years working in hardware store."

Rajalingam quickly scanned the letters of reference. This applicant looked trainable, not too bright, but a good follower—willing to learn, ready to do as he was told, without any preconceived ideas that might conflict with Rajalingam's methods.

"We're looking." he said, "for someone who can take orders and follow them to the letter. If you want the job you can have it, provided you are successful in performing the task I shall now give you."

Taking a sheet out of his briefcase he said, "Sign this agreement. Now your task is to take the 2 p.m. plane to Delhi and collect a very large air-conditioning unit in the name of Dr. Aiyapandian, whom you represent."

Rajalingam handed Doraiswami an envelope.

"These documents will identify you as his representative. A return air ticket and enough rupees to cover incidental expenses are in there also. My driver will take you to the airport. You must arrange for the equipment to be shipped by transport here directly to me at my bungalow. We shall pay the cost when it arrives. If you can successfully carry out this mission we shall sign a contract and the job is yours. Most important: discuss this matter with no one."

"You can count on me."

S

That night Steve spent two hours in prayer. He read his Bible, searching for an answer. The cooper bird let out a screech that startled him. An inner voice seemed to say, "This is the place."

He picked up a pen and wrote.

August 15th, 1971

Dear Andrew,

A very bizarre thing has happened. There has been a political shakeup here. Consequently, the Mission's Field Secretary for south Asia offered me the job of Chief Surgeon. In addition to training other surgeons, I would inherit a large research grant that will let me develop some ideas I have on how to restore sensation. It is almost like getting a university appointment.

However, I'm not sure I can work with the administration, which I now suspect are "the bad guys" in this battle. Still they can't be worse than Smithers in Dhanbad and, compared to other mission posts I've heard about, the hospital here is so modern it's almost beyond belief.

I'm going to accept. I hope this is what God wants for my life. Please pray for me as I suspect there may be some difficult days ahead.

I'm sending this to the address you gave me in Roodepoort, as you must have arrived there long ago. If you have written me at Dhanbad, nothing has been forwarded and I wonder how things are working out for you in South Africa. Keep in touch. We can be a great help to each other.

Yours in Christ,
Steve

Book Two

Six

Andrew Heath settled back in his seat and heaved a sigh of relief. At last they were on their way to South Africa—first stop London. He looked around to see how the others were handling it.

His eldest son John, in all his 13 years, had never ridden in an airplane. Neither had 10-year-old Edward. Andrew smiled when he saw John suck in his breath as the BOAC 707 accelerated down the runway and tilted sharply upward.

Toronto fell away quickly, becoming a city of model houses and Dinky toys. In minutes the earth vanished under a gray haze. The engine whine settled to a dull roar, the aircraft tipped forward into level flight, and John seemed to breathe normally again.

Andrew uttered a silent prayer, "Lord, you know he's the one I worry about. Please make this a great adventure for him."

Andrew remembered the fuss there had always been over moving, how John had objected when they sold their house in Kitchener to move to the prairies. But it was essential that Andrew get a good grounding in the Word of God to prepare for whatever they might have to face in Africa, even if it meant the kids had to say good-bye to all their friends. Then there were complaints when he had to leave them to go to linguistics school in Toronto. Roaming the countryside drumming up support money didn't help matters.

Andrew knew the kids never understood all the chaos. He hoped they would see what a difference their ministry could make in the lives of those poor black people and would then agree that it had all been worthwhile.

A tear trickled down John's left cheek.

"John, what's wrong?"

"Nothing." As he spoke the distortion of his face betrayed his anguish.

"He wants to go back to Kitchener," Nancy said. "He misses his friends."

"But John," Andrew pleaded, "you'll have a whole bunch of new friends."

"No, I won't. I hate Africa! And I hate the silly mission. I just want to go home."

Andrew put his arm around his son and hugged him close. "I'll make a deal with you. If you'll give it a try, a really good try, and then you don't like it, we'll have a family discussion and consider returning home."

Nancy's eyes widened in surprise.

"But I think," he added, "you'll find it a great adventure. We're only going for five years..."

"Five years?" Edward piped in. "I'll be all grown up by then."

"And I'll be ready to go to university," said John.

"Let me finish. Our first term, I mean for your mother and me, is for five years. Then we'll all go to Canada. How would you like it if we went to Kitchener?"

"Kitchener?" the boys shouted together.

"Yes, Kitchener. Then if all has gone well here in Africa we shall come back to South Africa. Wherever we are, you'll both be with us till you're old enough to leave home and go to university. But if we really don't like it here, we can go home anytime!"

John heaved a sigh of relief and wiped his eyes. Nancy sighed also.

"What was that about?" Andrew asked, looking at Nancy.

"I was just happy you defused the tension so nicely."

"Oh really?"

"Well," she added, "I never heard you mention any possibility we might come back as 'failed missionaries.' You're not a quitter."

"So how would it make you happier if I were?"

The cloud of tension he had so deftly demolished lingered over them again.

"I'm not happier," Nancy said. "But sometimes it's hard to keep up."

"Look, Andrew," Nancy said, pulling on his sleeve.

English countryside broke through the haze. Farms and villages drifted slowly beneath them. Within minutes the pastoral scene changed to sprawling suburbs, revealing roofs and chimneys that seemed to reach upward to the belly of the aircraft.

As the wheels contacted the tarmac, Nancy bounced against the seat belt like an excited child. "Andrew, it's like coming home! I loved England so."

"Hey, you weren't born here!"

"No, but I spent the two most wonderful years of my childhood here at St. Luke's, the boarding school near King's Lynn. I loved being thrust into another culture—Britain's upper classes and the children of the rich and famous from around the world."

"Is that why you want to go with me to Africa?" Andrew asked.

She eyed him curiously. "There'll be no upper classes there."

"I'm talking about loving different cultural experiences."

"I like to see different cultures, yes. But at King's Lynn, the girls were so sophisticated! That was what I liked there. We won't see any sophistication on the mission field, of that I'm quite sure."

Andrew nodded.

"But, Andrew, I'm happy you suggested that after we see London we rent a car and drive to King's Lynn for a visit to my old school."

"Your happiness means the world to me, Nancy."

They smiled at each other. Now it was Andrew's turn to sigh.

"Look alert Nancy! Time to go," Andrew said as he began pulling bags from the overhead bins.

London became a highlight in Edward Heath's young life. The city lifted even John from his melancholy. The family stayed in the mission's headquarters for the British Isles—another Victorian mansion, almost a duplicate of the mission's building in Toronto. They ate some meals in the dining room where the starchy silence and formal manners of the staff and British guests dampened Edward's natural effervescence. He fumbled with his knife and fork as he tried to copy the continental style of eating—fork in the left hand when it should be in the right. He watched his mother for a moment; she seemed right at home with her knife and fork clicking away on the plate. It was almost like watching a tennis player with a racket in each hand.

The minute Edward left the building his exuberance returned. For five days they went out each morning after breakfast. They rode the District Line of the underground to Victoria Station and walked to Trafalgar Square to feed the pigeons. One day they walked up Baker Street, past the fictional residence of Sherlock Holmes, to visit the Planetarium and Madame Tussaud's Wax Museum. With their missionary calling in mind, they searched through Westminster Abbey until they found David Livingstone's grave. With hundreds of others, they watched the changing of the guard at Buckingham Palace. Every day they ate at a department store lunch counter or feasted on burgers at a Wimpy Bar before continuing their exploration of old London on foot.

When he saw Tower Bridge, Edward cried, "Oh Dad, it's wonderful. It's so real! I always wanted to visit Disneyland, but it couldn't be anything like this!"

On day six, Andrew rented an Austin Maxi. After a few turns around the neighborhood to practice driving on the left, they headed north toward Norfolk and King's Lynn. They visited Castle Rising, took long strolls on the vacant beaches of The Wash, and stayed in a British pub, The Dirty Duck. It was when they arrived at Nancy's old school that they experienced the singular disappointment of their visit to England: St. Luke's school had closed.

"I feel abandoned," Nancy said. "I've not talked much about it, but those two years at King's Lynn seemed like an oasis in the desert."

Andrew squeezed her hand. "Was that when your parents were in the middle of...a...a..."

"Yes, the divorce. They had always quarreled, but when Dad's business went under and they split up, Mom couldn't afford to keep me at the school."

She remained silent for a moment. Andrew just waited.

"Back in Canada I clung to the memory of this place, but now I see it standing there vacant, deserted, and crumbling."

As Andrew embraced her and wiped tears from her cheek, he said, "The days of things crumbling and collapsing are over. We're off to a new life in South Africa."

Seven

The 707 winged across the deserts of north Africa. The day droned on in perfect sync with the aircraft's engines. Andrew reacted to the boredom by withdrawing and reliving the thrills and wonders of England. A glance at the boys suggested they might be doing the same.

He worried about Nancy and her disappointment at finding the school closed. He could see she had retreated into the pages of her journal, as she often did when things troubled her. She seemed nervous and, when their eyes met, quickly closed the book and locked it.

Nancy had never let him look in that book and Andrew wondered what secrets it contained.

Andrew didn't keep a journal, but he had made detailed notes relating to his dreams and expectations for his new work in South Africa. He kept them in a file folder tucked into his flight bag, now stored in the overhead rack. He couldn't easily reach the bag, so he visited it in his mind. In addition to his notes, he had also placed three specification sheets in the folder. One, an architect's drawing of the new press building he would soon see in Roodepoort. He had no actual photo, but the drawing from the original proposal, dated 1968, showed a long, low building with glass covering most of the front wall. He had never worked in a building so impressive.

The second sheet, a brochure really, contained pictures and specifications for his pride and joy—his precious Gevaert graphics camera. To Andrew the camera, his most valued personal possession, symbolized his professional status. The third item, a detailed instruction manual, gave operating instructions for the four-color printing press, a gift from a former employer. They had parted with it out of respect for Andrew, and because it had become surplus when they upgraded their facilities.

Both items, the camera as big as a kitchen range and the press the size of a refrigerator, now rested along with the Heath's household goods in the belly of a ship bound for South Africa. If any doubts existed about his family's ability to adjust to new surrounding, he had no reason to question his professional success with God's Word Mission.

The intercom crackled to life at the very moment the plane banked to the right. A few of the distorted words reached Andrew's lethargic brain: "Approaching Nairobi... landing in 20 minutes... refueling... one hour."

A murmur of voices swept through the aircraft, bringing Andrew upright in his chair. He swiveled his head to find the reason for the sudden animation in his fellow passengers, and gaped in wonder at the scene outside the cabin window. A snow-capped mountain peak protruded through a white blanket of clouds that otherwise hid the Kenyan countryside. The sun ignited the symmetrical cone like a great signal beacon. The aircraft banked left, wiping the view from the window, but not before Andrew could alert his family.

Andrew shook his head in wonder. "Wow, what a sight! Surely, God sent this as a signal to pull us onward to South Africa—to tell us we have made the right decision to serve him there."

Edward beamed at his father, but Nancy and John stared back blankly.

A few hours later, the airliner swung low over Roodepoort in the West Rand on a flight path that would take it north of Johannesburg's downtown toward Jan Smuts airport. Andrew's hands gripped the armrests and shook with tension and excitement. His thoughts raced and tumbled over each other. They would have a new life leading them each step along the way. He believed Nancy would love South Africa because of its cultural similarity to England.

Visible from the right side of the aircraft, huge mine dumps appeared, looking like desert mountains—golden peaks in the wilderness.

Edward grabbed his father's arm and pointed out tiny houses with red tile roofs. The late afternoon sun, slanting in from the northwest, glinted from hundreds of swimming pools like little mirrors, beckoning them to take a closer look.

Nancy tightened her seat belt and closed her eyes.

She's praying, Andrew thought, *that things will go well for us in our new home—our new life.*

After landing, it took the family an hour to clear customs and immigration, collect their luggage, and press through the crowds to the "arrivals" hall. There they stood, feeling like lost souls awaiting judgment.

Edward broke the tension. He swaggered a few steps from the group, looked toward his father, and drawled, "What do we do now, Mr. Dillon?"

Andrew studied the throng. "Son, someone is supposed to meet us here to take us to Roodepoort. I don't know who. And I don't know how he'll find us in this crowd."

John suddenly brightened. "Dad, look! Those people are holding a sign with a name on it. We can do that too."

Kneeling, John pulled a sheet of notepaper and pen from his carry-on bag. Placing the paper on the floor, he wrote, *HEATH, GOD'S WORD*. He didn't have room for the word *mission*. Andrew took the paper from him and held it high.

"Snap," said a short, middle-aged man, emerging from the crowd. He held a white card bearing the name *HEATH*.

"Ferguson, Jack Ferguson. Lila and I are your ride to Roodepoort."

Andrew barely had time to make introductions before Jack began picking up their baggage.

"Me Rolls is just over 'ere," he said in an exaggerated British accent. "Lila is parked illegally."

Outside, he motioned toward a VW minibus. "We brought the mission Kombi. That's what we call these things over here."

Lila jumped from the driver's seat and lifted the tailgate. "Put what you can in here," she said in an American Southern drawl. "The rest can go inside."

Lila joined Nancy in the middle seat. With the boys and the remainder of the luggage in the back seat, Andrew climbed in beside Jack, who had taken the wheel.

"We'll swing north of Jo'burg to miss the freeways and the traffic and enter Roodepoort through Allen's Nek," Jack explained as he skillfully broke into a line of moving vehicles.

"Good of you to come for us," Andrew ventured.

"It's a pleasure. In fact we're thrilled. Got to miss the annual field conference down in Durban. Both Lila and I find it a bore. You will too when you have to go next year. The rest of our coworkers will arrive back in three days. Just in time to prepare for Christmas. Don't get much done this time of the year. We all thought it silly of the Canadian office sending you out in mid-December, and in the middle of the field conference."

Feeling he had to say something, Andrew said, "I guess we were ready, so we came. Are you with the mission press, Jack?"

"Heavens no," Lila said. "We work with the translation department. We get things ready in Bantu languages, so you at the mission press can print them. I work with Sesotho and Setswana. Jack works in Zulu and related languages."

"We even speak different languages at home," Jack cut in. "She speaks American and I speak Cockney. We met on the field years ago and married after Lila had learned one native language and I another."

"Do you do the translations yourselves?"

"Yes we do, with a little help from African employees," Lila explained.

Andrew wrinkled his brow, but bit his tongue. At T.I.L. he'd learned that national workers must do all translation for it to be effective, for the readers to accept it as authoritative.

He changed the topic. "What's on for tomorrow?"

Before Jack could answer, he had to swerve the Kombi around an erratic driver. "Idiot driver! South African drivers are the world's worst—especially the black ones."

Andrew wanted to point out that the errant driver had white skin, but again bit his tongue.

"Now, about tomorrow. You folks get to do nothing for two days before the others get back from conference. I'll come by and show you around the station—the mission buildings. The next day Lila can take Nancy to the shops so she can get a feel for the place. Then on the following day at 8 a.m. you have a meeting with the station head and the manager of the print shop."

After escaping the cluster of buildings and tangle of roads around the airport, the Kombi gathered speed along a country road. Jack talked incessantly, pouring out information that Andrew and Nancy needed to know.

"You'll be living in the Ward's house. Tom and Sheila are home on furlough—due back in three months. They work with the schools department, placing Bibles and other literature in the Soweto classrooms. Mostly English, but some Afrikaans."

"Don't we get a house of our own?" Nancy asked. "The Canadian office told us—"

"Eventually," Lila said. "A newcomer lives wherever the field director can find a house. We moved six times in four years before we got a permanent house. You look a little pale, Nancy. Are you all right?"

"I'm okay."

"You can't go by what the Canadian office told you," Jack said. "They really don't know. But things work out eventually. Lila and I put some food in the fridge, and clean linens on the bed. You get to use Ward's things until your goods arrive from home."

The rough, uneven countryside with its red soil and weed-covered ditches looked foreign to the Heaths. The boys looked for what they considered evidence of Africa but saw little, except for the occasional African man walking on the roadside. The December summer sun burned down. The blast of air through the minivan's open windows felt uncomfortably warm against exposed flesh.

"Look at that!" Edward cried out, twisting in his seat to get a better view. "Those African men are wearing woolen hats and jackets in this heat."

Jack never took his eyes off the road to look, but answered, "You'll learn that natives do a lot of funny things—"

"Blacks," Lila said.

"Righto, Lila," Jack answered. "They want us to call them blacks now. As I was saying, they do a lot of things differently. Don't be surprised by anything."

The Kombi left the open country and followed the road into a narrow gap through a ridge of hills.

Jack glanced back at his passengers. "This pass is called Allen's Nek. Roodepoort, your new home, is just beyond this ridge."

The Kombi struggled though the twisting roads of the pass, came down a steep descent, entered modern suburbs and turned onto a side street.

John shook his head in wonder. "Houses just like in Canada!"

"More like England," Edward said. "Look at the tile roofs and the low walls around most of the houses."

Jack wheeled the Kombi through an open wrought-iron gate into a driveway. "We're here, your temporary home on Honeyball Avenue. They call this subdivision Discovery. Most of our missionaries live in this area. In fact, so many mission organizations have homes here, the local people call it Missionary Hill. Even the post office recognizes this designation."

As the family members carried their bags inside, Jack continued talking. "Discovery Primary school is just two blocks away, and Florida Park High School is less than two miles. The boys may want to walk past them tomorrow—get the lay of the land before the new school year starts next month. I've left a map in the house. Both are English-language schools, but you boys will have to study Afrikaans."

ॐ

The next day Andrew and Nancy sat in the kitchen drinking coffee. John and Edward had taken Jack's advice and gone out to explore the community. The parents felt alone in a strange house in a foreign land.

"Somehow," Andrew said, "I thought things would be very different. I'll never understand why they let us come during field conference with everyone away."

"That's a minor problem. Why didn't they tell us about this musical-houses routine? They said we'd have a house. Our boys need stability, a place where they feel secure."

Andrew took time to drain his cup before answering. "I'm not sure that's the biggest problem. Jack and Lila seem to have strange racial attitudes for missionaries. Oh, well, we won't be working too closely with them, and today we get to see the mission facilities."

Nancy shook her head. "I'm not going. I'd better be ho...here when the boys return from exploring."

"I guess that's best," said Andrew, pulling a drawing from his travel case. "I brought the architect's conception of the new press building, although I don't suppose the finished product looks exactly like it. Dr. Hamilton-Jones bragged about it as though it rivaled the Taj Mahal."

"Has he ever seen it?"

"Must have. He visited South Africa recently."

Jack pulled into the yard, driving a white Peugeot, horn tooting. "Hop in," he called. "The mission departments are housed in an old factory building just off Van Wyk Street, Roodepoort's main street. All of the departments have come together there in the last few years—the translation department, the correspondence group, the literature sales people, a small audio studio to record cassette material, and of course the mission press."

Andrew opened his mouth to speak, to remind Jack that the press had a new building, but he held off as an uneasy feeling flooded his mind. He suspected there was an air of resentment between mission departments. Also he wondered why Jack wouldn't take him to the press building first.

Jack drove down a street lined with shops, turned down a narrow lane, and stopped the Peugeot in front of a gray cement structure. A small sign, at eye level beside a door protected with a metal security gate, said *Welcome, God's Word Mission.*

As Jack unlocked the gate and door, he said, "We need the security in this part of town."

In the dimly lit office, Jack threw a switch, flooding the room with florescent light that revealed a variety of mismatched desks, chairs, and filing cabinets.

"The corner office belongs to the field director. Through that door, a passage leads to the translation and correspondence departments. I can show you them if you like."

Andrew hesitated. "The press—"

"Yes, you want to see the press. The door to the left leads to the school ministry. Straight ahead takes us through the literature department to the press room."

Andrew's lips tightened; the earlier feeling of unease returned, sending a quiver through his whole body. "The press room?"

Jack frowned but led on. "This way."

They walked between shelves of literature and books to another door that bore a one-word sign: *Press.*

Jack paused at the door, "Now watch yourself. We go down three steps. The press room began its life as the boiler and engine room tacked onto the back of this old factory building—hence the high ceiling and lowered floor."

Jack threw the door open with a flourish. "Behold, your department, the mission press."

Andrew looked down a short stairway into a windowless room about 30 feet long and 12 feet wide. The door and steps entered in the middle of the long wall. A glass partition walled off a small office across the narrow end to the right; a layer of dust covered an old graphics camera on a trestle table inside the office. An ancient wooden desk, two worn office chairs and a battered filing cabinet filled the rest of the smaller room. In the main room, a small photocopier backed up to the glass wall.

Andrew turned and looked to the left end of the press room. An ancient press stood against the far-left wall. Right across the long wall opposite where he stood, piles of paper spilled from wooden shelves mounted askew across its length. Two mismatched desks and chairs vied for space with an assortment of filing cabinets and a worktable in the middle of the room.

For a full minute, Andrew could not speak as the truth dawned upon him. He wanted to step down into the room but his legs wouldn't move.

"So we haven't occupied the new building yet. When is that supposed to happen?"

Jack frowned. "Not before they build it. And I doubt that will happen this decade. That dream originated with the press manager, Gordon Muir. Then your Canadian secretary, Dr. Nicholas Hamilton-Jones, picked up the idea and started touting it. As far as I know he hasn't raised more than 10 percent of the funds—and the councils in America and Britain aren't interested in helping."

Andrew's legs weakened and he sat suddenly on the top step and blurted, "It's like a dungeon. Oh, dear God, what have I got into?"

The following day, when Lila arrived to take Nancy to the shops, Andrew gave her special instructions. "Lila, take her to the stores, but also visit the mission building. She needs to see it herself, before we meet with the brass tomorrow."

To Nancy he said, "Enjoy yourself."

Andrew and Nancy sat under a cloud of gloom engendered by their visits to the mission complex and prepared to meet their immediate superiors. Following breakfast, they had sent the boys exploring and fortified themselves with a second coffee.

A Kombi decorated with Scripture verses pulled into the yard. Trying hard to mask his bitter disappointment and sense of foreboding, Andrew opened the front door, thinking, *Here they come, we haven't met them, and I'm ready to resign.*

"Andrew and Nancy! So good to meet you at last. I'm Gordon Muir, the press manager, and this is our field director, Peter Fowler. I'm originally from Toronto; Peter Hails from Atlanta, Georgia."

They shook hands. Nancy forced a smile. "Oh, isn't Lila from Atlanta?"

"She certainly is, certainly is," Peter gushed. "In fact, she's my sister. It's too bad Lila and Jack missed the field conference. My, how we experienced the blessing of God down there! But then someone had to meet you folks. In retrospect, I wish it had been me."

"Well, sit down," Andrew said, pointing to the chairs around the dining room table. He could feel the tension.

Peter must have detected it too, for he got right to the issue. "I understand you have experienced some disappointment since arriving, Andrew."

Searching carefully for words, Andrew said, "A disappointment, yes...more like a betrayal...we spent months telling people about the work of the mission press—how it had a new building and needed new equipment...."

Gordon Muir interjected, "Andrew, I'm sorry. You obviously got misleading information from our Canadian office. I considered calling you last week, suggesting you wait until we had a real need for you."

"Last week?" Nancy exploded. "By last week, we had already left."

Gordon flushed and looked at Peter.

Andrew placed his hand on Nancy's arm. "Based on that misleading information, I talked my old employer into contributing a four-color press and I brought my most prized possession—a Gevaert graphics camera. They're on their way here with our household things. But there isn't even room to install them in that hole you call the press room."

"We'll have room someday. Maybe you can help raise money for the new building," Peter suggested.

"No. I think we should resign. Admit we misinterpreted God's leading in our lives, and go home."

"And apologize to all those good people who supported us," Nancy added.

"No. Don't do that. We can use you here. There is great work to do. We need people in most departments. You can work part-time at the press to spell Gordon off. When that new equipment comes, we can find a better place to install it, and then you'll be able to fully use your artistic and graphic skills."

Andrew stood up. "I'm an artist, not a pressman. Give Nancy and me a day or two to think and pray about it."

The visitors left. The cloud of gloom blackened and settled even lower.

Not ten minutes later, John and Edward burst into the house with such energy it cut quickly through the gloom still gripping their parents.

Edward spun around on one toe, like a ballet dancer gone berserk. "Man, that was wild, really wild! Just three days in Africa and the ruddy thing nearly killed me."

"It didn't nearly kill him," said John as a crooked smile broke across his face.

"It did so. Did so! Did so!"

"No Mom! No Dad! It scared him, but he was at least three feet from getting killed."

"You didn't even see it, so you don't know what happened—."

Nancy's mouth gaped open and seemed stuck there so Andrew waved his arms in front of the boys and cut in with, "Stop it, boys. Tell us what happened."

"I did so see it. I was running along the path through the field, saw it curled up on the path, and jumped over it. My dozy little brother stopped to pick it up."

"But I didn't pick it up. It uncoiled and looked me in the eye. I ran just a second before it could start spitting."

Nancy finally got control of her vocal chords. "What are you two talking about?"

"A cobra, Mom. A real, live, African spitting cobra. And it didn't nearly kill Eddie boy. When it saw him it slithered off into the tall grass."

Both parents sat still for a long moment. Andrew felt an icy feeling run down his back. Finally, Nancy said, "Boys, this is Africa. Be careful."

John looked toward Andrew. "Dad, have you ever seen a cobra?"

"No, Son, you have something on me. But I really don't want to meet one."

John turned to Nancy. "Mom?"

Her brow wrinkled and she nodded. "I think we might have, although I'm not sure I can tell one kind of serpent from another. I think two of them left the house just before you two characters came bursting in."

Andrew felt his mouth gape open. He managed to stammer out one word, "Nan-Nancy!"

During the next few days, in an attempt to make a decision, Andrew and Nancy visited many of the missionaries of God's Word Mission. They discovered discouragement, apathy, and tensions between the missionaries and their leaders. But their spirits rose when they found two couples who radiated joy, who loved their work, and who praised God for calling them to the mission.

When Jack and Lila suggested they join them on Sunday to attend a local church in the white area of Roodepoort, they declined, thinking they really should visit an African church, but didn't know how to go about it.

On the Wednesday of their first full week in South Africa, they sat alone in the lunchroom of the mission building following tea break.

"Some of these people," Andrew said, "these so-called missionaries, need a lot of help, but not the kind I'm prepared or able to give."

"But Andrew, some are dedicated, wonderful people."

"True."

"But I still believe we should go home."

Neither heard the approach of a middle-aged African woman. She sat opposite them and through sparkling black eyes studied them carefully. With a voice pitched low and in musical tones, she said, "I couldn't help but overhear. Maybe you should go home."

Andrew stared at her in stunned silence.

"My name is Mumsa Makunyane. I work in the translation department, fixing the bad translation work done by missionaries. I'm a Zulu."

Taken aback by this unexpected approach from an African woman, neither Andrew nor Nancy thought to introduce themselves.

"I know who you are," said Mumsa. "Everybody talks. I have also watched you going from one missionary to another, asking for advice. Tell me, did you come here to work with black people or white people?"

"African people, black people," they answered in unison.

"Then talk to us about your problems. Don't make decisions without consulting us. If we want you to stay, we'll tell you."

"How do we go about that?" asked Andrew.

"Don't make a hasty decision. Go to Mr. Fowler and ask him to get you permits to enter Soweto. Then come to my church on Sunday. My husband is pastor. We like missionaries who identify with the people. If you don't have a car by then, we'll come and get you in the church's Kombi."

"We'd like to come," said Nancy. "But we could ride out there with one of the other missionaries."

Mumsa laughed, a sound that rippled upwards from somewhere deep inside, slowly rising in volume and pitch until her ample body shook to the same rhythm.

"No," she said, beaming, "you will not likely do that. Most of them go to the white churches in Roodepoort or Johannesburg. Whether you have the permits or not, we'll come for you this Sunday. No one will notice."

Andrew nodded. Mumsa took it for agreement and said, "Be ready at nine o'clock Sunday."

Andrew and Nancy said little on the long walk back to Honeyball. As they neared the house, Andrew said, "I think we should stay for now. Maybe we do have something to offer."

"If that's what you want, Andrew, I'll stay."

"I think that's what God wants. But I'm sure this won't become a lifetime commitment. We'll do well if we can last through our first five-year term, let alone come back for a second."

Eight

Gordon Muir and Andrew sat in Gordon's glassed-off area at the end of the press room. In his fifties and somewhat overweight, Gordon had a slightly crumpled look, as though his body and clothes had come from the same tailor. Piles of papers and books on the desk and shelves carried the same imprint. Andrew liked Gordon, in spite of his deep disillusionment about the situation.

Andrew's eyes swept the room, finally stopping on Gordon. Thoughts continued tumbling through his brain, summing up Gordon: middle-aged, middle-class, and middle-of-the-road.

"Andrew, I saw you talking to Mumsa," Gordon said. "She is a fine person, as is her husband Thomas. But they often take radical positions on issues—not always in accord with mission policy or practice. So just be cautious until you get a better feel for things here."

Nonplussed by Gordon's comment, Andrew murmured, "Ah... okay."

Gordon leaned forward in his chair. "We need to talk about your assignment here. As I explained, we don't have enough work in the mission press to keep you busy. And about the only graphics work involves a few paste-ups and the occasional task helping other missionaries create posters and promotional material. So I'd like you to look around the other departments to see if you can find something to do until things start happening around the press. I would think we can begin to expand in a year or two if Hamilton-Jones succeeds in raising the money for the new press building he promised you."

Gordon seemed to relax, as though exhausted by his long speech.

Andrew nodded. "I've looked over the printing we're doing and think I could improve things by changing the layout or format of most pieces. We often use inappropriate fonts and don't always use graphics or photos in a way that would make the product more appealing. I think I could keep myself busy for six months in that way—then maybe spend about half time in the press until we get new facilities."

"That sounds like an excellent plan," Gordon said. "Put together some sample layouts and we'll talk to the other departments about sprucing up their stuff."

He began to shuffle a stack of papers, signaling the end of that part of the conversation.

"Oh, before you go, I do have two other things to mention. We have a practice here to assign new missionaries to weekend ministries for their first month on the field. After that you make your own decisions. I suggest you take your boys to a local church in the white community. That way they can get established there, because I have you booked to preach in an Indian church for the next three weeks. They called us asking for a speaker because their pastor is ill. The East Indian township, Lenasia, is just a few miles out of town. I have a map here for you."

Gordon pulled a photocopied map from the middle of the stack. "I've written the details on the back."

Andrew frowned. "How will I get there? I may not have a car by then."

Gordon reached into his desk drawer, withdrew a key, and held it out to Andrew.

"I'm sorry. I should have thought of that sooner. The press has an old Kombi. You can use that until you find something."

As Gordon returned to his papers, Andrew stood to leave, but hesitated. "You said you had two things?"

"Oh, yes, yes. We have a number of young African women who work for the mission and find it difficult to travel in from the township every day for work. So we assign them to missionaries' homes. They live in the *ekhaya* or servant's room. The missionary supplies them with food and the room in exchange for a few hours' work. They do the dishes in the evenings or housekeeping on Saturdays.

"We have one new one who will need accommodation. Lucy starts work the month after next. Talk it over with Nancy."

With Nancy? Andrew had instant concerns about Nancy's attitude to another woman in the house.

72

"I'll talk to Nancy," he said.

They had always wanted a daughter, though never expecting one fully grown. On the positive side, she could make contact with the African community that seemed otherwise difficult in apartheid South Africa.

After leaving Gordon, Andrew headed for Mumsa's desk to tell her the visit to the African church they had planned would have to wait a few weeks. By that time he hoped he would have his own car.

"What on earth is it?" Nancy asked as she looked at the car Andrew had just driven into their driveway.

"It's an Austin 1800." Andrew grinned as he stepped from the driver's seat.

"I thought all Austins were little like the one across the road," she said, pointing to a small two-door model. "This thing with its flat nose and wide body looks like an English bulldog."

Andrew threw open a rear door. "My artistic personality tells me it looks great. And see all the room inside—it'll hold six full-sized people, yet it's small on the outside. It's ours if you like it. Take it for a spin."

Nancy wasn't sure. "Why does it look so...odd?"

Andrew pulled up the hood to reveal the engine. "It has a transverse engine—meaning the engine sits sideways compared to most cars—that's why it has such a short nose. It also has front-wheel drive. The mechanic told me that every car will be built this way in 15 or 20 years, but I find that hard to believe."

Andrew tossed her the keys. "Quit frowning and try it out."

Nancy hadn't driven more than three blocks westward along Ontdekkers Way when she said, "Andrew, I love it! Let's keep it. It's better than anything we've ever had."

They turned away from the built-up area and into the country with the big-little car gliding along at highway speed.

"Our own car again." Nancy bubbled with excitement. "I'm almost feeling like this is home. I don't mind that we had to wait so long for it."

"And when we got our things from Canada in January," Andrew said as he placed his hand on her knee, "it was almost like having a second Christmas."

"Hey! Get your hand off my knee. I need that leg for working the pedals. This thing isn't automatic, you know. Actually, Christmas in a strange place without our things and with different customs, just wasn't Christmas. Imagine having a barbecue and going swimming on Christmas day."

"A *braaivleis*," said Andrew.

"A what?"

"A *braaivleis*. That's what South Africans call a barbecue."

But Andrew's mind wasn't on the barbecue. As his thoughts went back to the Christmas pool party Jack and Lila had thrown to introduce them to many of the other missionaries, he recalled the admiring glances from the men and the envious expressions on the women's faces when Nancy appeared in a two-piece swimsuit. He knew some wondered how that homely little Andrew had captured a beauty like that.

Andrew himself had never found a good answer to the question he assumed ran through other men's minds. The thought of Nancy in her swimsuit, coupled with that touch to her knee, sent a surge of testosterone through his system.

Would her excitement over the car make her receptive? He wondered. *Would she cuddle up to him tonight?*

Nancy seemed to have less carnal ideas in mind as she swung the car onto a side road to turn around. "Sunday we finally get to visit the African Church," she said.

As they moved back onto the main road, Andrew nodded. Their stint at the Indian church had lasted weeks longer than planned. He wondered what they had gotten into. It had kept them away from learning more about Africans.

Nancy broke the silence. "We did get one good thing from the Indians—a liking for curry."

"Nancy, you amaze me. At the same time you skillfully shifted through those gears like a sports car driver, you read my mind."

The following Sunday, Andrew and Nancy drove to a large African church in the heart of Soweto. Mumsa met them as they got out of the car and said, "Follow me."

Andrew kept her in view as he and Nancy weaved through the crowd toward the back of the cinder-block church building. Mumsa shooed away a group of teenage boys and girls sitting on a bench against a back wall.

"Sit here," she said, "One on each side of me. That way I can interpret so each of you can hear. Those kids should not sit here. I told them to go to their own sides."

Andrew watched the crowd as people continued filing into the building. The African men all sat to the left, the women on the right. Adults filled the rear third of the building, with teens ahead of them and children at the very front.

"We sit separately. It's the way we do it. But we save the back two rows for visitors and married couples who want to be together. So you aren't breaking any rules by sitting here," Mumsa explained.

People continued entering and squeezing onto the benches, always making room for one more.

"You put ten people where we would seat only five!" Andrew whispered to Mumsa.

She grinned back. "The service is about to begin."

The murmur of voices dropped, but Andrew could see no one preparing to lead the service. Pastor Thomas Makunyane, Mumsa's husband, sat on the men's side. Three latecomers slipped into an overcrowded row. The church became silent.

To Andrew and Nancy's complete surprise, Mumsa threw back her head and in a rich mezzo voice filled the building with the first line of a Zulu hymn:

"Hlengiwe-limnandi lelizwi..."

Even before she finished the line, 300 voices began thundering out the words.

"Hlengiwe-limnandi lelizwi,
Hlengiwe ngegazi leMvana,
Hlengiwe ngomusa nothando:
Ngenziwe sengaba umntwana."

Bass, tenor, soprano, and alto meshed in superb accord. Andrew and Nancy had sung in church choirs, but had known nothing like this. Thundering, powerful voices beat together to fill the room with rich four-part harmony. Mumsa's voice soared above them all, leading, encouraging, worshiping in song.

By the third line of the hymn, Andrew had taken control of his emotions, recognized the tune, and joined in with the English words:

"Redeemed through His infinite mercy,
His child, and forever, I am."

They sang three more choruses and hymns, passing the leadership around the room as though guided by some mysterious order known by all.

Pastor Thomas prayed, gave announcements, and invited the people to give. The congregation, starting with the children, filed to the front to drop money onto a plate as they sang, "*Bonga, Bonga, Bonga...*"

Mumsa, Andrew and Nancy went last, singing the words in English, "Thank you, thank you, thank you."

Following three more choruses, Pastor Makunyane returned to the front and stood behind a table. A middle-aged African man stepped up beside him.

Mumsa whispered, "Thomas will preach in Zulu, while Daniel interprets it into Sesotho. I'll try to keep up by giving you the English words."

Without warning, Pastor Makunyane fired out a line in Zulu, his powerful voice filling the room. Clicks, a characteristic of the Zulu language, shot from the roof and sides of his mouth like rifle reports. Before he finished the first sentence, Daniel began his interpretation in a softer tongue that, to Andrew, sounded much like French.

76

They continued with tremendous energy, overlapping each other, yelling, commanding, whispering, pleading. Daniel, standing slightly behind the pastor, mimicked every gesture. When the pastor imitated a woman walking seductively along a railway platform, Daniel copied every hip-swinging wiggle, looking like the second person in a chorus line. The congregation echoed its approval with bursts of laughter.

Toward the end of the sermon, Pastor Makunyane began to describe the crucifixion. He grabbed Daniel by the wrist, spun him around, and bent him backward over the table. His free hand imitated a hammer pounding nails into the hands of the prostrate Daniel cum Jesus. Even as they dramatized the scene, the pastor preached rapidly in Zulu while Daniel, lying on his back, fired Sesotho interpretation toward the ceiling.

As the awful scene grew in intensity, Daniel's voice became husky and tears running from his eyes fell on the table. Ultimately a great sob choked off his words.

Pastor Makunyane released Daniel and stepped back, freeing him to spring to his feet and wipe tears from his face. The staccato preaching with its echoing interpretation resumed as the two pleaded for everyone to come to the cross of Jesus.

Gripped by the drama of the event, Andrew heard very little of Mumsa's whispered English interpretation. He glanced sideways to see tears rolling down Nancy's cheek.

Andrew guided the Austin along the road from Soweto to Roodepoort. Neither he nor Nancy spoke for the first few minutes. They barely noticed the Peugeot taxi lying on its roof in the ditch, the litter that had collected along the fence, or naked teenagers swimming in a pond.

Andrew spoke. "We did our stint with the Indian Church, but I think we have found the place God would have us—in the African church."

"We could just go to the church in the white community like most of the other missionaries. But I'll go where you want," Nancy replied.

Andrew slowed to steer around a big pothole. "We can visit the other churches for their evening services, but I really believe God called us to work with Africans."

Nancy sat quietly for a moment. "Well, the really good news is that we are making this trip in our own car."

Andrew braked sharply to avoid an elderly man on a bicycle who swerved into their path. He wore a tattered suit jacket, a woolen cap, torn pants, and mismatched shoes. A bottle protruding from a brown-paper bag rolled back and forth in the bicycle carrier.

Nancy screwed up her face. "Drunk."

"Nancy, we'll have to find ways to communicate the gospel to these people."

"Isn't that the church's responsibility? You're an artist. I'm a housewife and part-time mission office worker. I could never talk to most of these people. Mumsa is okay, but most of them are so, so different."

"Maybe the new African girl will help us learn to communicate. She's due next week."

Nancy screwed up her nose. "Are you sure about next week? They said she'd be here last month."

Andrew laughed. "Have you seen anything work out exactly as this mission says?"

"And Andrew, don't you go sounding like one of those old missionaries by calling her 'the African girl.' Her name is Lucy."

Eight days later, Andrew sat at a trestle table at the back of the conference room on the top floor of the mission building waiting for the other missionaries and African workers to arrive. Nancy had chosen not to come; she found Monday-morning staff meetings a drag.

Today Andrew would present his plan for improving the format and appearance of mission documents. He had prepared 20 overhead slides suggesting changes in everything from letterheads and envelopes, to correspondence courses, from standardized posters to time sheets, from booklet covers to appropriate page layouts, from a chart recommending proper use of the mission logo, to individual business cards. On a table near the door, he had piled photocopied examples of his designs, enough for each person who would attend.

The missionaries drifted in, taking seats around tables toward the front of the room. Most of the Africans gathered at two tables near Andrew.

As he watched the 40 or so people arrive, his mind raced back over the difficulties and disappointments of the last few weeks. They had faced such a whirl of activity, getting used to a new country, registering the boys in school, opening bank accounts, and shopping for a car. Everything demanded five times the time and energy required in Canada.

A movement caught his eye. A tall, slender African girl paused in the doorway, then moved toward the table occupied by the African workers. She walked with a gentle hip-swing that brought the word *feline* to Andrew's mind. Each foot landed on the floor directly in line with the other. She wore, with all the class and grace of a fashion model, a form-fitting dress with a geometric print of gold and red on a green background.

As she arrived at the table, Andrew heard a babble of conversation as welcomes and introductions swept round the table. He looked away and immediately sucked in his breath; he had stopped breathing during the passage of this black goddess. He felt a patina of red creeping up his neck. He covered his face with his hands as though in a moment of contemplation or prayer, hoping to hide his embarrassment.

Still berating himself for reacting to another woman with feelings he had vowed to reserve for Nancy, he barely noticed the field director open the meeting. Peter Fowler's words came through to him like the signal from a fading radio station: "Welcome...all of us...now something new...Andrew Heath now has a presentation for us."

Now fully alert, Andrew scooped up his overhead transparencies and started forward. But his mind was still on that gorgeous creature and he almost forgot his well-rehearsed speech.

For the next 15 minutes he felt in a daze and hoped he had covered everything. He remembered saying, "Because people can read it more readily, we must use a serif, or Times Roman, font for all the main copy, employing sans-serif fonts only for headlines. And never use more than two or three females, I mean fonts, on each document..."

He also talked about the mission logo. "We have a good logo—it needs no change. We can easily reproduce it in any size, big enough to fit a billboard or small enough for a business card. It is our identity, our signature as an organization. It should never change. This overhead proposes the size, position, and color."

He paused and glanced at the new African woman, imagining the geometric designs on her dress transforming into mission logos of all sizes. He looked back at his notes and had difficulty finding his place.

To himself he said, *Andrew, keep your mind on the task at hand,* and then stumbled on with his presentation. "Er...headquarters has specified the Pantone number for the shade of blue in the logo, but I found six distinct shades on various documents..."

He also touched on general layout. "Our book and correspondence course covers show no unity. They should bear a family resemblance as this slide suggests..."

Andrew closed the presentation by saying, "You'll find photocopies of these overheads on the table at the door."

As Andrew stepped aside, Peter asked, "Do you have any reactions to Andrew's presentation? Any questions?"

Andrew had noticed Fran Jamieson squirming in her chair. He knew very little about this wiry oldster, except that she had spent 40 years on the field with God's Word Mission teaching Zulu to new missionaries, had never married, and had a reputation as a curmudgeon.

Her bony wrinkled hand shot up and stood out like a dead branch on a flower-covered Bougainvillea tree, fingers writhing in the air to attract attention.

"Yes, Miss Jamieson," Peter said.

She spoke without rising. "I don't think God blesses our attempts to dress up letterheads and carry fancy business cards. We came here to proclaim the gospel through the written word. I'd be just as happy if we went back to the old Gestetner machine."

Andrew choked back a retort.

Peter glanced about the room and asked, "Any other questions?"

80

Andrew saw a few people exchange sly grins. Most looked down to avoid his eyes. Then Jack Ferguson volunteered, "I don't think we should push ahead with these changes. We can talk about them in our own departments, maybe form an interdepartmental committee."

Peter nodded. "Let's move on. Thank you, Andrew."

Andrew returned to his seat feeling like a burst balloon. He heard very little of the proceedings that followed.

Finally Peter's voice broke through to him. "I did forget one little item. We have a new employee in our midst. Lucy Bambisa will be working in our translation department and staying with Andrew and Nancy Heath. Stand up, Lucy, so we all can see you."

Andrew looked up to see the gorgeous African woman rise to her feet. He gulped and felt his heart skip a beat.

When Peter dismissed the meeting, Andrew hesitated between manning the table bearing the sample layouts and meeting Lucy. He didn't have to make the decision. Lucy stepped up and extended her hand.

"Hi, I'm Lucy. I believe you have a room for me at your house."

Andrew held her hand briefly, long enough to note its warmth and feel a tingle in his own. "G-good to meet you. Yes, yes we do. Nancy, the boys, and I have been looking forward to your coming."

She flashed a smile at him. Her dazzling teeth stunned him for a moment.

When he recovered he said, "I've got my own car now, so I can take you and your things to the house when you are ready to move in."

"I'll see you then," Lucy said, turning to go.

As he watched Lucy's retreating figure, his mind began playing tricks. Like a multi-media presentation running amok, it dissolved between pictures of Nancy and Lucy in various circumstances and wearing everything from swimsuits to formal gowns.

Andrew shook his head, fired off a prayer for forgiveness, and turned toward his table. Most of the African workers, including Lucy, had gathered around it to pick up samples. While he watched, the missionaries filed past the table and out the door. Only Jack and Lila stopped to pick up materials. Few others even looked at them.

As Andrew gathered up the remaining pages, Gordon Muir said, "I guess we have a little convincing to do."

Andrew nodded. "The African folk liked what I proposed, but not the white missionaries."

Gordon looked even more crumpled than before as he said, "Unfortunately, the white missionaries make all the decisions."

Andrew kept his thoughts to himself. *Do we really have a place here? Surely, Nancy will want to leave.*

He decided to write to Steve and get his opinion, but at the same time wondered if Steve had found a place where he could serve God effectively.

Book Three

Nine

Steve had just finished morning devotions in his bedroom when he heard a knock at the door. A dark-skinned bald-headed man with thick glasses stood in the doorway.

"Good morning, Doctor. I am Doraiswami, the new hospital manager."

"*Vonacum-ai-ya,*" Steve said, with his palms placed together.

"Well, well now. You speak such fine Tamil. You know how to say hello to a man in such a respectful way."

"I only know a few words," Steve said. "Since I'm going to stay here, I must take many lessons."

The screen door squeaked as Steve opened it and Doraiswami entered.

"It is about your appointment as Chief Surgeon that I have come to talk to you, sir. You must move into a house as soon as possible."

"Move? But I like it here. My room has excellent cross ventilation, and I love the food served in the Guest Quarter's dining hall. Where do you suggest I go?"

"Two houses are currently vacant. You may have your pick. Each has two bedrooms."

"But I'd be lost in a big house, and would have to spend all my time looking after it. You must know I don't have a wife."

"What about Nurse Johnson?" Doraiswami's eyes twinkled.

Steve's nose wrinkled up like a rabbit sniffing rotten cabbage.

"You'll have maid service and a gardener provided, of course."

"I'll take the maid and the gardener, but leave out Nurse Johnson. Perhaps in time I'll find someone else. Some of your South Indian women are extremely attractive." Now it was Steve's eyes that twinkled.

Doraiswami responded with a foreboding look. "Now be ever so careful on that one, Doctor. Emotional entanglement with foreigners is frowned upon. Laws have been passed about color and caste to make all things possible. But social customs remain. Please, I implore you. Remove all such thoughts from your mind."

"So I really must move?"

"If not, what place will the next surgical trainee have?"

"He can go into one of the big houses. It's a great idea. Perhaps if he has a family, it will be better there for him than for me?"

"No. There would be too many fans. These vacant houses each have four fans. A trainee must have only one. I myself have a house with three fans. I am not worthy of a house with four. But you are—and so you must take it."

Steve found this whole situation quite amusing. He wondered how far he could push it. "How about two fans, and replace my bicycle with a car?"

Doraiswami's face flushed.

Steve realized he had overstepped the bounds. "Sorry, I shouldn't give you a hard time. You are doing your job, and very well, I must say. I was joking about a serious matter. I shall start getting ready to move this evening."

"You could speak to Dr. Rajalingam about a car. He will occupy Dr. Aiyapandian's house after the air-conditioner I have brought from Delhi is installed."

"Oh, so he's worthy of an air-conditioner, is he? I thought that was supposed to be for the mice."

Doraiswami gave him a puzzled look and turned to walk away. "One more thing," he added. "You will need to interview for a new secretary. Victoria is having a baby and has resigned her post."

Steve watched Doraiswami go down the path between rows of white jasmine and yellow-flowering oleander trees, thinking, *So much depends on your station in life here.*

He decided to look into the operating room on his way to chapel, to see if it looked any different, now that he was in charge. As he pushed open his front door and stepped onto the veranda, the morning sun shone brightly into his eyes and warmed his cheeks. He took a deep breath and smelled again the scent of jasmine that he loved so much.

He was happy these things had not changed.

Just outside the O.R., he saw a scruffy looking woman wearing a drab, dirty sari sweep dog droppings into a small bucket. How glad he was he didn't have to do these things. At home, everyone did whatever was necessary. But here in India a doctor wasn't supposed to pick up a broom or even make a bed. It would deprive someone of a job and upset the order of things. It was a strange world, and he had to adjust to it.

The next scene was beyond adjustment. He watched in horror as, barefooted, this same woman carried her bucket and broom into that inner sanctum of sterility which had so recently been placed under his command.

"Stop!" he screamed at her in English. "You can't go in there."

Hearing the foreign outburst she spun around and gracefully bowed her head in his direction. She could have no idea what it meant or to whom it was addressed, but even the sweeper seemed to realize he was more important now than he had been just the day before.

She placed her dirty bucket on the operating room floor and began sweeping. Brother Yesudasan, R.N., Operating Room Supervisor, looked curiously at Steve from the other side of the room.

"Is there a problem, sir?"

"Problem?" Steve blustered. "Can't you see? She's filthy. She comes in here to make things cleaner and brings in more dirt than anyone could remove with a bucket of detergent."

"But she is a sweeper. Sweepers sweep. That is what they do. Surely, you would not ask nurses to sweep the floor. Who then do you suggest should do it?"

Steve took a deep breath. He had been given an important job to do and feared he might mess it up if he was considered too much out of step with Indian culture. But there had to be some changes that were right and proper.

"Suppose," he began, "someone came with a dirty wound, oozing pus and maggots. Who would clean the wound?"

"That would be a nurse's job. We do it in the septic O.R."

"I fully agree. The human body must be treated with such respect that only a nurse is good enough to care for it in this way. Now in this room, human lives are put back together again. Don't you think this room should be treated with similar respect?"

"When you put it that way, sir, it makes perfect sense. I shall try to get the other nurses to see it your way, sir."

Steve smiled. "You don't have to call me *sir*."

"Alright, s... doctor. I shall inform the others of your feelings about that also."

"As your name is Yasmina Ali Khan you must be a Muslim," Steve suggested.

He'd been interviewing women most of the afternoon, trying to find a suitable secretary to replace Victoria. Of the seven applicants, this last one seemed the most qualified. She was also quite beautiful.

"That might be a reasonable conclusion, sir—"

"Please don't call me *sir*. Call me Dr. Manley."

"My father, Ali Khan, is a devout Muslim from north India. My mother was a Hindu before she married him. I was raised to respect all faiths. When I attended a Christian boarding school, I accepted Jesus into my heart. I am a truly born-again Christian."

"Your mother must have been South Indian. That would explain your delicate facial features."

Yasmina blushed. "You are so perceptive, doctor."

Steve knew he had gone too far again. *But how beautiful she is,* he thought, *with that dusky tinge to her smooth, café au lait skin, the tiny nose with slightly flared nostrils, full ruby lips...*

"You have the job," he said, inwardly not daring to explore how far he might like her duties to extend. "I hope you can start tomorrow," he added.

"I shall arrive promptly at 7 a.m.—Dr. Manley." Her eyes twinkled as she looked directly at him for the first time. "I am extremely grateful for this opportunity."

Yasmina rose from her seat, pivoted, and passed through the doorway, all in one graceful motion. Her hips swayed from side-to-side as she glided down the hallway. Steve thought about his old movie-star flame, Ava Gardner, and wondered if she ever wore a turquoise sari like this one?

Rajalingam gently opened the door and put his head inside the animal lab. "Thomas, are you in there?"

"Over here, sir. Don't be afraid to come in. The mice won't bite you."

"I've come to talk to you about your research."

"There is precious little to report. With no air conditioner, we simply can't get leprosy bacilli multiplying the way Aiyapandian claimed, although I do everything else exactly as he did. I thought you said you would be getting a large air conditioner from Delhi. Didn't Doraiswami go there to collect it?"

"That wasn't for the lab. It was for my house. I've moved the south Asia headquarters here so I can keep a closer eye on things. I'm not used to the heat like you southerners, and there is much work to be done."

"But what about the lab research? It simply cannot be done if the skin temperature of the mice rise above 36.5 degrees Celsius."

"Thomas, you should spend less time in the journals and more time reading the newspapers. Today's *Hindu Times* claims that some Dr. Jorgansen in Sweden has just done everything Aiyapandian was babbling about a few weeks ago. So this lab work you're doing isn't necessary at all. You could spend your time more profitably treating the sick."

Thomas put one hand on each side of his head and shook it from side to side. One word at a time, and very slowly, he said, "If we can grow the bacilli in mice we can test other drugs to see if we can find something better than DDS. That is what this is all about."

Rajalingam frowned at first, but then bobbed his head loosely from left to right and back again, indicating he understood. "Your idea has some merit. We'll save money on the closure of the south Asia office in north India. I'll see what I can do."

Within a week of his appointment as Chief Surgeon, Steve was surprised to find, at the end of a busy operating schedule, a portly but distinguished-looking gentleman waiting in his office. He had a wisp of curly gray hair that embraced the back of his shiny brown skull, and a grin a mile long.

This man had come without an appointment and Yasmina had apparently ushered him in without objection. Perhaps she wasn't as smart as he'd thought. He decided he must straighten her out on policy.

As though she had read his mind, Yasmina appeared in the doorway that separated his office from hers. Steve noted that today she was wearing a tangerine sari that swept from her shoulders down across her full bosom to end at a pair of delicate ankles.

My, but she is gorgeous. How can I not forgive her for this small mistake?

"Dr. Manley," she said, flashing him a smile, "this is Professor Srinivasan. He is anxious to meet you, and has intimated to me that he has something to say that will be of great interest to you."

Steve smiled back at his new secretary and offered his hand to the professor. "How good of you to take the trouble to come here, Professor. I believe you are the Professor of Orthopedic Surgery at Madras University. I've heard many good things about you. Please be seated."

"It is because of my association with Madras University that I have come today to make your acquaintance. You may be knowing that Dr. (Mrs.) Aiyapandian has, until her untimely departure, occupied the post of Assistant Professor in my department. It was her custom to visit us once per month, to hold seminars or teach the residents about leprosy surgery. I have come today with the request that you might take her place with respect to these duties."

"Could this be done in English? I've not yet had a chance to learn Tamil."

"English is what we speak. Even the staunchest nationalist will

90

agree that the British have united India and made one nation out of many. They have done it in two ways: with a network of railroads and a common language."

"But the patients, for the most part, only understand Tamil."

"That will not be a problem. You would not be seeing patients, only doctors and medical students."

"I think I would like to give it a try. And the remuneration...?"

"Ah now, there I must confess we have a difficulty. Government regulations forbid us hiring a foreign national. Payment would imply you were hired. We must offer you only an honorary appointment. But you would have free use of the library and such-like amenities. You would also be granted a parking space at no charge."

"Well now, that would not be necessary. You see I do not have a car."

"Why then, we shall send someone to collect you. Would the first Thursday of every month be convenient?"

"That sounds fine. I hereby accept an appointment as Honorary Assistant Professor."

Professor Srinivasan blushed, and for the first time his smile faded. "For one so young, an appointment as Lecturer would be more appropriate, would it not?"

"Whatever. It's your department."

The two men shook hands and the professor left.

Steve felt uneasy about the whole encounter. He suspected the real purpose of this man's visit to Janglepit was to develop a relationship that put him three rungs on the ladder below him. *Do they consider me such a threat to the establishment that I must be boxed in like this?*

After supper, Steve sat on the upstairs balcony of his house and reflected, as he often did, on the day's activities. *Surely, this appointment matter could have been completely handled by correspondence. Did the professor have to come here, look into my eyes and see my reaction when he told me I don't really measure up to the stature of the woman I've replaced?*

The evening air was sticky. Somewhere it was raining—but far away. In Janglepit the sky was clear. Venus shone brightly above a low range of old mountains behind which the sun had dropped an hour ago.

A light-brown lizard wiggled along the top of the balcony railing, stopped to gaze a moment at Steve, flicked his tongue to catch an insect, and disappeared into the night.

That lizard got what he wanted, and I suppose the professor got what he wanted—some political end no doubt.

Steve recalled that St. Paul had once said that the three greatest gifts are faith, hope, and love, but the greatest of these is love. He fantasized about Paul coming to India and in his mind heard him say, "There are three great problems here: poverty, disease, and politics, but the greatest of these is politics."

During the next six months, Steve relished his work in the operating theater and enjoyed the challenges he found in the clinic. At the end of a busy day, he returned to his oversized house to relax, alone.

As he went up the two steps to the veranda that almost circled the house, his maidservant stood with the screen door open and a big smile on her dark brown face.

"Hello, Sakundra. It's always nice to come home to this cool house. You keep it so clean and tidy."

"It is my duty, Doctor. Have letter for you."

Steve took the letter, examined the postmark, and frowned. "They've had this letter sitting in Dhanbad for nearly a year. That's disgusting!"

The letter from Andrew told about racial tension in South Africa and the devastating effect it could have on the missionaries' attempt to communicate the gospel. As Andrew tried to show the love of God to those he came to serve, he was surprised to find himself physically attracted to a young African woman. The letter ended with...

Steve, it is good I have you to talk to about this. The missionaries here see everything in terms of black and white, but always from the white point of view. It is so hard to know what is best to do in this situation. We could dissociate ourselves from this group and come home, but that wouldn't help these African people at all. So for now at least we'll stay on and try to make a difference.

However, being here raises another problem. I worry about the natural attraction I have for Lucy. I mustn't let my emotions get out of hand. Please keep us in your prayers,
    Andrew

Steve folded the letter, held it between his palms, bowed his head, and said a silent prayer for Andrew.

That night he had a vivid dream, a weird dream in Technicolor. He was watching an Indian movie at the local cinema. A bevy of scantily clothed women wiggled their hips as they pranced across the screen. The one in a turquoise half-sari looked familiar. As the camera moved in for a close-up, he recognized the face. It was Yasmina. From that point onward, he couldn't get his eyes off her figure as she undulated and gyrated across the screen.

Slowly he became aware of a woman sitting to his right, about his own age, perhaps a few years younger. She had beautiful, rust-colored curly hair. Her soft emerald green eyes shone like lights in the darkness, mysteriously drawing him closer. It had to be Jennifer, the love of his life, the one who had refused to come with him to India. He put his arm around her, moved his mouth close to hers—and woke up.

Ten

Steve's front garden was a patch of light brown sand. Two trees commonly called "Flame of the Forest" thrust their limbs skyward. From these dark gray branches, the old leaves had recently fallen, pushed off by young buds bursting forth from their hiding places deep within. Before new leaves were visible, orange-red flowers erupted, wafting a tantalizing aroma to the many insects buzzing around in search of food.

The scent of spring hung in the air.

"How beautiful is the handiwork of the Lord," Steve said aloud as he made his way to the chapel before morning rounds. Hope blossomed within him, a hope that he could really accomplish something very useful here in Janglepit, a scientific development that would improve the lot of leprosy patients worldwide.

Doctors came regularly from various parts of Asia for surgical training. During the first three months, he gave each new trainee his undivided attention in the operating room. They watched him operate and did the same procedures under his guidance. Then at level two they would assist the senior trainee and learn from him, before finally moving on to become the next senior trainee in the last third of the nine-month program. "See it, do it, teach it"—a policy Steve had been taught when learning orthopedic surgery in America—seemed to work well in India.

During the chapel service he began to reflect on these accomplishments.

His research on sensory nerve regeneration had been less successful than he'd hoped. He learned how to transplant an island of skin from one finger to another while preserving its blood and nerve supply. The transferred tissue was in each case three or four centimeters long. It brought sensitivity to that location, but he'd hoped the nerves in the island would sprout and grow into the neighboring insensitive skin. Well, they did, but for just a few millimeters.

At Washington University, St Louis, Missouri, a few years earlier, a research worker he knew had isolated a substance that makes nerves grow. At his request, she had sent him some of this "nerve growth factor." But when he injected this into the skin around the island it didn't seem to help. This chemical only worked on nerves to blood vessels, not the kind that carried sensation. He had to find another way.

Sitting in chapel on such a lovely day, a brilliant idea formed in his mind. At least, he thought it was brilliant. He recalled that when a nerve to a particular area of skin was cut, the surrounding nerves sprouted branches that grew into this numb skin. His "brilliant idea" was that there must be some kind of chemical messenger, a nerve growth factor that attracts these little sprouts to this denervated area, and this must be a different nerve growth factor than the one developed at Washington University.

The first stage would be to denervate skin in rabbits, and then try somehow to isolate the chemical that this skin produced. He would need a lab. Thomas controlled the only one. He must think of a successful way to approach him.

Lost in thought, he failed to notice the others leaving, or the small boy who approached him until he heard, "Dr. Manley, everyone waiting on ward."

"Thank you," he replied. He rushed off to the male surgical ward to begin morning rounds—and found Yasmina waiting for him just outside the entrance. The sun lit up her dazzling white sari. She looked like an angel on top of a Christmas tree.

Steve choked when he saw her and silently prayed: *Lord, help me concentrate on the work you have for me to do today.*

Yasmina, as usual, took notes to type on the patients' charts as Steve, two trainees, and the ward nurse went from bed to bed. This day there seemed to be more flies than usual. One man had developed a post-operative infection.

Steve sighed. "An infection like this has never happened before. It must be the flies. This year they're worse than usual. There are too many large open windows. We need screens."

He turned to Yasmina. "Take a note to Doraiswami. Better yet, I'll go and talk to him."

After rounds, he crossed the courtyard and entered the administration building. The always-jovial, soft-spoken Hindu hospital manager had become a close friend. A personal chat was more appropriate than a formal memo.

Steve barely reached the doorway when Doraiswami said, "Come in, Steve. You are always welcome. What can I do to help you?"

"Put screens on the wards to keep the flies from infecting my surgical cases."

"Oh, oh. Money. Have you discussed this with Dr. Rajalingam?"

"I can't expect much from him. He won't even let me learn Tamil. Says a surgeon just needs to cut, not talk. That's why I've come to you for help. Perhaps he will listen to you."

"I'll try. Now about the language. You must learn it. You seem to have a natural gift for languages."

"He tells me there are plenty who can translate for me. But I want to communicate directly—hear the cry of the soul, and respond."

"Ooh. Now you are a poet, isn't it? I think he may be a little jealous of you. So he doesn't want you to speak Tamil better than him. Any South Indian language is as hard for a north Indian to learn as it is for the English...sorry...Americans. Why don't you ask one of your translators to teach you," he added with a twinkle in his eye. "But don't ever tell, don't even hint, it was my idea."

Before the end of April, pale green screens covered all the windows, and screen doors closed the doorway openings. Perhaps he could make a difference here, Steve thought. Far beyond helping individual patients, he might also raise the entire standard of hospital care. Who knows? Perhaps one day he could even become hospital superintendent. Rajalingam could go back to north India. Life would become very pleasant.

But his joy quickly evaporated when, one hot afternoon in June, he made post-op rounds with Yasmina and two surgical trainees. He almost screamed when he saw the beautiful screen doors that kept out flies propped open by chairs placed against them.

"What is this all about, Yasmina?" he asked.

"It is getting warmer now, Dr. Manley. The screens block the wind that keeps them cool, so they open the doors."

"But it's so unsanitary! Don't they know anything about flies and germs?"

"Most of these villagers have only one or two years of schooling. They only know about leprosy germs, and that is because they learn about them here."

"Yasmina, if I could talk to them, explain things in Tamil, I could teach them so much, even find out what motivates them. But without knowing Tamil I feel like I'm shut up in a tower, dropping notes to people and never getting any reply. Every missionary must learn the local language. It's just common sense."

"And you can learn Tamil."

"No, I cannot. Dr. Rajalingam says that because I've already spent four months in language study, I have no right to take time off now to learn Tamil. But it was Bengali I studied. That's no use here. Sometimes he makes me so angry."

"I could teach you, Dr. Manley. I'd be happy to stay for an hour after work each day."

"What a wonderful, kind woman you are, Yasmina. I'll see that you are rewarded in some way for this."

Taking her aside where others could not hear, he added, "But what you do will have to be kept a secret, just between us. Perhaps you could come to my house and my serving-woman could make us tea."

"Thank you, Doctor, but coming to your place of residence would not be appropriate. People would talk. I believe that working overtime at the office would be more acceptable."

Rajalingam sat in Aiyapandian's former office with his feet up on the desk, puffing a cigar and reminiscing. He was moderately satisfied with the way things were going and had developed a workable timetable. He spent the cooler morning hours in the old medical superintendent's office taking care of hospital business. In the afternoon, he retired to the house the Aiyapandians had lived in, where he'd installed the new air conditioner in one of the spare bedrooms. This and the room next to it had become the office of the Field Secretary for south Asia of the Mission to the Outcast. There, in what for him alone could be called the cool of the day, he supervised almost one-quarter of the mission's hospitals worldwide.

It was very clear to him that in Janglepit, the elaborate spending of recent times had to be sharply curtailed. There was no money now for the detailed record-keeping system that had been so highly praised by the W.H.O. Without the extra funding from Aiyapandian's three research projects, the budget had been cut by 60 percent. His was a responsible job that required a cool head. Air conditioning was essential for him and certainly not a luxury.

He thought about putting in private beds, calculated savings if he reduced the quality of the food, and worked on a scheme to discharge patients earlier. User fees and less expensive drugs were considered. He picked up a pen and wrote a note to Thomas, suggesting that he get some research funding or see his privileges curtailed.

Thinking of research reminded him of Steve. *It's a good thing we have this American surgeon to carry on the project Mrs. Aiyapandian began. That pays for fifteen staff members. But he's so arrogant and opinionated.*

His reverie ceased abruptly when he heard a knock on the door frame. He quickly put his feet under the desk as a face appeared in the open doorway.

"What do you want this time, Steve? Another request to make this place more like home for you?"

"Perhaps I just came to say hello, sir." Steve grinned. "In fact, this place is very different from my home, as you must know. But I've learned there are many ways of doing things, and most of them work quite well. But having flies on the wards isn't one of them. Oh we can't kill them. They could be reincarnations of somebody's relatives. And it's too hot to keep the screen doors closed. So we need fans. That's what I came to talk to you about."

Rajalingam began to boil inside. He resisted the urge to throw a paperweight at Steve. After three deep breaths he said, "I knew it was a crazy idea to install all those screens, but I did it to please you. These patients of yours don't have screened windows in their villages. Yet somehow they survive. We are a nation of tough people. We don't need all those amenities you foreigners indulge in."

Steve smirked and shrugged. Rajalingam could call him a foreigner but he knew what he was. He was an American. They were the foreigners.

"Perhaps now," Rajalingam added, "you can see why we do things the way we do. Our civilization is thousands of years older than yours. We've developed ways of doing things that work. Then you come along and upset it all. I hope this will be a lesson to you. Now run along. I have serious work to do."

Thomas was looking down a microscope when Steve entered the lab with a surgical trainee.

"I hope you don't mind us coming in like this," Steve said. "The door was open. I have a special favor to ask, and also I would like you to meet our new team member. Ragout is a doctor from West Africa. He wants to learn more about what you're doing."

He turned to a tall, slender African wearing horn-rimmed glasses. "Ragout, this is Professor Thomas."

"Hello, Ragout." Thomas reached out and shook hands.

"Normally, as Dr. Manley knows, you could not just walk in. This lab would be under lock and key with restricted entry to avoid germs being brought in. But we don't have any thymectomized mice at the moment."

"Why thymectomized?" Ragout asked.

"We remove the thymus gland in newborn mice so that they will not develop natural immunity to any germs. Then we can inject them with leprosy bacilli and see the effect of new drugs. But they would also be susceptible to all infections, so you couldn't just walk in here."

"How does that work, Professor? I mean what does the thymus gland really do?"

Thomas looked up at the ceiling. *Where did he go to school? I wonder.*

"It's a key player in the immune system," he answered. "You know some of the white blood cells are called lymphocytes, I suppose?"

"Oh yes," Ragout said, "we learned that in the first year of medical school."

"Well, there are two types of lymphocytes, B and T. When the T lymphocytes circulate through the thymus gland they are programmed to identify certain things as foreign, things the white cells should attack. Now normally in all mice and in 95 percent of humans, these T lymphocytes learn to attack leprosy germs and destroy them. But if we remove the thymus gland we can inoculate these mice with leprosy bacteria and later determine which drugs are most effective."

"Oh," said Ragout, "I like it. Now this is real science."

"There's more," Thomas said. "This strange disease will only grow in tissues that are at 36.5 degrees Celsius. So we must keep the mice in an air-conditioned environment—and right now, we don't have a large enough machine to do the job."

"But leprosy grows well in people in a hot climate," Ragout said. "How is that?"

Thomas was speechless for a moment, long enough for Steve to enter the discussion.

"Body temperature is 37 degrees Celsius, too hot for these bacteria to multiply in *most* people. There are exceptions. Now in a cold climate, with most body parts well-covered, the skin temperature comes close to the body core temperature. But when it's hot we expose more skin, which is cooled by sweating, cooled enough for leprosy to thrive in the arms, legs and face, exactly where the nerves are attacked by this disease."

Thomas looked surprised at Steve's explanation—the viewpoint of a surgeon—one he as a pathologist had never known or even considered.

"Wow!" said Ragout. "Now it all makes sense."

"Professor Thomas," Steve said, "I see you have a lot of unused space and I wonder if I could do some animal experiments here."

"Just exactly what did you have in mind?"

"No one has ever been able to restore sensation in skin whose nerves have been destroyed by leprosy. Yet we know that to some extent the neighboring nerves do try to branch out and get into this damaged area. I think that there must be some chemical signal coming from the skin itself, directing the nearby nerves to sprout and send branches to it."

Steve leaned against a counter, his eyes swept covetously over the unused space, and he continued. "As a pathologist yourself, you must know that another pathologist at Washington University discovered a substance that promotes nerve growth. But this nerve growth factor, as she calls it, only works for the nerve fibers to blood vessels, not those that carry sensation. I think that if I cut skin nerves in a rabbit's leg, the end organs of those nerves might elaborate a messenger hormone that would attract the cut nerves to reconnect with them. We could use this sensory nerve growth factor to enhance recovery of lost sensation in our patients."

"Now Steve, what could an orthopedic surgeon possibly know about nerve growth factor? You are way out of your league on this one."

"You obviously don't know, Professor Thomas, that when I was in training, I spent a year doing research with the world's greatest authority on electromyography. Together we published the first paper on the development of the neuromuscular junction in mammalian fetuses. We worked with rabbits. I am an expert on the development of rabbits and that is why I want to do this work on rabbits."

"Well, we shall have no rabbits in this lab! They could bring in germs that would easily kill my mice after their immune systems are disabled to allow the growth of leprosy bacilli. I intend to do a lot of research with these little friends, and I can't let you jeopardize it."

Steve recognized that, just like Rajalingam, Thomas was jealous of him and for this reason would not allow him to work in even one of the many empty rooms in the lab. Afraid he might say the wrong thing, he held back his words, turned, and left without even saying good-bye.

It was lunchtime but he had no appetite. He trudged slowly up the path that led to his house at the base of Elephant Hill. As he entered the front yard, his eyes focused on something he had never really thought about before. It was the chicken coop he'd never used.

His mind raced into overdrive. He could keep his rabbits in the chicken coop. And turn one of his unused bedrooms into an operating room. Then Yasmina could come to the house and take down a record of operative procedures. He'd never been able to get her into his house. This might be a way of getting to know her better.

Thoughts of Yasmina restored his appetite.

By October, the intense heat of the summer was slowly melting away. Yellow flowers on the oleander tree brightened Steve's spirit as he walked up the path to what he now thought of as his home. He began to whistle. A small brown bird joined in the chorus. The smell of spices told him his lunch was ready. Unknown to him, something even more enticing awaited him as he entered the living room. On the table beside his favorite chair was a letter from Andrew.

September 23, 1972

Dear Steve,
I can't believe that I haven't written to you for over 1 1/2 years, even though you have written me quite often. Time has flown by at a tremendous rate. We are just approaching our hottest season of year as your weather is cooling off. We are south of the equator and you would say our world is upside down. I agree, but in a different sense altogether.

When I think back, I can't help but wonder if we made the wrong choice only days after arriving. The general missionary attitude here leaves me cold.

However we have experienced some bright spots, some real

blessings from God. You'll remember how I told you about the African girl the mission assigned to us. I shouldn't say girl. That's a no-no here, I should say, young woman. Anyway, the mission expected us to put her food on a tray and send her to her room. That smells of racism.

The rest of the letter told of problems faced and problems overcome, or mostly so. Andrew's wife, Nancy, seemed to be the backbone of Andrew's life, a stalwart warrior who always seemed to know which side was the right side in the struggle against evil.

Good for you, Nancy, Steve mused as he folded the letter. He saw in Andrew and Nancy's mission board the Pharisees Jesus had condemned, and in Nancy the spirit of Christ, who had said to those who claimed to be His followers while treating others as inferiors, "Depart from me, I never knew you."

Eleven

Christmas in South India was very different from Christmas in Minneapolis. Without snow, it didn't seem like Christmas at all. No spruce or pine trees grew within miles of the hospital. Instead, the staff erected a limb of a cassia tree, whose sagging branches could hardly support the colored paper ornaments fastened on them. Santa would soon arrive, riding in a cart drawn by men dressed up as reindeer. To any decent Hindu, Jesus was just one more of all the many gods they had. Some said there are more gods in India than people. But Santa was special to Hindus and Christians alike. Everybody loved Santa Claus.

It was the coolest time of the year. The temperature at night could dip to 70 degrees Fahrenheit even though Janglepit was just eight degrees north of the equator. It was cold enough to turn off the fans in the daytime and put blankets on the beds at night. With ocean on both sides of this part of India, summer and winter temperatures were less extreme than further north. Acclimatization was much easier and, as Steve approached his second winter in India, he looked upon 80 degrees as pleasantly cool.

But visitors would not find it so. Steve remembered how hot he had felt when he first arrived here after Bengali language school in Darjeeling. This added to his concern about the visit of a team of research investigators soon to come from America, worried they might find it too uncomfortable. It was so important to make a good impression. This team of experts would decide whether or not the large U.S.-funded research project he'd inherited from Mrs. Aiyapandian could continue.

The Indian Council of Medical Research had expressed concern that money donated by America to fund Indian research would actually be used for research conducted by an American. It seemed to them that this implied Indians were not capable of doing this research. The U. S. government had agreed to investigate and was sending over a surgeon, a physiotherapist, and a statistician. If what they found made them unhappy, the funds would be withdrawn and offered to another Indian organization.

For reasons unexplained, the visit was delayed until mid-January. The weather was dry, not yet hot, but growing warmer day by day.

Just before their arrival, news came that prohibition in Tamilnadu had been lifted. Until then, alcohol had been available in many states of India. But Tamilnadu was one in which only those with special permits could imbibe. These were available to foreign nationals. Steve had been offered such a license when he arrived, but declined it. He didn't want to stand out in the crowd as one who did things society disapproved of. It was not a stance that would bring glory to God.

Now the social climate had changed. It was time to order some beer. It might prove useful if the project investigators became thirsty.

When they did finally arrive, after a few hours' rest, Rajalingam put on a special party to welcome them. This "function," as they liked to call it, began at 5:30 p.m., just as the sun was ready to take its quick plunge below the horizon. In the center of a grove of coconut palms, eight rows of chairs had been placed, with a ten-foot square space in front of it for those who preferred to sit cross-legged on the dry sandy ground. Beyond this was a small raised platform with five chairs on it. A 70-foot wide banyan tree provided the backdrop. From its green-leafed branches, gray, pillar-like roots descended, some of them eight inches in diameter.

After Rajalingam welcomed the visitors and introduced to them important staff members, a group of musicians took the stage to entertain everyone with traditional Indian music. They played the sitar, hand organ, flute, and a pair of drums called a *tabla*. Stars shone in the dark moonless sky above. A sweet fragrance drifted on the gentle breeze.

A young woman rose up to speak, her dark brown skin contrasting beautifully with her lime green sari. She spoke in Tamil, with a young physiotherapist translating her words into English.

"I would like to sing for you a song I have composed. It is a sad song about a happy place. Sad because now that I have leprosy my family has disowned me, and I can never return there. But in the end I have found joy, for now as a staff member here I have a new home, a new family, and the joy of serving God in this place. So I have written this song that begins with joy, becomes very sad, and returns to a joyful sound. It is in Tamil, but the music will tell the story."

Steve recognized her as the sweeper he'd forbidden to work in the operating room, and wondered if he'd been unkind to her.

The music was at the same time sweet and mournful. It began on an upbeat, with loud joyful sounds on the drums and organ, and then switched to a minor key as the sitar and flute took over the melody. Gradually the tempo increased. Softly the hand organ re-entered the scene. The beat of the drums grew louder and louder as the song reached a triumphal conclusion. The audience broke into applause. Steve clapped louder than most. Tears filled his eyes.

After 30 or 40 minutes of music like this, the chairs were cleared away. Everyone sat cross-legged on the ground to eat. Each was given a banana leaf to use as a plate. After the hospital chaplain said grace, servers came along with large buckets of rice and three varieties of curry.

"We have forks and spoons," Rajalingam announced, "if anyone wants them. But food always tastes better when eaten with fingers."

Steve was sitting on the ground next to Dr. Mark Evans, the surgeon on the investigating team.

"Let me get you a fork," Steve said.

"Thanks, but no need. This is my third trip to India and I quite agree with Rajalingam, the food tastes better this way."

"But, pardon me, Mark, you're using the wrong hand to eat with."

"I'm left-handed. Is there a problem with that, Steve?"

"It seems that in India they use the right hand to eat and the left to wipe their bottoms. So eating with the left hand is considered a dirty habit."

"Well, thanks for that bit of cultural advice. I wash my hands more often in a day than 99 percent of the rest of the world. But I can't afford to let anyone think I'm dirty."

"Creating a good impression is most important, Mark, and I hope you'll get a good impression of us. Tomorrow you'll be with me in the O.R. for the first operation, a new procedure I've devised to restore the natural curvature of the hand. The surgical trainees you met tonight will do the rest of the operating. We'll join the other members of your team for ward rounds and finish the day giving all of you a report on what we've done, and plan to do, with the money your organization has so generously given us."

"I am prepared to be impressed, but the rest is up to you."

Rajalingam accompanied the team on ward rounds the next afternoon. He tried to make it look like this was a frequent occurrence for him, but the fact was, he'd never been on the wards before. He looked at the screened windows and shook his head in disbelief.

"Kind of warm in here, even in January, isn't it?" Mark said.

"A person gets used to it in a year or two," Steve replied. "People born here find it so cold they sometimes wear scarves around their necks at this time of year. The hot months are April, May, June."

"Gosh, what do you do then?"

"Keep the doors open," answered the ward sister, "and let the breeze blow through."

Steve grimaced. Rajalingam raised his eyebrows.

"That must let all the flies in too," Mark said. "Why don't you install some fans?"

"No money," was Rajalingam's quick response.

"Read the fine print on the contract," Mark said. "It says that up to 10 percent of the $15,000 you get each year can be allocated to necessary capital expenses. That would include equipment like this. After witnessing such brilliant surgery this morning, it's clear to me that keeping flies off the wards is essential to the success of such innovative work."

Steve and Rajalingam exchanged glances. Steve's lips formed the words, *I was right.* Rajalingam turned his head away, as if he hadn't seen.

Immediately after lunch they reconvened in the training room auditorium. The research investigation team said they were quite satisfied with the outpatient rehabilitation program started by Mrs. Aiyapandian and continued by Steve after her departure. There was much concern expressed about the reduction in quality of record-keeping. But, while this created problems regarding medical compliance and leprosy control, the rehabilitation research project was not compromised.

Steve's plan to enhance recovery of sensation impressed them the most. He told them he had 24 rabbits in his chicken coop, and that next week he planned to start trying to isolate a sensation-specific nerve growth factor. All the team members were excited about this research, and he was assured the funding would continue for the next three years. There was even the possibility of a new contract for five years beyond that if all went as anticipated.

When the meeting ended, Steve said, "Come to my house for some refreshment."

"I could sure use a drink," Mark answered. "You wouldn't by chance have some ice-cold boiled water, would you?"

"We don't keep our water in the fridge," said Rajalingam. "It gets too cold to drink. The Indian way is to boil the water and store it in a semi-porous earthenware jug. Evaporation on the surface makes the water cool and pleasant to drink, never cold."

"I've got ice-cold water," Steve said, "but not boiled. I guess I've developed immunity to all the local bugs. How about some ice-cold beer?"

"Wonderful," they all said at once. All except Rajalingam.

Sneering he said, "You've got beer on mission property? I'll discuss that with you later."

The visitors departed that evening. Steve's joy was tempered by misgivings over Rajalingam's parting shot.

Before heading off to bed he went over to the chicken coop to thank his wonderful rabbits, whose existence had helped so much to maintain the research funding.

He found them all dead.

Twelve

The air conditioner on the operating room wall hummed reassuringly. Though it was just February, the temperature outside was increasing daily. But heat was forbidden in this hallowed area. Surgery required an atmosphere characterized by "no sweat."

"You're doing very well, Cherian," Steve said to his young Indian surgical trainee. "I'm going to leave you to finish up this operation with Saing. You can teach him some things you've learned from me so that, when he returns to Burma, he'll be as good as any of us. I have a paper I must finish writing for the American Journal of Hand Surgery."

As Steve stepped into the change room, Yesudasan, the operating room supervisor, approached him.

"Doctor, may I tell you about one of my villagers, Poothu? He has a problem."

"Of course. Perhaps I can help."

"He has been afflicted with leprosy, but a good boy—."

"Brother, you are a Christian and a trained nurse. You know leprosy is not God's punishment, as many villagers think."

"I know. And leprosy is not the problem. His disease, thank God, has been arrested with DDS therapy. In fact, he was one of your first surgical patients. He is so grateful to you and this hospital that he has dedicated his life to helping others with this dread condition. So he asked Dr. Rajalingam to give him a note saying that he would be hired to work in our village outpatient program if he successfully completed the government-sponsored training program for paramedical workers. And he got such a note. See, here is the note."

Steve examined it carefully.

"But," Yesudasan continued, "when he completed his training, Rajalingam said there was no job for him, that he just gave the note so he could get the training. Even Ramamurty agreed there is no vacancy for a PMW just now."

"Ramamurty? What's Ramamurty got to do with it? He's the hospital chaplain."

"Not for long, Doctor. Next week he's being moved to Chitoor as general supervisor of paramedical work in the whole district for which we are responsible to the government."

"Then who will be the chaplain?"

"No one seems to know that. Doctor, could you please speak to Dr. Rajalingam on behalf of my friend? I have taken the liberty of asking Poothu to wait to see you in your office. Would you be so kind as to speak with him?"

"Of course I shall speak to him, and try to help him. I'll do what I can but the outcome may still be the same."

Steve had a brief discussion with Poothu. He couldn't believe it was true till he heard it first-hand. Even then it sounded implausible. He knew people often got the wrong idea and when things are not written down, there can be misunderstanding. But he had just seen it in writing—a letter signed by Rajalingam guaranteeing this man a job.

He felt his neck getting warmer as he crossed the open area between the inpatient block and the administration building. He paused at the open doorway leading into the office marked *Medical Superintendent* and said, "May I have a word with you, sir?"

Rajalingam looked up from a letter he was reading and smiled. "Steve, you really impressed those Yankee visitors. Perhaps it's not so bad to have one of their kind here. Not only did they advise the Indian Medical Council to let us continue your research, they have increased the budget by 20 percent."

Steve was doubly pleased. It had been a long time since he'd seen this man smile.

"Too bad about your rabbits though."

"What do you know about my rabbits?"

Steve had always suspected that possibly Rajalingam, or even Thomas, especially Thomas, had sabotaged his research.

Squinting his eyes, he pushed his face toward Rajalingam as closely as he dared. "Do you know who killed them? They had no marks on their bodies. It was not a wild animal that killed them. Someone must have poisoned them."

"Steve, that hill behind your house is full of rocks where snakes hide. We have cobras in India that kill by spitting poison into the eyes. That's what killed them. You need to get yourself a mongoose to kill all the cobras."

Steve slumped into a nearby wicker chair, wondering if it could be true. But in India, all strange things seemed possible. At the same time he knew Rajalingam was a liar. He had long suspected this but now he had proof.

It was a few minutes before he could speak. Rajalingam just stared at him, as though waiting for a response.

"Sir," Steve said, "I came here with two questions. First, I would like to know who will be the new chaplain if Ramamurty becomes Paramedical Supervisor."

"We won't have one for a while. Ramamurty's needed for a much more important role and is well-qualified for the job. We need to develop a practical, inexpensive record-keeping system. The number of DDS-resistant leprosy cases in our area has increased dramatically, and the government has threatened to withdraw its 10 percent funding if we don't do something about it, or at least explain the situation."

"But sir, the chaplain conducts ward services for the patients who can't come to chapel. If this part of our witness is missing, how do we preach the gospel to them? Why are we here, if all our good works are not followed up by preaching of the gospel?"

"Steve, our specific mandate is, as Jesus said, to 'heal the lepers.' Didn't he also say that if we failed to preach the gospel 'the very stones would cry out'? Well, let the stones cry out till we can afford a chaplain."

Steve felt his blood pressure rising. *Have I come to this place to serve the Lord, or to work with the Devil?*

It was getting very stuffy in this office. He would have to complete this errand quickly and get out, into the sunshine, out where the air was fresh. It seemed to him there was a very bad odor in this room.

"Sir," Steve said, "the second matter concerns a local villager, one of my former patients. He trained as a paramedical worker on the understanding you gave him that there would be a job waiting for him here on completion of that nine-month program."

"So what is the problem?"

Steve rose out of the chair and glared at Rajalingam. They were about the same height and stood nose to nose. "After promising him a job you told him there wasn't a job for him, that he should look elsewhere."

"So? I did him a favor. Without that note he couldn't get the training. He'll find a job."

"You lied to him. That's what you did. We are here to represent Jesus Christ, and you, on behalf of our Lord, lied to one of those for whom He gave His life!"

Rajalingam slammed his fist on the table. "Who set you up as a watchdog over me?" Softening his tone, he added, "Steve, what has happened to you? The first time we met, you were so anxious to please. I thought you were a team player. But now you're a crusader—always trying to change things. Why? Why?"

"I didn't know what was going on then, sir. But now I do and I don't like what I see. Yes, I am a crusader. I'm on God's side in a battle, to quote St Paul, 'against spiritual wickedness in high places.' Whose side are you on?"

Rajalingam stared at him in apparent disbelief.

Steve stared back. Without another word he turned and walked out. He knew he had spoken the truth, and deeply regretted he'd had to say it. There was no going back.

Outside the administration building the sun was shining. Here the air was fresh, warm, and dry. But the ugliness of this scene remained in his mind. It had to be neutralized by something of beauty, and urgent action was needed to control this bizarre situation. Yasmina could help with both. He would write immediately to Head Office in London.

Rajalingam is the man in charge here—and he's totally out of control.

"Why Dr. Manley, you look as though you have just lost your best friend."

"I can't say I have. But I do need a friend. Yasmina, would you be my friend?"

She smiled at him in such an endearing way that he thought she would say yes. But for what seemed like half an eternity she remained silent.

When those full ruby lips parted, Steve heard her say something totally unexpected. "Jesus is my dearest friend, and I want to share his friendship with you."

Yasmina reached out and took his hand in hers.

Steve was shocked. First Rajalingam, now this. Indian women don't hold hands with men in public, even with the one they love. But this was not in public. Unaware of it, he had closed the door after entering Yasmina's office.

"When I take notes for you on ward rounds," she said, caressing his hands till his spine tingled, "I see how you hold the hands of the patients. What a blessing this is to them, particularly to the older women. They long to be touched. But no one will touch someone with leprosy. These women are so longing for love they will accept the advances of any man. All they want is for someone to touch them. That is why the women's ward must be locked at night."

"Really? I never knew."

"Oh, yes. My father tells the story of when he was young and lived for a time in West Bengal. There was a real scandal. During the war with Japan, there was an American naval base near Calcutta. The sailors used to sneak into a nearby leprosarium and violate the women."

"No! I can't believe this."

"Oh yes, but it is the truth. One night one of them was caught by a missionary, who threatened to report him if he ever returned. He did return, but this time he brought a gun. He crept up to the missionary's bedroom window and shot him while he was saying his prayers."

"Oh! This can't be true."

"Dr. Manley, are you alright?"

"I think I've had too many surprises today."

Placing her left hand on his right shoulder she fixed her eyes on his and said, "We all need love. What I want to do for you, dear doctor, is to give you love—from Jesus."

"Yasmina, you truly are an angel of the Lord."

As he looked into her chocolate brown eyes, they sparkled in the late afternoon sunshine. "Would you, could you please, call me Steve?"

"I would like to, but I cannot."

Her dark eyes glistened more intensely as tears welled up beneath her light brown lids. Long moist eyelashes fluttered to clear them as they spilled out and rolled slowly down her tan-colored cheeks, leaving in their path thin streaks of black mascara.

"I have been given to another, and cannot really be the kind of friend you want."

Steve handed her a Kleenex.

She wiped her eyes, blew her nose, and added, "Besides, you are my boss. I have a duty to my family and a duty to my employer. I have no life of my own. I am here only to take dictation."

"Then please type this letter," Steve said, swallowing the lump in his throat. "It's to the General Secretary in London."

Thirteen

Steve spent the month of May, as usual, in the hills. This year he wanted to be as far away from Janglepit as he could. He headed for a place in the high foothills of the Himalayas north of Delhi called Landour, Mussoorie. At 6500 feet above sea level, he was not quite as high as he'd been in Darjeeling, but the ascent had been much quicker. His legs felt weak as he got down from the bus.

The paved road ended just beyond the village of Mussoorie. On the last stage of the journey, the track to Landour was so steep that no motorized vehicle could climb it, not even a Jeep.

Nor could he. The thin air left him exhausted after just walking along the flat areas. His chest heaved when he climbed a small hill. It seemed impossible to carry on. Three men passed him with a grand piano on their collective heads. It was upside-down, each head at a corner of this somewhat triangular load. Bells on their ankles tinkled to warn people to get out of their way.

As he struggled up a forty-five degree slope, four men came running toward him. Together they carried a wooden chair large enough for two people, supported by two long poles. Each man had the end of a pole on his shoulder.

"Sahr!" one of them said, gesturing to Steve that he should get on board.

He knew he would have to be carried up in this four-man rickshaw. It was most embarrassing, but there was no other way. It reminded him of ancient scenes of royalty, of a king sitting in a wooden chair carried on the shoulders of four slaves. As the men struggled to climb a particularly steep part he felt so disgusted with himself that he wanted to throw up.

After nearly an hour of climbing they stopped in front of a yellow cottage with white trim. When a wrinkled-faced elderly Tibetan woman smiled at him he knew he'd arrived. Steve was happy to pay the men twice what he'd been told the fare would be.

We foreigners can't live in India without servants. We must be the weaker race. It was the first time he'd thought of himself as weak or foreign. He noticed his fingers tingling and wondered if he might be getting mountain sickness from so rapid an ascent. He was tired and his head ached.

Steve smiled back at the old woman when she offered him a bed to rest in.

"You sleep till food come," she said. "*Amara nom Sangria.*"

"You said your name is Sangria. You speak Bengali? "

"No, Hindi. Bengali sometime same."

Steve flopped onto the hard bed and closed his eyes. The buzz in his head made sleep impossible. He was glad when told it was dinnertime.

Golden beams from the setting sun filtered through the steam rising from a plate of goat curry and vegetable *biryani.* The smell of cinnamon and coriander made him hungry. But after a few mouthfuls he'd lost his appetite.

"Very good food," he said to his servant woman, "but somehow I can't eat it."

"Okay," Sangria replied. "Always like this first time. Mountains not like foreigner. First make suffer, then better."

Steve went outside and sat on the front porch. A chorus of chirping tree frogs greeted him. The sun had set, and a dramatic panorama lay before him. The southern sky was a curtain of stars that descended to a dark floor, an ancient sandstone mountain range called the Siwaliks. In the foreground lay pinpoints of light from the civilization he'd just left behind. Streetlights in the steamy villages far down the steep mountainside twinkled like stars. The town of Dehra Dun was more than half a mile below him—almost straight down.

Cool mountain air filled his lungs, giving him a sense of peace and serenity. His spirit revived and his headache almost disappeared. But his legs still felt wobbly. "Tomorrow I want to see the Himalayas," he told Sangria.

"Humph," she said.

❦

Next morning he went out on the back porch. The house was built on a narrow ridge that allowed an unobstructed view in both directions. To the north he could see a long thin white line that stretched from left to right along the horizon.

Could this be the Himalayas?

He went to a small shed at the back of the garden to ask Rajpoo, Sangria's husband. The door was half open and Steve edged his way in. A pungent haze filled the room. Rajpoo sat cross-legged with an opium pipe in his mouth. By the glazed look in the man's eyes Steve knew there was no point in asking the question.

Sangria told him what to look for.

"See that long line of white?" She pointed to the serrated horizon Steve had seen.

"If moves, is cloud. If not move, is mountain."

It would have to do. He stared at the horizon for ten minutes, long enough to convince himself he'd seen white things that didn't move, and went back indoors to write a letter.

May 4, 1973

Dear Andrew,

Here I am in north India. The political climate in Janglepit has turned sour. I find the administration lying to people and putting the financial needs of the hospital ahead of the spiritual needs of the patients. I wonder if they believe in the same Lord that we are trying our best to serve. I'm taking my annual holiday as far away as possible. Here at least the air is clean and the view is refreshing.

When I was in Darjeeling, at the opposite end of the Indian Himalayas, I went to Tiger Hill to see Kanchenjunga, the world's third highest mountain. But I didn't really see it. All I could see was the mist surrounding it.

I should have taken the six-day hike in the Himalayan

foothills to get a glimpse of Everest, like many other language students did. But I was so keen to learn Bengali that I stayed behind to work on my lessons. Now in Tamilnadu, what good is it to me?

The road in the valley before me, as I look northward toward the Himalayas, passes to the right to reach Tibet. It was the one the Dalai Lama took to India when he fled the Chinese invasion 15 years ago. As soon as I can, I'm going to hike toward Tibet, just to see how far I can get. But because of the altitude, I must acclimatize first.

To the south they have an interesting-looking bazaar, down the road in Landour. When my legs are strong enough to climb back up the steep winding path that runs between the village and my house, I'll spend some time there. It will be good exercise too. When I arrived here yesterday, I actually had to be carried up the hill. That's how steep it is, and how strong you have to be to live here. I tell you the people here are amazing!

God bless you, Andrew. Write when you can. Stories of your success will make my own difficulties more bearable.

Steve

Two weeks later, Steve felt strong enough for the hike. He began his trek at Happy Valley, a Tibetan refugee camp northwest of Landour. Smiling children ran to greet him with tiny hands outstretched. He'd come prepared and gave each one a pencil. They jumped and shouted words he couldn't understand.

"Thank you for helping our little ones."

Steve looked up to see a monk in saffron robes and shaved head approaching him. "Such small things seem to mean so much to them," Steve said. "And it means a lot to me to be able to talk to you. How wonderful it is for me to be able to carry on a conversation in English again."

"I have a Ph.D. in English from Oxford," the Tibetan replied, smiling. He was a little shorter than Steve and about the same age. "Please join me for a cup of tea. I will leave shortly for Tibet, but would like to thank you for your kindness before I go."

"You're going to Tibet? I'm hiking in that direction for the next two days. It's too far for me to walk all the way there, so I'll walk as far as I have time for, and come back by bus. By the way, my name is Steve Manley. I'm an orthopedic surgeon doing leprosy work in Tamilnadu."

"And mine is Loa Pang Dow. You can call me Lou. I'm off to teach English in Tibet."

They entered a small stone hut with a thatched roof and sat down on wicker stools opposite a gray oven that looked as though it might be made entirely of clay, or possibly cement. Without a word being said, a young woman placed two small brass cups before them.

Steve looked at the brown liquid with drops of grease swirling around on top and asked, "This is tea?"

"Yes, butter tea. We prefer adding gee rather than cream. It's a kind of butter so we call this butter tea."

Steve knew it would be yet another new experience for him in this land of never-ending surprises, and sipped it cautiously. It tasted as greasy as it looked, almost rancid, and was quite salty.

"Ah, very refreshing," he said, quickly adding, "is there such a need for English in Tibet that so highly trained a person as you should go there?"

"I could put a similar question to you. But if you will allow me to accompany you on your journey, we can discuss these things along the way.

"Wonderful! I'd love your company. You're not walking all the way, surely?"

"Oh no. I'm not as strong of body or spirit as is our Dalai Lama, to walk such a distance. It is more than 300 kilometers. But a short walk is good for the soul. Perhaps as we talk together we can learn from each other."

"Nothing I'd like better."

As they left the village, Lou attached a white cloth to a pole that held many more. "A prayer," he said, "for the soul of my father, who was killed during the Chinese invasion of our country."

Steve wanted to ask, *what good will that do?* but held his peace for fear of offending this gentle man.

Together they walked along the dusty road and over many hills, often with a steep hill to the left and a large canyon dropping away to the right. Each man carried a packsack with food, fresh clothing, and plenty of water. They planned to spend the night in a government-run tourist bungalow known to the locals as a dack house.

"I love the pine trees you have here," Steve said. "They are so slim, so straight and tall."

"They point upward to God," Lou replied, "so we call them *deodhars*, which means 'trees of the gods.'"

"You believe in one god or several?"

"Oh, there are many gods, I am sure. But they do not rule our lives as the Hindus think, and we do nothing to appease them. We say we are responsible for our own destiny. Buddhism is a philosophy that grew out of Hinduism, but we reject many of their beliefs, like the caste system."

"I'm glad to hear that."

"Some Hindu ideas we do accept. For example we believe in reincarnation, and that what we do in this life determines the future—just as I think you do."

"I don't believe in reincarnation."

"You believe in a future life in heaven, do you not? And are you not rewarded there for how you conduct yourself in this life?"

"To some extent that's true."

"And did not your leader, Jesus of Nazareth, teach many Buddhist ideas? Did he not say you should give to the poor, live a life of purity and discipline, be moderate in all things, speak well of all those who do right? We believe in these same principles."

"The practice of Buddhism shares much in common with Christianity. But one essential element is lacking. That is Jesus Christ."

"How could the Buddha know about Jesus Christ, born as he was four centuries earlier?"

"God won't hold that against him. But the only way we can please the one true God is by acknowledging Jesus as the Son of God and asking God, in the name of Jesus, to forgive our sin."

"I told you already, I don't want to please any god. I just want to live a good life, and that I am doing."

Steve realized their discussion had come to an impasse and said nothing for the next ten minutes. As the road went up a small hill and around a corner an amazing sight came into view: four bundles of sticks, each with two legs.

He put down his backpack and quickly pulled out his camera. As he stood ready to take a picture, the piles of sticks rolled off the legs, the legs became people, and the people began throwing stones at Steve.

Before he could get a picture Lou shouted, "Run for your life. These villagers are Animists. They think that if you have their pictures you also possess their souls. They intend to kill us."

"And I'll bet they can run like the devil they worship," Steve replied.

Though fearing for himself, he considered his camera more vulnerable but had no time to put it away. Camera in hand, he raced up the road and after ten minutes caught up with Lou.

"My legs may be longer than yours," he said, panting, "but my heart is not as strong. Let's sit down for a bit if you think we're far enough away now."

While they rested Steve brought up the subject of Animism and Lou began to explain it to him.

"These people believe there is a spirit in everything—not just in people and animals, but also in trees and mountains."

"Aha, so that's why my servant, Sangria, said the mountains were making me sick. She thinks of the mountains as living things that can do things to people, even take their lives."

"Yes and they do, don't they? That is why Buddhist Sherpas pray to the mountains before trying to climb mountain peaks like Everest."

"So," Steve chuckled, "they do want to please a god, the god of the mountain."

"No, no, no. The mountain is not a god but a spirit. And all we want to do is to be polite to all. To you, to the mountain, to all animals, to everything on this planet."

"Well, that's wonderful. I'm sure Jesus would approve of that attitude. But I think you are also something of an Animist. Do all

Buddhists believe as Animists do?"

"Not at all. There are many kinds of Buddhists, just as there are many kinds of Christians and Muslims. Those of us who live in the mountains believe a little more like animists than those who live in New York City. But I don't feel as they do about photographs. If you took my picture I would not think you'd captured my soul."

"Then I'd like to," Steve told him.

After he took Lou's picture they resumed their journey.

"Lou, you haven't told me much about your purpose in going to Tibet. Of course, it's not my business. But I'd like to know if that's okay with you. Are you going to live in a monastery?"

"Like you, I am a missionary, but to my own people. I'm not a monk though I may look like one to you. I intend to teach English to Tibetans just across the border. No one can predict when the Chinese will stir up trouble again. And when they do, many will flee to India. But life in a refugee camp should not be the goal. They must find good jobs to support themselves here, and English will be essential."

"But what about Hindi?"

"I know a little Hindi and will teach that too. But I don't have a Ph.D. in Hindi." Lou turned his head and smiled at Steve.

"Ha, you're joking of course," Steve said. "Look at me. I work in Tamilnadu and only know a few words of Tamil."

They remained silent as they climbed a steep gradient, but Steve's mind, as always, churned with ideas. He imagined this man with such a great heart and sense of humor would become a powerful missionary for God in Tibet, where Westerners were forbidden to enter, if only Steve could bring about his conversion. Then a doubt arose. Was he being too narrow-minded? Didn't Jesus say that whoever does the will of His father we should call brother or sister?

As they continued their journey, Steve told Lou about his reason for going to India. He also tried once more to win him over to Christianity, but Lou declined with extreme politeness. Both seemed happy to reach the dack house at the end of the day.

After hot food and a good night's rest, they were ready to go again. This day Lou did most of the talking, and Steve learned more than he really wanted to know about Buddhism.

124

"No doubt you have seen the Ganges River," Lou said.

"I crossed it on my first day in India. Took nearly half-an-hour in a hand-drawn rickshaw."

"Where we stop tonight you will see it again. It is but a few miles from the source, and not many feet across. Here we call it the Ganga River. Some call it Bhagirathi."

As evening drew near they came to a gurgling stream hardly more than 30 feet wide. Yellow-brown water, with tinges of green, poured across huge gray-brown boulders, leaving on the top of each a white deposit of lime.

"Why," Steve asked, "is the water so brown this far upstream?"

"It is melt water from the Gangotri Glacier a little north of here, and these Himalayan Mountains are made of sandstone. One day they will be washed away. The Siwaliks, south of Mussoorie, were once much higher than the Himalayas. Now they are so small we call them hills. Mountains are like people. They live, die, and are reborn."

Humph, Steve said under his breath, *there's that reincarnation again.*

On the far side they saw a small wooden shack with a corrugated tin roof. It was set back from the road up a steep incline. Closer to the road a man in a red robe sat cross-legged, facing the setting sun, meditating beside a large waterfall.

Their shadows reached far ahead of them as they crossed the wooden bridge. The rushing of water made further conversation impossible as they turned left and walked upstream to the dack bungalow.

Inside the building the sight was familiar: a stove against the far wall, two wooden bunks along each side, and a low table in the center surrounded by four wicker stools. But this time the food was less than appetizing. Though he disliked the greasiness of butter tea it did seem to warm his body. But the night that followed was bitterly cold.

About midnight, Steve could take it no longer.

"Is there an extra blanket?" he said, without really knowing whether the person in charge was even in the building.

A match flame lit up the darkness, developed into a lamplight, and moved toward him. A boy's face appeared above it.

"Problem?"

"Cold. Blanket *hai?*" Steve said in broken Hindi.

"No blanket."

"Hot-water bottle?"

"Will look."

Ten minutes later the light reappeared and the boy said, "Hot...water...bottle."

Steve reached out a trembling, grateful hand and took from the lad a square glass bottle. It was pleasantly hot. By the light of the lamp he read, *Johnnie Walker Red Label Scotch Whiskey.* It was indeed a hot water-bottle.

The food next morning tasted much better: brown rice, hot fresh-made Tibetan bread and some aromatic sauce to dip it in. Steve couldn't identify the ingredients but liked the spicy flavor. Breakfast was just over when they heard the honking of the bus to Mussoorie. It sounded quite far away. Steve quickly thanked his host, paid his bill in rupees (about one dollar U.S.), added a generous tip for the hot water-bottle, and said good-bye to Lou.

Before he could get out the door, though, it seemed the circus had come to town...an Indian circus playing Indian popular songs. An ancient rickety-looking blue bus came trundling down the road, its sound system at full volume. There were so many passengers that even the luggage rack on the top of the bus was full of people. A man in red, white, and blue pajamas stood on a window ledge outside the bus, hanging onto the luggage rack.

The driver waved his right hand out the window at the crowd standing on the road, telling them to get out of the way. Slowly the vehicle came to a stop, well beyond the expected place. Steve saw smoke oozing from the wheel rims, but no one seemed to care. *Doesn't look very safe to me. God help us.*

Though some got off, more got on. The only place for Steve was the luggage rack. No one asked for his fare. He just had time to scramble up the ladder at the back of the bus before it took off.

He managed to find a place where he could hold on with both hands, but this meant his head was over the edge. He had a good view of the side of the bus and the road below. Sometimes there wasn't very much of the road to see as the bus swung around sharp corners at high speed. Deep valleys filled most of his view many times. He fought to hold back his breakfast. Sweat dripped from his forehead.

When the road curved the opposite way, dust churned up by the wheels filled his nostrils. He would sometimes see a steep hill rising before his face. He knew then there must be a steep drop on the other side of the bus. There was no way of knowing if they were already over the edge.

Steve worried that the driver might take chances. Perhaps he didn't like his present life, and would be happy to end it so that he could be reborn. Steve had no intention of dying. He had many things to do in this life before entering the next.

In three hours they covered the distance by bus he'd taken two days to walk. He didn't die, but later wondered if in one sense he did, and was somehow reborn before the driver arrived at Happy Valley. His conversations with Lou had given him a new way of thinking about other religions.

Fourteen

On his arrival back at Janglepit Steve was pleased to find a letter waiting—an invitation to give the keynote address, November 1973, at a meeting of the Indian Plastic Surgery Association's annual conference in Bombay.

They wanted him to accept an honorary membership in recognition of his many contributions to the development of reconstructive surgery.

"Wow! Can you believe that?" he said aloud. "I'm an orthopod and they want to make me a plastic surgeon."

He knew that tendon transfers were in the domain of plastic surgeons in many parts of the world. Also, some of his work involved face-lifts and nose reconstruction to correct the deformities of leprosy that created such a social stigma. So in that sense it was logical—but still a great honor.

He decided to collect the results of his new operation to restore the natural curvature of the hand. He knew they'd love it. It brought the little finger to the thumb, allowed a five-finger pinch that was so essential when eating rice with the hand, and also gave a natural appearance to the hand.

Over the next three months he interviewed all the patients on whom he had done this operation to see how well they were doing. He wished he had a colleague to review the paper and give him some feedback. He was about to get some from an unexpected source, but for a very different reason. As he was writing the final paragraph, Rajalingam called him into the office.

"I want you to go up and welcome your new surgical assistant, Steve. He's just moved into that unoccupied building next to the swimming pool in 'A' Quarters."

"New assistant? No one told me about this. Am I out of the loop or something? Why was I not told?"

"We do everything through chain of command in this organization. When London received a letter from you, the Board of Directors was immediately concerned about your health. They suggested sending us a British surgeon to relieve the strain for a while. Of course I agreed. His name's George Atkinson. He brought his wife. She's from Sweden, a former model. Fine-looking woman they tell me.

"After you've trained him, you might like to take a few months off, put things back into perspective you might say."

"And the letter? What did they say about the letter, about its contents?"

"They forwarded it to me, asked me to deal with it. That's what I mean by chain of command. Everything in proper order—just like in the army."

"And how do you intend to deal with it?"

"I'll incorporate much of it into my report, that's what I'll do. It says a lot about your attitude, goals, sense of loyalty, and all that. Impressions that I'd formed myself have been confirmed by your own words. Now run along and meet the Atkinsons."

Steve dragged himself up the road that led toward his own house and beyond, thinking he would probably be replaced in a year by this newcomer. Nevertheless he resolved to be polite, knowing this surgeon was not to blame but only wanted to help—just as he had when he replaced Dr. (Mrs.) Aiyapandian.

As he approached the stone cottage nestled against the side of the hill on the other side of a 10 by 20-foot swimming pool, he saw what the day before would have been a most welcome sight. It was a sleek gray rodent, about three feet in length, including its very long tail. It just had to be a mongoose. No more need to worry about venom-spitting cobras.

But it was too late now to think of breeding rabbits and re-innervating patients' hands. It would take much longer than a year.

With the prospect of an early return home, those dreams were now gone forever.

Steve ducked under an overhanging arch of pink bougainvillea to knock on a sky blue door. He was surprised to note that the door and all the windows were shut as though no one was in there.

The door opened inward to reveal a bald-headed man slightly taller than Steve, with a black handlebar mustache, and sweat dripping from his very long forehead.

"Hello, I'm Steve Manley, Chief Surgeon here. Welcome to Janglepit, Tamilnadu, and the finest leprosy hospital in India."

"Ah yes, Tamilnadu—home of the Tamils."

"Not Tamils. Those are the Tamil-speaking people of Sri Lanka. Here they call themselves Tamilians."

"Please come in, my good chap. Name's Atkinson, George Atkinson. I'd like you to meet my wife, Yolanda."

All the fans were running full-blast but not a single window was open. They shook hands in the dim light of a single overhead bulb.

Steve noticed her delicate pale hand was cold. Her blond hair hung down halfway to her waist. As she brushed it aside, her weak smile seemed to say, "Please, help me."

"What a bloody hot country you've got here," George said. "We had no idea."

"October's not the coolest month," Steve said. "The second monsoon rains will come in a couple of weeks or so. Then it gets a little cooler. Till then, it'll be hot and sticky. Let's open some windows and let the breeze blow through."

Steve slid the bolt on a nearby window and opened it wide.

"No. No. You'll let the bugs in," George hollered. The right side of his face began to twitch.

"Look. The windows have screens. Bugs can't come in here."

The twitching stopped.

"Except in May," Steve added.

"May? May? What happens in May?"

"That's when we have the tiny gnats that get in everywhere."

"Everywhere?" The twitch returned at double-speed.

"Don't worry about May. We foreigners will be off to the hill stations. It's too hot here for all but the locals."

The twitch completely stopped, well almost.

"The rest of the year," Steve said, "all you need to worry about is snakes and scorpions."

"S-snakes and s-s-scorpions?"

Steve thought he had never seen such twitching. *Was it a twitch or a facial seizure?*

"Sorry this talk makes you nervous. Forget about the scorpions. They only come out after we go to bed. They fall in the pool and drown. All I've ever seen is dead ones. We fish them out with a long-handled net before we go swimming. Come outside—I'll show you."

George looked nervously over his left shoulder at Yolanda, as though he was afraid to leave her unattended. He picked up a large straw hat to cover his nearly bald head and followed Steve out into the bright sunshine.

"Wow," George said when they stood at the edge of the pool. "I've never seen water like this. What makes it so blue?"

"Copper sulfate. That's what we use to kill germs. With the constant sunshine here, chlorine only lasts a few hours."

"Much less smell, too."

"Watch this, George." Steve picked up a long-handled scoop-like net and fished out a light brown scorpion about five inches long.

"See, it's dead, poor thing. Can't swim. Can't breathe under water. It was in the wrong place at the wrong time, and made the wrong move. Maybe there's a lesson for us all in that."

George began to twitch again. "Are you saying we made the wrong move by coming here?"

"Not at all. Although lately I've wondered if perhaps I did. But let's not get into that. This is neither the time nor the place. Here's what's important now. Snakes and scorpions can never get into your house because you have screens covering the outlets where water flows from your kitchen and bathrooms to the drainage ditch. Come on. I'll show you. "

They walked over to an opening in the wall beneath the kitchen window and also inspected the water outlet from the bathroom. There were no screens.

132

S

Steve continued his Tamil lessons with Yasmina. He was doing so well that now they just met once a week—on Fridays. Learning to communicate was no longer the goal. He studied just for the love of it.

"It" was the way Yasmina's lips moved when she demonstrated how to form the sounds correctly. His favorite sounds were "oh," "oo," "poo," "bu," and "cue." Over and over he would ask her to demonstrate these sounds, and others that she could only make by putting her little pink tongue behind her pure white teeth.

Yasmina giggled. "You don't need me to go over these basic sounds at the start of every lesson. You speak Tamil beautifully."

"I love to watch you say 'be-u-ti-full-ly.' I enjoy this time with you so very much, and I know you do also. It's the only time I see you laugh."

"Yes, I do enjoy it. When everyone else leaves, they seem to take the whole world and all its silly rules with them. I feel freedom I never had at home in my village. It's as though I have entered another world, a land of fantasy where anything can happen. Do you know why Indians go so much to the cinema? It is to escape the drudgery of everyday life."

"Well said! Here it's like you're at the cinema, living another life. You are no longer a secretary in a hospital in Janglepit. You're a language teacher in Minneapolis, teaching Tamil to a little boy named Steve. Call me Steve."

Yasmina gave him a sly look and abruptly changed the subject. "What's she like, that Mrs. Atkinson? I hear she has long blond hair, eyes blue like the sky, delicate features, and skin like fresh milk."

"You know, I've been in India so long I can't tell one white woman from another."

Yasmina frowned.

"Sorry, that's a bad American joke twisted upside down. Please forgive me."

"I forgive you, Steve. Oops. I said your name. Now I must beg your forgiveness."

"There is nothing to forgive. But to answer your question properly, she is much too pale for my liking."

"You don't like white?"

"No. I much prefer brown. Chocolate brown." He surveyed her body from head to toe, stopping to pause in all the right places.

"I like white," she said. "I wish I had whiter skin. Tamilians are darker than those in the north. Light-colored skin makes people think you are higher caste. Even though Indira Gandhi made discrimination on the basis of caste illegal, high caste still gets preference."

"But, Yasmina, your skin is much lighter than most Tamilians. You look high caste."

"That's my father's influence. He's from north India, Rajasthan. I have my mother's bone structure and his skin."

"Tell me about your father. Has he been good to you?"

"His name's Salim. He's quite short. So is his temper. Something seems to be troubling him. He says he has been bullied a lot. Three years ago he bought a Lee-Enfield rifle. He says it is to protect the family. By now he is an excellent marksman."

"Then I guess I'd better be good to you. I wouldn't want him to be mad at me."

"Steve, you have always been good to me. But I must warn you. He doesn't know we meet like this. It would upset him if he knew. He is a very jealous man and can sometimes be quite vindictive."

Steve glanced at his watch. "It's getting late. You'd better go now, and not make him suspicious. Your brother will be waiting outside to walk you home. But wait a minute. Can he be trusted? "

"Absolutely. He is most discreet, and we have always been best friends. I shall go now. Goodnight, Dr. Manley."

Steve suspected he might be leaving India soon, a country to which he had devoted his life. He wondered if he was developing feelings for Yasmina, feelings that went far beyond the love of Jesus that she'd said she had for him.

He said good night and watched Yasmina walk away. He just stood and watched, feeling confused. There had been a time when he had very definite plans. He knew what he wanted from life and exactly how to get it. Now he seemed to be less clear about everything, and didn't have any idea what to do next.

The door was open in front of him. He walked through it, and out—into the night.

$$\mathbf{\sim S}$$

A full moon shone through the branches of the palm trees as Steve scuffed his sandals on the sandy soil of his front yard. Somewhere to his right an owl hooted. A large fruit bat flew close to his head. He hardly noticed these things. Yasmina totally consumed his thoughts.

This language lesson with her had lasted longer than usual. Now he was 30 minutes late for dinner. Sangria met him at the door.

"Hard day working, Doctor?" she said, smiling as always.

"Not really. I'm sorry to keep you waiting. Why don't you go home to your family—and take the food with you? I am not that hungry tonight. Just leave me a bowl of rice. I'll eat it later."

"I leave some curry too. Is very good. Fish curry...you like it, I know. Letter come. Maybe feel better later." Bowing slightly and with palms pressed together, she added, "Thank you, Doctor. I go now."

A few minutes later she walked down the path with a large stainless steel bowl under each arm. Steve sat down in his favorite chair and began reading the letter.

September 11, 1973

Dear Steve,

Greetings from the land of Apartheid. That word apartheid *means separateness. Somehow, separateness seems an appropriate description of many things that have happened here.*

They call Africa the Dark Continent. As a kid I thought the term referred to the native people. Before I came here, I assumed it had something to do with the lack of the life-changing gospel. On arrival, I discovered that Africa is one of the most Christianized areas of the world.

Now I've come to a shocking conclusion. The darkness, as I now see it, has settled over the minds and hearts of many of my coworkers—my fellow missionaries!

Nancy and I seem to be swimming against the tide here. I believe we are in the will of God. We are just treating our neighbors as Jesus said we should. But the other missionaries don't see it the same way. Right now I am somewhat confused. I'll write again when I have a clearer idea of what the Lord wants us to do.

Your friend in Christ,

Andrew

~S

Book Four

Fifteen

ndrew skipped a step or two as he led Lucy from the car to his front door. Holding it open for her he called out, "Nancy! Come and meet our new boarder."

Lucy sidled past him and bent to lower a small suitcase to the floor. In that moment, Andrew couldn't avoid seeing her dress cling more tightly. Its large angular pattern did nothing to camouflage the exquisite figure beneath. Andrew averted his eyes to see Nancy entering from the kitchen. Flour whitened her hands and apron front, and streaked her face. She had fastened her hair back in a bun and wore old house slippers. The tightness of her apron emphasized a tummy no longer flat.

"Hello, Lucy," Nancy said. "Do come right in."

Lucy stood in the entryway, glancing uncomfortably about.

"She didn't want to come in the front door, but I insisted. She said she's a servant and should come only to the back door."

Nancy smiled. "You're a house guest. You can use the front or back doors as you choose."

They all stood awkwardly for a moment until Nancy said, "Andrew, show her to the *ekhaya*. I'll have dinner on in 45 minutes."

Andrew led Lucy across the front room, through the kitchen, and out the back door. The *ekhaya*, or servant's room, stood alone in the back yard against the garden wall. Andrew pulled open its door and motioned Lucy in. A cot stood against the wall opposite the door and beneath a tiny, high window. A rough wardrobe stood on the left side, a tiny washbasin jutted from the wall on the right. Beside the basin, a tied-back, plastic curtain revealed a narrow doorway opening on a toilet and shower.

"You must have re-painted the room. It looks wonderful."

Andrew's body tingled. Blushing, he said, "See you at the house in 45 minutes," and slipped outside.

Walking slowly back to the house, he wrestled with his feelings. He loved his wife, he intended to remain faithful to her, but Lucy fired up his carnal nature. He had to get a grip on himself. Nancy couldn't see what was happening inside him—but the Lord could.

As he entered the kitchen Edward sat at the table, licking a mixing spoon. Nancy slipped a casserole into the oven and turned to Andrew.

"Husband, bring your thoughts into subjection now we have such a fascinating house guest. Just remember it is illegal here for whites to get mixed up with blacks. I think you know what I mean. And next time you have a bath be sure to put on the Zulu bathrobe I bought you. No more running around here naked, not even half-naked."

Edward's tongue, extending for another lick, snapped back into his mouth. "Mom, why is Daddy standing there with his mouth open?"

Almost an hour later, Lucy stood at the entrance to the dining room shaking her head.

"No, I can't eat with you at the table," she said. "Let me take my food to my room."

"It's perfectly proper for you to eat with us. You're our house guest, not a servant," Nancy pleaded.

"I can't. We don't do it in this country. The mission leaders will give you a problem. The police might come and you'd have to leave the country. They don't want the races to mix."

"All right," Andrew relented. "We'll give you your food in the kitchen, but you must eat it there."

Lucy's lips trembled. "I... all right, *Baba*. I just don't want to create trouble for you—for any of us."

The following day Andrew sat opposite Gordon Muir in his dusty office.

140

"I want Lucy to feel like a family member," he said. "We're supposed to demonstrate Christian family living to her, and we can't do it any other way. She must sit with us at the table."

Gordon wagged his head. "It's not done here. The girl won't do it. You would upset mission practice. Goodness, at home in Canada, you wouldn't have a servant sitting at your table. Here in South Africa, you just don't entertain other races at your table. Let her eat in the kitchen."

Andrew's throat tightened. "She might do some work for us, but that doesn't make her a servant. She's a house guest. And besides, in Canada, on the farm, helpers and farmhands always sit at the table with the farmer and his wife."

Gordon shrugged. His mouth moved, but no words came out.

"And if I heard someone had treated a daughter of mine like an outcast, I'd get mighty upset."

"Remember," Gordon warned, "this is South Africa. The politicians forbid too much interracial collegiality, and our whole missionary endeavor could be compromised."

"But should we not take a stand for Christian principles no matter the cost?"

Gordon threw up his hands. "Do as you will, but I warned you. Some of our missionaries, when they have a visit from an African pastor, give him his tea and food in a tin cup and plate and send him to the back stoop."

The days slipped by. Lucy continued to eat in the kitchen. On Saturdays, she helped with the household duties, but right after chores or meals, she returned to her room. One month after her arrival, Andrew poured out his heart to Mumsa in a quiet corner of the cafeteria.

"She sits in the kitchen, listening to our conversation and laughing at our jokes, but she won't sit with us at the table. Is it wrong to want to make her a member of the family?"

"No, it isn't wrong. You must not listen to missionaries who work here but show with their lives that they don't love us. And the police will not come. Eating with black people might be against some people's customs, but it isn't against any law."

"Then what can we do to get her to the table?"

Mumsa pursed her lips, then spoke. "You are living in South Africa. You need to do what South Africans do. Don't ask her; tell her. She will obey you."

That night Andrew piled Lucy's cup and cutlery on her plate but left everything on the kitchen table. Andrew, Nancy and the boys took their places in the dining room but with an extra chair for Lucy.

When the outside door opened and Lucy entered singing, Andrew jumped to his feet and entered the kitchen from the dining room.

Before Lucy could sit down, he said, "Lucy, you'll see that your place isn't set there. I want you to pick up your things and bring them to the dining room. We have a space for you at that table."

Lucy stopped singing. She looked from Andrew to her old place at the kitchen table and began to tremble. For almost a minute, she stood quivering like a willow tree in the grip of an earthquake. Snapping out of the trance, she grabbed her things, threw her head high, marched past Andrew into the dining room, and sat in her new place.

While Lucy beamed and Nancy and the boys clapped, Andrew thought, *Now she's more like a family member, like a daughter. I must start thinking of her in those terms.*

Soon after Lucy's arrival, two other Africans began to put in regular appearances at the Heath household, working part-time. *Mama* Bertha came once each week to clean the house. For this service Nancy gave her lunch and three Rands for the day. *Baba* Joseph came one day weekly to work in the garden and maintain the lawn. He asked for three Rands per day, but Andrew insisted on giving him four.

The first time Andrew paid him, he thought, *Four Rand is less than six dollars. No one should work for so little. I should ask Nancy to give Mama Bertha a raise too. Who could have imagined we'd one day have a cleaning woman and a gardener?*

The Christmas break and the annual missionary conference had come and gone. Andrew and Nancy had tried to opt out, but Gordon Muir and the field director insisted they attend. At the conference, they felt like aliens in a strange world. While the missionaries praised God for the way He had blessed them, Andrew shook his head in disbelief. He failed to see anything of God's blessing. Nancy chose to keep her own counsel.

Now back home from the conference, and well into their second year, Andrew agonized about their future. They just didn't fit! *When it comes to the Africans,* he thought, *most of the missionaries don't seem to give a . . .* It shocked him that in his mind he'd almost used his father's favorite swear word.

Andrew did have a few things to thank God for. Going to the African church almost made everything worthwhile. Lucy had become an integral part of the family. The boys had easily blended into the South African school system without major adjustments, apart from having to trade hockey and baseball for soccer and cricket. They made good progress learning Afrikaans as a second language. Edward quickly made friends, but John seemed to retreat into himself.

Andrew had managed to keep busy, but still had no feeling of being "in the perfect will of God."

One day as they sat around the table, John said, "I still want to go back to Canada. I miss Canada. It was bad enough leaving Kitchener when we moved to Saskatchewan, but that was still Canada. I made new friends there. Then we left them when we moved back to Kitchener before coming here. I just feel like I don't belong anywhere."

"Don't you love us?" Lucy asked him.

"I like the people... I guess."

Nancy looked directly at her son. "You just guess?"

John blushed, stole a glance at Lucy, dropped his eyes, and answered, "I like some people—especially some black people."

Andrew's forkful of food stopped halfway to his mouth. *Oh man,* he thought, *someone else is having trouble with his hormones.*

"Well, I like soccer," Edward said, reaching for another piece of *boerewors.* "We didn't play soccer in Canada."

"And you didn't have this wonderful South African farmers sausage you're eating," said Lucy.

Andrew climbed to the third floor of the mission building where Gordon had found him an unused office that suited him better than the dingy press room. Here he had installed his graphics camera, built light and drawing tables, and completed the decor with an old, discarded roll-top desk.

Today he had a challenging assignment—to design a new logo for Med-Help, properly known as Medical Help South Africa, a Christian Medical Mission. In addition to the logo, he would prepare a folio of related designs for letterheads and other mission documents.

The fee for the job would go into the fund for the new press building. Andrew had little hope of ever seeing construction begin, but the challenge of the graphics assignment had raised his spirits higher than at any time since coming to South Africa. He pulled a collection of letters, booklets, magazines and other material from a large manila envelope and spread it on the table. Before beginning, he would study the history and culture of Med-Help.

A small book caught Andrew's attention. The title read, *Med-Help, Sub-Sahara, and its World-wide Affiliates.* He began reading.

"*Sa'bona,* Andrew, mail call," said Elizabeth, the black, effervescent general girl-Friday and secretary to the field director.

She flashed Andrew a toothy smile and disappeared as quickly as she had come. She was a chubby little creature who always bubbled with fun.

Andrew smiled. Everybody seemed to like Elizabeth. What a sweetheart. If she were their house guest, he could have enjoyed her without the improper thoughts of Lucy that troubled him. But he knew he could not easily give up Lucy.

The mail consisted of one item—a memo from the field director, Peter Fowler. It announced an all-missionary meeting two months hence. Andrew read the words, "We need to discuss goals for closer cooperation with the African Church. Bring your ideas to this key meeting."

Tossing the memo into his in-basket, Andrew spoke aloud to the empty room, "We talk, we discuss, we plan, but we do nothing. Unless this signals a change, watch your attitude, Andrew."

Andrew again began reading the book on Med-Help, but hadn't got beyond the first page when he read this statement:

"Med-Help is the South African operation of Greater Missions International (GMI). GMI also gives general direction to its other semi-autonomous divisions: Mission to the Outcast worldwide, and Medical Asia in the Far East."

Andrew put down the book. He stared at the ceiling as he remembered the contents of Steve Manley's last letter. He worried that Med-Help might be something like Steve's group and worse stick-in-the-muds than the leadership at God's Word Mission.

Andrew's ambition evaporated. He placed the Med-Help information back in the envelope and again stared at the ceiling, losing track of time. He could see his idealistic dreams of missions and missionaries dissolving into a pile of rubble.

He wondered if all mission agencies ran like the one he and Nancy had become involved with—or Steve for that matter. He recalled the instructors at the Toronto Institute of Linguistics hinted about tensions between missionaries and nationals, but professors at Bible college had portrayed mission life as satisfying and fulfilling, with never a negative outlook. Slowly the truth dawned on him—most of the college faculty had once been missionaries!

"You missed the tea break."

Andrew swung around to face the doorway.

"Mumsa, you startled me!"

"I thought I should check up on you," she said, sitting in a chair opposite.

He noticed the twinkle in her eye. *She is just like a mischievous sister, but a very wise one.*

"I'm feeling discouraged, Mumsa. What do you know about the

Med-Help mission?"

She pursed her lips, as though pulling some words back inside, words that were better left unsaid.

"They have some very good people, both missionaries and Africans. But like our mission leaders, they have some difficulty accepting Africans as equals. They take their orders from head office in London."

"They have asked me to do a job for them."

"Then do it! Your help will be a blessing to them. You might even teach them something."

Andrew pulled a memo from his in-basket and handed it to Mumsa. "I guess this also upset me a little. This is a memo from the field director calling for a meeting to discuss our relationship with the African church. Nancy and I are the only missionaries with God's Word who regularly attend an African Church. How can the rest know what's wrong with our relationship to the African church?"

Mumsa read the memo and returned it.

"Do your husband and the other pastors plan to attend?" he asked her.

Mumsa's ample body began to shake. A gurgling, rippling, starting deep within, emerged as infectious laughter. Her eyes sparkled and her teeth flashed. She clapped her hands.

"No... no... no," she said, her words skipping out between fits of laughter. "Did you ever see any of us at a field conference? They don't invite us to anything. We might embarrass them by telling them what they don't want to hear. This is apartheid South Africa, you know."

Andrew could not decide whether to laugh or cry.

Finally he blurted out, "How can we get along with people we keep at arms' length?"

Now Mumsa looked dead serious. "You are new here; they haven't yet tainted you with their bad habits. You haven't yet soaked up South African racial attitudes—"

"And I won't!" Andrew said.

"I hope not. But usually people who come here with fresh ideas don't last. They will think of you as a troublemaker and send you home."

Maybe we should have gone home immediately, Andrew thought. Aloud he said, "What can we do?"

"Be yourselves. Keep working with the African church even if others don't. Be positive. God will bless you."

Andrew and Nancy arrived late for the meeting called by the field director. As they approached the meeting room door, they met Jack and Lila Ferguson peering in. When they saw Andrew and Nancy, they stepped back from the door.

"They're doing devotions. Better wait a few minutes," Jack said.

Nancy smiled at Lila. "I'm glad we're not the only ones late."

"You all know how much Jack and I hate conferences and business meetings," Lila said. "We thought by arriving late we'd find it over."

Keeping his voice low, Andrew said, "Jack, you always say something worthwhile."

A grin spread across Jack's face. "Only to suggest a compromise and get the meeting over."

Nancy peeked into the meeting room and whispered, "Peter has just finished the Scripture reading and begun to pray. Let's all slip in when he says, amen."

Andrew took the opportunity, with all heads bowed, to step inside and look about the room. He could not see one African staff member or church representative.

At the end of the prayer, the four of them slipped into seats at the very back. Gordon Muir, just one row ahead of Andrew and Nancy, turned to look at them and gave Andrew a vigorous thumbs-up.

Leaning back, he whispered, "I just talked to Dr. Hampton from Med-Help. He says your sample graphics are great—like a breath of fresh air."

"Well done, Andrew," Nancy whispered.

Gordon gave another thumbs-up signal and turned to the front as Peter began the business part of the meeting. Without Africans there, the meeting seemed pointless to Andrew. His mind fled the room to dwell on the designs for Med-Help.

He only half-heard the discussions on missionary housing and the disparity between support money for American versus British workers. Information related to salary levels for African workers jerked him back for a few minutes. An unnamed family had increased the rate paid their one-day-a-week gardener from three Rands to four per day. Someone suggested that now all missionaries would have to do the same for gardeners and maids.

"That's going to cost us a lot of money," an American piped up. "We have a maid for three days per week and a gardener for two."

Andrew noticed the speaker and a good many other people looking his way. He squirmed in his chair thinking, *Next month I might raise him another half Rand. That's still only the equivalent of six dollars per day.*

Peter Fowler redirected the meeting to a less acrimonious matter: co-operation with other mission organizations in South Africa.

I'm already doing that with Med-Help, and they like what I'm doing.

After another 15 minutes of day-dreaming, Peter's voice again aroused Andrew. "Enough about general issues. Our main purpose today is to discuss our relationship with the African Church. The meeting is open to general discussion."

A male voice with an Australian accent spoke up. "I've made some friends with the missionaries of the All Africa Fellowship. They have an affiliated African church with 30,000 members. Their mission has been in southern Africa for 50 years and has only 12 active missionaries on the field. On the other hand we have been here for nearly 100 years and have 97 missionaries. Yet we have planted an African church with less than 6,000 members, and a church among the Asian Indians with a following of 1,200."

The speaker paused as if to gauge his impact. No one spoke, and he continued. "I'd like to suggest we do a study of the All Africa Fellowship. Find out what they have done right and compare their procedures with our methods."

A murmur of voices swept across the room. Andrew caught disjointed words from the dozen conversations that had erupted:

"They're charismatic...don't pay their missionaries a living stipend.. a paternalistic group...make the Africans do all the work..."

When the babble lessened, the Australian stood up again. "Mr. Fowler, I have something else to say. If we came here to discuss the African Church, why didn't you invite the Church leaders?"

Andrew poked Nancy and whispered, "We have a supporter in the crowd."

Peter sputtered, coughed, and finally said, "This is a meeting of missionaries. We have to make decisions for ourselves. What do the rest of you think?"

A deep silence fell on the group. Andrew could be quiet no more and rose to his feet. "I came here to work with African people, not to push a mission agenda. With all apologies to those of you from Britain and Australia, we are demonstrating North American arrogance when we make decisions for other people. I agree we need the African leaders here to give us their viewpoint. By not inviting them we just reflect the culture of South African Apartheid."

During his mini-speech, Andrew watched the faces that turned toward him. Some showed animosity, others surprise. The majority reflected a lack of understanding.

The body language of at least two said, "Does this upstart who overpays his servants want to run the mission?"

Andrew sat down, thinking that for good or bad he'd said his piece.

The discussion ranged back and forth, with only half of them supporting the concept of involving the African leadership in decision making.

Jack stood up. "We're getting nowhere. I suggest we adjourn, talk about it in our departments, and then deal with the issue at another meeting."

Andrew sprang to his feet. "Let me make another suggestion. Before we meet again, let us each ask our African friends for their thoughts on mission-church cooperation. Ask them what they think we should do to help the church."

Peter raised his hand to stop further discussion. "That is a great idea. That's your assignment before we meet again. I declare the meeting closed."

But the meeting hadn't completely ended. Everyone in the room heard Fran Jamieson say, "That's ridiculous. I don't have any African friends."

Andrew drove the Austin home, through the open iron gates, and parked in front of the garage door. He had rejected the local custom of closing the gates at night. Many householders also turned a large dog free at night to "keep out the Africans." He was glad he didn't have a dog.

While Nancy headed for the back door, Andrew walked around the front yard to inspect the work the gardener had done the day before.

It looked good for a six-dollar-a-day worker.

Passing the dining-room window, shaded by a six-foot poinsettia, he entered the front door. The display on the living-room floor stopped him cold.

Lucy, John, and Edward lay on their stomachs on the floor, heads together around a textbook. Lucy was speaking, one finger tracing the words on the page.

"*Verlede week het mnr. Van der Merwe sy motor na die motorhawe geneem.* Work on the pronunciation and you will sound less like Canadians and more like *Afrikaaners.*"

Edward, chin propped on hands, asked, "What will our white South African teachers say if we copy you too closely and sound like Zulus speaking Afrikaans?"

"Or worse yet," John added, "we might sound like Zulu women."

Lucy grabbed the textbook and struck John across the head, causing the tutorial to dissolve into a session of laughter. Chuckling, Andrew carefully stepped over the prone bodies, walked through the dining room, and entered the kitchen.

He spoke to Nancy who had already begun the evening meal. "The mission may not have its relationships straight, but we've begun to build an interracial family whether they like it or not."

"Andrew, we'll have to talk more when the kids can't hear us. But after that meeting, I've lost all faith in the mission. I want to go home. It's wrong, it's immoral, to take support from people overseas when we're not doing the job we came to do."

"We are doing good work with Mumsa and Pastor Makunyane's church. They want us to help start an outreach ministry to maids and gardeners who live in the white community."

Nancy sighed. "We can work in our church back home."

"Okay, we'll talk about it again. What's for dinner?"

"*Boerewors*," she said.

Sixteen

"Andrew, I want to do some letter-writing," Nancy said as she disappeared into the bedroom where she kept a writing desk.

Andrew looked around the living room. The boys had taken their regular positions on the floor around a pile of homework.

John had a South African history text open. He scowled at his dad, "I never heard of Jan van Riebeeck before we left Canada. Now he shows up in every history lesson."

"Who is he?" Andrew asked.

"He brought the first load of settlers from Holland in 1652. *Afrikaaners* who can trace their ancestry back to that ship are true South African blue bloods."

Edward groaned. "John, forget your dumb history and help me with my stupid arithmetic."

"Only until Lucy finishes the dishes and comes to help with Afrikaans."

Andrew watched the boys settle into Edward's arithmetic lesson, then turned away. Tonight he would have watched television if they had it in this forsaken country.

Lucy's voice, singing a Zulu chorus, drifted from the kitchen. Andrew walked in behind her and pulled open the bow on her apron.

"You sound happy," he said.

"And you are more mischievous than your sons!" she answered, while fumbling to retie her apron strings.

Andrew picked up the tea towel and began drying a plate.

"Put that down," Lucy pleaded. "This is my job. You can't help me."

"I can and I will."

Lucy watched as Andrew put the plate in the cupboard, then

grabbed the towel. "Give me that!"

"No. I'm helping."

"You must not. Let go," Lucy said, pulling hard on the cotton cloth.

When she grabbed for Andrew's end of the towel, he sidestepped, propelling them both around the kitchen like two exotic birds in a mating dance.

On the third spin about the room, the towel tore into two pieces, sending Andrew backward into the refrigerator and Lucy against a wall.

They both laughed gleefully until they noticed Nancy and the boys watching from the doorway.

"Maybe we need to get out two new towels," Nancy said. "Andrew and I will both help with the dishes while the boys get back to their homework."

The South African green summer faded into a brown winter. Andrew's disposition didn't improve with time—frustration seemed to walk side-by-side with every small victory. And there were a few small victories. The correspondence department had asked him to redesign their gospel tracts.

Andrew's phone rang just as he had arranged the elements of a tract on the copy table beneath the camera lens, causing him to jump, knocking the pieces askew. "Drat, who needs telephones?" he muttered aloud as he stepped across to his desk. "Yeah!" he snapped into the mouthpiece.

"*Cor*, you sound angry," said a man with a cockney accent.

"Jack, I'm sorry. I'm trying to get this tract put together for you, and the phone keeps ringing. First, Peter Fowler phones with a request for a quarterly report. Then the mechanic tells me my car needs brakes. Now you're about to bug me for this job."

"I'm doing nothing of the sort. I called to ask a favor of a friend."

"A friend? Well in that case, ask away."

"Lila and I are off to Kruger Park for three days—a bit of an escape from the daily grind. Can Elizabeth come over and eat with your Lucy for three days? We'll be back Saturday night. She can stay in our *ekhaya* at night and keep an eye on the house. Should I have called Nancy? "

"No, don't call Nancy; she'll be happy to help out. Elizabeth is such a sweetie, we'll enjoy having her." Andrew hung up and returned to the camera to check light levels and aperture.

"Sa'bona Baas! Mail call," said a voice from the doorway a short while later.

Elizabeth stepped in and dropped an envelope on the desk.

Andrew smiled. "Don't call me *Baas.*"

"Okay, *Baba.* I hear I'm going to be your servant girl for three days."

"How did you hear that so soon?"

"Baba Jack Ferguson was sitting on my desk when he called you. You spoke so loudly I heard both sides of the conversation."

"Oh. But you won't be a servant; you'll be a house guest."

"Oh, thank you, *Baas!*"

Andrew shook his head. "I said don't..."

"Sorry, sorry, *Baba.* I won't call you *Baas* if you'll quit telling the world I'm a sweetie."

Elizabeth bubbled out the words and slipped away in a shower of giggles.

Two days later, when Lucy entered for the evening meal, Elizabeth came with her.

Nancy greeted her in the kitchen. "Welcome, Elizabeth. Go right through with Lucy to the dining room. We have a place set for you."

Elizabeth hesitated, but Lucy caught her arm and led her to her place. Andrew sat at the head of the table opposite Nancy, with the boys to his left and the girls on the right.

Andrew's eyes swept around the table.

"I always wanted a balanced family," he said. "Now we have it, two boys and two girls. Let's ask God's blessing on the meal."

It seemed that God had indeed blessed. Andrew found the food excellent. The *boerewors* seemed especially good. The whole family had taken to this spicy South African version of farmer's sausage.

With a different person at the table, everyone acted more subdued than usual. Andrew watched Elizabeth with concern. She had lost her bubbly disposition. She didn't say a word during the meal, yet she knew everyone. Andrew wondered if she had just had a bad day at work.

The following evening Elizabeth's bright disposition began to return. She chatted easily when someone directed conversation her way.

By the third evening, she had become the center of attention.

"Edward, could you please pass the *beetroot slaai?*" Elizabeth asked.

"Red stuff coming up." he answered.

"And while you're at it, please pass the peas. All the good food seems to have accumulated around your plate."

As he passed it across the table, he said, "*Accumulated?* Big word. And you seem to want all the brightly colored food. Do you have a thing about color?"

"I do. 'Having a thing about color' as you say, is the way we live in this country. You notice I didn't ask for more potatoes," she said, throwing up her hands, palms outward and eyes enlarging, "because potatoes are white."

Edward chuckled, then recovered to say, "Hey, Black Girl, I guess you don't like rice either."

While the two white boys and the two young black women laughed, Andrew continued eating. He could hardly believe what he'd heard—laughing together about problems they faced living under a white government.

When he glanced at Nancy, he detected perplexity on her face.

Elizabeth turned her attention to John. "Do you play the piano, John?"

"I play a bit. I'd like to take more lessons."

Elizabeth pointed a finger at him. "We should take lessons together. We could learn to play apartheid piano."

She paused for effect.

John's brow furrowed, looked from his mom to his dad, and then back to Elizabeth. "What?"

"Sure, it would be easier for both of us. If we played apartheid piano, I would play the black keys and you would play the white keys."

This time both Andrew and Nancy added to the laughter that danced around the table.

❧

John Heath sat in his room flipping through the pages of a North American road atlas. He stopped at Ontario and began to trace his finger from Kitchener along Highway 401, then north on routes 400 and 69, and west on 17. When he reached the Manitoba border, he turned the page and traced his way across Manitoba and into Saskatchewan. There, somewhere west of Moose Jaw he stopped at the Bible college his dad had attended.

He remembered with joy that trip and the return journey to Ontario.

Then they came to South Africa. The visit to England and the arrival in Roodepoort had been the highlights of his life. But now he wanted to return to Canada—to Kitchener, the place he still thought of as home even though he hadn't lived there for years.

He hated South Africa. His idealistic spirit rebelled against apartheid. He had memories of Kitchener as idyllic. Mom and Dad were happy there. Here the tension began the day Dad learned the mission had lied about the press building.

John opened his door. At 10 o'clock, Edward would be asleep, and Mom likely reading in bed. He heard someone in the living room.

"Dad?"

"Yes, John," Andrew replied in hushed tones.

"Can we talk?"

"Sure."

Andrew entered John's room, closed the door, and sat on the bed.

John jumped right in. "Dad, are you and Mom happy here?"

"No. Things haven't gone the way we expected. But I think you know that."

"Then why don't we go home? Now?"

Andrew squirmed.

He doesn't have an answer, John thought.

It took Andrew a full half-minute to answer. "I...I don't know. One day I feel we should, the next day something good happens and I want to stay."

John placed his hand on his dad's knee. "Well, I know. I want to go home now. I could live with Aunt Marjorie and Uncle Mack. When I finish high school, I could attend the University of Waterloo. Can I do that?"

Andrew slowly shook his head. "Right now we couldn't afford it. But we will go home for a furlough in a couple of years. That'll be about time for you to begin university."

John threw the atlas onto the floor. Color rose in his cheeks. "Dad, Mom is unhappy here. I'm unhappy. Even Edward wants to go home. The only reason you won't go back to Canada is because you don't want people calling you a missionary failure."

Then, as he watched his father fight for control, John wondered if he'd pushed him too far.

Andrew stood up to leave, then sat down again. "Son, I need to know God's will for my life—for all our lives. When God says 'Go home,' we'll go home."

John picked up the atlas. His peak of anger had passed, but a knot of stubbornness remained. "Why do you have to know that? I believe the rest of us already know. Don't we get to have a say?"

"The Bible doesn't talk about families as democracies. It gives leadership to the husband and father."

John didn't feel quite ready to give up, so he tried again. "The Bible also says that parents shouldn't provoke their children."

Andrew frowned and rose to his feet. "Let's talk about it another time. But I am glad you let me know how you feel."

John watched his father leave the room with his shoulders sagging. His dad wasn't the person he'd known in Canada. He wanted to go home. Tears flowing down his face dropped onto the map of Ontario.

"You wanted to see me?" Andrew said to Gordon Muir as he entered the office behind the glass partition.

Gordon squirmed in his chair, brushed down the wrinkles in the front of his shirt, and cleared his throat three times. Without looking directly at Andrew he said, "Well, you've done it again."

"Done what?"

"You had Elizabeth at your place for three meals last week. She has gone around the building saying, 'Did you know Lucy eats at the table with the Heaths?'"

Gordon squirmed again, but Andrew said nothing.

"Only you and I and Lucy knew about it. And none of us talked—not even Lucy. You got all the missionaries mad at you when you raised your gardener's pay and they had to follow. Now they're seething because all the blacks are talking about the way you and Nancy deal with Lucy. The Africans are waiting to find out what the rest of us will do."

Andrew tried to control his emotions, but a note of anger crept into his voice. "All of you could start treating African people like fellow humans!"

Gordon wrung his hands, recalling in Andrew's mind a picture of Pilate washing his hands at Jesus' trial. Gordon said quietly, "I don't have an African employee staying at my place. I'm not sure what I'd do if I did."

"Okay, Gordon. It's happened. What do we do next?"

"A committee of unhappy people met with me and the field director this morning. They want the field council to deal with it. The council meets next month. They figure if we have a general meeting of missionary personnel it will cause serious disruptions."

"What's Peter's attitude?"

"Very unhappy. His wife, Sarah, is particularly upset. She said, 'How can I have an African eating at my table and then expect a white neighbor to eat off the same plates?'"

Andrew shook his head. "She said that?"

"Yes, she wants to have a good Christian testimony in front of her neighbors."

Andrew continued shaking his head. "But Gordon, we came here to minister to African people. That attitude is...it's racist."

"I know. You've shaken us up, Andrew. Obviously, we need it, but I fear the outcome. You have to toe the line set by the politicians—even if your name is Mahatma Gandhi."

Without another word, Andrew walked out of the office and went straight to Mumsa's desk.

"*Sa'bona, Mama,*" he said, sitting down on her desk.

"*Baba*, you look ill," she said, completely ignoring African tradition by not continuing the greeting exchange.

"I am. You must have heard."

She smiled and a heavy chuckle echoed deep within her ample bosom. "Yes, the talk started going around yesterday."

"I seem to have caused a bit of a stink."

Again, a chuckle preceded her words. "Good for you. It is time someone shook them like naughty children. About half the missionaries are mad at you and the other half feel ashamed of themselves. But all the African staff think you and Nancy are wonderful."

"It's the field council that will send us home, not the African staff. They have turned it over to field council."

This time Mumsa's chuckle exploded into full laughter. "Then you have nothing to worry about for now. They won't get around to a decision for six months or a year."

"That sounds like the story of my life—hurry up and wait," Andrew said, preparing to take his leave.

"Don't go yet. I have a favor to ask."

"Mumsa, I'll do most anything for you."

"Do you know Rebecca Tsatsi? She works in the Sesotho language department."

Andrew nodded.

"She's a single mother and must work this Saturday. Her boy, Daniel, will come with her. She doesn't want to leave him alone in the township—he might get into mischief around the building all day with no playmates—"

Andrew interrupted. "Most boys create mischief when they have playmates to encourage them."

Mumsa chuckled. "He is about Edward's age. Can he stay at your place for the day?"

"I believe so, but I'll check with Edward. He has no African playmates; it's so difficult here to have friends of another race."

Andrew left with a warm sensation vibrating through his system. He had gone to ask for advice; she had given it. Then she had turned his mind from himself by asking him to help someone else.

Edward felt a tension pressing against his temples as he sat on the front stoop, thinking Dad would soon arrive with the African kid. He wondered if he could speak English, and whether he'd be dumb and slow.

Many of Edward's white playmates at school claimed Africans didn't think as quickly as white people. They also called them dirty and insisted you could get lice from them.

The Austin rolled into the driveway. A small black boy climbed out. He wore a red shirt and black shorts—almost identical to Edward's clothes—and he had a soccer ball under one arm. Under the other he carried a toy car. He placed both items on the ground. The car had wheels made of jam-can lids and a body of twisted wire that simply outlined the car so you could see right through it. A long wire, like a straightened coat hanger, came up from the front wheels, through the open body, and ended in a crude steering wheel at waist-height to the boy.

Edward didn't move from his seat on the porch. His dad and the African boy approached on the walkway to the front door. The boy held the steering wheel in one hand and pushed the lunch pail-sized car ahead of him. It bumped along, zigzagging from side to side.

"Son of a gun," Edward exclaimed when he noticed the steering wheel turned the front wheels like a real car.

"Edward, meet Bonga Tsatsi," Andrew said.

"Hello, Bonga, how are you?"

"I am fine. How are you, Edward?"

"I'm fine too," Edward replied, remembering to complete the greeting in a formal African way. "Can I try your car?"

"Sure," Bonga said, as he stepped from behind the wheel.

As Edward pushed it along, he could see through the skeleton-like body to the clever wire mechanism that controlled the front wheels. He pushed it to the driveway and back to the stoop where Bonga waited alone. Andrew had gone inside.

"Wow, where did you get this wonderful car?"

Bonga looked down, shrugged, bounced his soccer ball three times, then said, "I made it."

"You made this? You must be very clever. I could never make anything like this."

Bonga shrugged again. "Let's play soccer."

As they kicked the ball around in the back yard, Edward felt like an amateur playing with a World Cup champion. The ball seemed to become part of Bonga, as it rolled up his body, bounced from knee to head to foot.

When they tired, they went indoors and stretched out on the floor in Edward's room to read books. Edward couldn't help but notice that Bonga read English and Afrikaans with ease.

"I'm sorry I don't have any *Sotho* books," Edward apologized.

"That's all right. But the language is called *Sesotho*, our homeland is *Lesotho*, and I am a *Basotho*."

Nancy stuck her head into the room, "Lunch time, boys."

"Let's go," Edward pleaded with a reluctant Bonga. "In our house, our African friends eat at the table with us."

The rest of the day went well as the boys rotated between outside and indoor games. Much too soon, Bonga said, "I must meet my mother at the Georginia Station at 4:30. I must leave in a half-hour."

"Let's go early and explore the park on the other side of the tracks," Edward suggested.

The boys raced along the streets toward the station. While Edward pushed the wire car, Bonga skillfully hoofed the soccer ball, sometimes dribbling it like a basketball. Edward felt a tremor of unease when he noticed housewives in the all-white neighborhood stopping their activities to watch them pass.

He thought these ladies needed to get African friends themselves.

From the station platform duplicate pedestrian bridges stretched over the twin tracks to connect with the opposite platform. The sign at the entrance to one said, *Whites Only*, the other bore a sign saying, *Non-Whites Only*.

Bonga headed toward the non-whites bridge. Edward hesitated in front of the one intended for white people, then turned away to join Bonga and said, "The heck with their stupid laws. I'm crossing with my friend."

Shoulder-to-shoulder the two dissenters crossed the non-whites overpass. As they arrived on the opposite platform, four white boys playing near the station saw the act of defiance and jeered at Edward. He merely waved at them and called, "You guys want to play soccer?"

The mockers hesitated but turned away as a lone African woman approached on a pathway through the park.

"Bonga," she called out.

"Hello, *Me*," Bonga answered, then to Edward, "My mother is early. I must go. Can I visit you again sometime?"

"Yes, you'll have to come again."

"I will. Good-bye, my good friend."

"Good-bye to you, Bonga...my friend."

Edward raced home, pleased that he had an African friend, surprised that he had made that tiny protest against the status quo. He felt a little afraid when he considered what might have happened—and a touch of anger at the racist attitudes he met everywhere.

At the dinner table he spilled out his story, what a great day he'd had with Bonga. He put particular emphasis on his boldness at the railway crossing.

His dad beamed. "Edward, I'm proud of you, taking a stand against apartheid. Most adults here won't do that."

Edward thought of the kids who had jeered at the crossing and his anger returned. The muscles on his face tensed as he blurted out, "And I'd do it again!"

~S

Nancy slipped the big Austin into third gear and merged with traffic on Ontdekkers Way. After three miles, she would exit left into Florida Hills to pick up Bertha and Johanna. The car responded smartly despite the three women already in the back seat.

Each one alone weighed twice as much as she did, Nancy realized. It never ceased to surprise her how so many African women not only carried excessive weight, but gloried in and laughed about it.

Nancy liked driving. She had adjusted to driving on the left without difficulty. But more than driving, better than the sense of freedom delivered by steering wheel and open road, she loved her involvement with the Tuesday-night maid's meeting.

When she and Andrew had volunteered to help Pastor Makunyane and Mumsa start the outreach program, she hadn't planned on driving all over suburban Roodepoort to pick up people. But now she saw that as an added bonus. Mumsa had insisted that Nancy drive, not Andrew. It wouldn't look good for a white man to pick up a carload of black women.

To Nancy and Andrew's surprise and pleasure, the Methodist church in Discovery had willingly made a small chapel available.

It amazed Nancy that they allowed thirty African people to use their building. She'd expected they might think like some of the missionaries, believing Africans would contaminate a whites-only facility. South Africa never ceased to surprise her.

The women in the back seat echoed a cry of delight as Nancy exited left a little too quickly onto Pindus Street, and then right onto Cotswold. Pulling up in front of a house, she expected the ladies in the back would make a lot more noise when Bertha and Johanna got on board.

The two came through the iron gateway as the car stopped. Johanna, young and slender with hair in an Afro, looked anything but the typical African maid. She slid to the center, sitting on the divide where the front seats met.

"Sa'bona, Mama, Sa'bona, everyone," she said.

Bertha, who also weighed less than her sisters in the back seat, followed Johanna, but not before reaching over the seat and shaking hands with those behind.

Nancy fumbled for the gearshift. "Johanna, if you don't move your leg, I will have to shift gears with your knee!"

Johanna pushed Bertha against the door to reveal the hidden shift lever. Nancy grabbed it and said to Johanna in a not-too-quiet whisper, "Good thing you and Bertha weigh less than the *Mamas* in the back seat, or we'd have to hold the meeting right here."

Another squeal of delight erupted from behind.

As Nancy pulled away, she wondered if a passerby might think the squeals emanating from the car came from overburdened tires. Who would realize it came from five African women within? Women joyfully expressing pleasure on this special night out, exhilarated by the thrill of riding with a white woman who accepted them as equals, even to the point of joking with them.

In her humble way Nancy wondered how she had bridged the cultural gap when others had spent 40 years without doing so?

They barely got back onto Ontdekkers Way before Johanna had everyone singing a lively Zulu chorus.

"Mbonge, mbonge, Mbonge ekuseni, Mbonge nasemini,
Mbonge, mbonge, Lize lishoni 'langa."

Rich harmonies thundered off the walls of the car. Windows, door handles, and dashboard joined in sympathetic song. Nancy used English words to add her alto voice to the mix.

"Thank you, thank you, thank you in the morning..."

Nancy couldn't look away from the road to see which one of the ladies was adding that fabulous bass line.

When they reached the church, the women hadn't quite finished the last verse of a hymn, so Nancy took the car three times around the traffic circle before stopping. On one of those circuits, she saw Andrew and Lucy walking toward the church.

The women exited the car with cries of *"Siyabonga, Mama"* and headed for the chapel door and their friends inside.

Waiting beside the car for Andrew and Lucy, Nancy thought about the things she'd learned to love in South Africa: the African people, the maid's meetings, the African church services in Soweto, the great friends she had made—people like Pastor Makunyane and Mumsa. She even loved the Austin. They'd never had a car so classy at home.

She looked up to see Andrew and Lucy approaching across the traffic circle, heard their voices, but not the actual words. She studied Lucy's liquid walk—almost like a panther creeping up on its prey.

As Andrew and Lucy drew near, her mind raced. She thought now of things she disliked about her missionary experience: the culture of apartheid, racism, and the paternalistic missionary attitudes.

A stream of thoughts tumbled through her mind. Andrew should not drive black women around in a car in this sick country. A man shouldn't walk down the street with one—especially one like Lucy. Neighbors would talk, might even call the police. And, God forbid, even worse things might happen.

Seventeen

Andrew and Nancy struggled on with mixed emotions—torn between an expanding love for the African people and a growing estrangement between themselves and the mission hierarchy. Indeed, the two seemed to bear a direct relationship. The closer they got to the African community, the greater the gap that opened between them and their fellow missionaries. The eruption over their relationship with Lucy had certainly marked a turning point. They had waited for weeks to hear from field council but heard nothing. The weeks became months. Then it happened.

Andrew sat with Gordon Muir behind the glass wall. Gordon's clothes had the usual slightly disheveled, uncomfortable look, but with something else added. With his right hand tidying his shirtfront, he drummed with his other hand an uncertain beat on the arm of his desk chair. Ripples ran across his clothing as he shifted within them.

He's squirming again, thought Andrew, prompting him to ask, "What's wrong?"

"Wrong? Nothing really. Well, maybe. Peter Fowler wants to talk to us. That's why I called you down. He should arrive at any minute."

"What does he want?"

Gordon shrugged and looked at his watch. "I guess he'll tell us when he gets here."

At that moment, as though choreographed by an outside force, Peter stepped down into the press room and crossed to the office behind the glass wall. He lifted a pile of papers from an otherwise vacant chair and sat down.

"To what do we owe the pleasure?" Gordon asked, obviously fighting to sound casual.

Peter looked straight at Andrew. "It involves you to a great extent, so I thought I should tell you first before I announce it at the staff meeting."

Andrew sucked in his breath.

"The field council met and made a decision regarding the African employees that live in missionary's homes. We feel the practice has caused some ill feeling, so we decided to make a change."

Andrew stared at him, expecting the worst.

Peter looked down at a paper in his hand, apparently to avoid his gaze. Then he raised his eyes but looked toward Gordon as he spoke. "We have arranged to lease a hostel in Soweto for the girls. We'll arrange to have a Kombi, unless you think a larger bus would be needed, to pick them up and take them home each work day."

He turned to Andrew and continued. "I know you and Nancy have become attached to Lucy, but we felt this move necessary to keep peace in the mission family."

Bloody racist fools. Andrew almost let the words slip out. His whole body stiffened, his hands gripped the edge of his chair seat, but he said nothing.

Peter stood to leave. "I must get ready for the staff meeting. See you there shortly."

Andrew and Gordon sat in silence for a full minute before Gordon spoke. "Andrew, I am sorry. I know how much Lucy means to you and Nancy. But I guess we can't buck mission tradition and leadership."

"Thanks anyway for your sup-support," Andrew answered, stumbling over the critical word.

Andrew took his usual seat in the staff meeting, at the back near the door. Peter made the announcement about the new worker's hostel without adding more to what he had previously said, then moved on to other business.

Andrew slipped out before the meeting ended and headed home to share the bad news with Nancy. She had the car for grocery shopping, so he walked home, covering the distance in record time, his anger rising with every step, his mind racing.

Only idiots would stay here! he thought. All his life he'd wanted to be a missionary. And he'd always wanted a daughter. Now when he'd got one, a beautiful, mature young woman, the hypocritical mission leaders wanted to take her away. He'd miss her smile, the way she walked....

Was it for the best? He wasn't sure.

As Nancy carried the grocery bags from car to house, she saw Andrew approaching the gate. Even a cursory glance revealed his clenched fists and a stiff, rapid walk.

Something's wrong, she thought, dropping the groceries on the kitchen counter. The front door slammed and she heard Andrew's agitated footsteps cross the living room to the kitchen doorway.

"Andrew, what's wrong? You look, you look—"

"I think it's time to go back to Canada," he said, banging his fist into his palm.

Nancy stepped forward and grabbed his hands. "Andrew! Relax. I haven't seen you so agitated since you thought I was going to refuse your marriage proposal."

Nancy watched his facial muscles relax as though internal pressure had eased. As he stepped inside the kitchen, she pulled out a chair. He dropped into it, placed his elbows on the table, and rested his face in his hands.

"You're right. I need to relax. The world hasn't fallen into an abyss, even if our great missionary dream is teetering on the brink."

"What happened?"

"They're taking Lucy away from us. Putting all the African workers in a hostel in Soweto."

"Oh!"

She dared not let Andrew see the relief that flooded her being—relief followed by a wave of guilt, like tears washing over her soul. She knew this harsh decision on the part of the mission would deeply hurt Andrew. But she also felt Andrew's emotional tie to Lucy could develop into something serious—something that could wreck their marriage.

Struggling with conflicting emotions, she finally said, "Even though she won't be living with us anymore, she can come back any time for a visit. We can keep the room just for her."

Andrew rose to his feet and hugged Nancy. "Good dependable old Nancy. Always ready with a practical answer." He kissed her on the cheek, and left the room.

As Nancy watched his retreating back, her thoughts became hopelessly entangled with her emotions. Did he picture her as plain "old Nancy" who gets just a peck on the cheek, compared to "young Lucy"? Did Andrew feel guilty? Was she just jealous? But she'd seen the way they looked at each other... She knew she must confront Andrew... but not now.

The mission bureaucracy moved with uncommon speed. Within one week, they had arranged for Lucy, and all those like her in other missionary homes, to move to Soweto. Nancy walked with Andrew to the waiting Kombi to say good-bye on a Saturday afternoon.

As she pulled shut the minibus sliding door, Lucy called out, "Thanks for everything. I'll see you at work; and I will come back."

She never even looked at me—she said that just for Andrew, Nancy thought as they turned back to the house. She noticed Andrew's shoulders sag as he entered just ahead of her. Steeling herself, she followed him in, thinking, *Now is the time to confront him.*

She waited until Andrew sat on the sofa, then took the chair opposite.

"That ends another chapter in our lives," he said.

Nancy bit her lip, delaying her challenge only for a moment. "I hope so, Andrew, I sincerely hope so."

He looked directly at her, but she saw only confusion and questioning in his face.

"You're in love with her," she said spitting the words out more harshly than she had intended.

His face reddened. "I am not!"

"You may not have realized it, but you are. I know you—I can read your body language."

Andrew's face fell, his eyes staring at the floor. Neither spoke. She watched the inner struggle reflected on his face.

"I...," he began. "Maybe in some way you're right. I didn't realize it. But it doesn't mean I don't love you."

His last words sounded like the pleading of a hurt child. When his eyes came up to meet hers, she nodded. "I know, Andrew."

No more words came, so she rose and headed for the kitchen, her heart racing and her mind in turmoil as she asked herself, *But do I know that? I don't even know what to think. Oh God, why is this happening to me?*

The fallout of the Lucy debacle cast a shadow of discouragement over both of them. In Andrew's mind, it didn't come between them personally. Unhappiness with missionary life in South Africa fueled their desire to go home, but their attachment to the African community and their fear of appearing as failures kept them there. Life went on much as before.

They continued worshiping each Sunday at the African Church—dropping the boys off at the local white Baptist church before driving to Soweto. In addition to the pleasure they experienced there, they gained great satisfaction by working with the maids' meetings, and 40 maids now attended regularly.

Other mission agencies had become aware of Andrew's artistic skills and contracted more work—more logos, letterheads, fund-raising brochures, and even some book covers. But he made only limited headway in improving the printed material within his own group. The boys fared well at school. They now spoke Afrikaans with fluency and had even mastered a few Zulu expressions.

Although she never came to the house, Andrew still saw Lucy from time to time at work. Their meetings stirred something inside him he didn't want to recognize—a mix of anger, frustration, and a sense of lost opportunities—feelings reminiscent of early adolescence.

He regularly visited with Mumsa at her desk. He and Nancy both valued the bond that had grown between them and Pastor Makunyane and Mumsa.

"You have become like a brother, Andrew," Mumsa said one day as he sat opposite her. "The missionaries and even some of the African staff have commented on our relationship. I tell them, 'Andrew is my brother,' so leave us alone. But you are wise to avoid spending time chatting with Lucy. That might really start tongues wagging."

Andrew tensed slightly, thinking, *She is good at reading people—she can see deeper inside me than she lets on. I hope my face isn't red.*

"So," Mumsa said, "I hear you have won one battle."

"Which one is that?"

"*Baba* Makunyane and I have been invited to represent the African Church at the next mission planning meeting and at International Council when they meet here in Roodepoort early next year."

Andrew's mouth dropped open. "I hadn't heard that. I've been chipping away for what seems forever. Somebody must have been listening."

Mumsa began to chuckle. "Maybe the Lord was listening. But don't get too excited; they'd like to send you home. All the good missionaries get sent home—they show up the rest who spend all their energy following the real and imaginary rules of apartheid."

"We're on the verge of going home without any push from them," Andrew admitted.

Mumsa shook her head. "Don't do that. You love the African people and they love you. You have a good ministry in the church and through the maids' meetings. That's why God brought you here. You didn't really come to draw nice pictures—you came to draw hearts to God."

Andrew wanted to hug Mumsa, but that kind of demonstration of affection between black and white, between missionary and national, would just not do in South Africa.

Again she seemed to read his mind. "Cheer up. South Africa will change. So will the mission. At the international council things might happen with the new international president, Dr. Ralph Sommers, in charge. You have an expression in English that says, 'A new broom sweeps clean.'"

Feeling almost elated, Andrew left Mumsa, pleased that she always managed to cheer him up. She had made a good point: Sommers, a New Zealander, might have a different outlook on life. He might have new insights—and the courage to bring about change.

The weeks slipped by without any great alteration in their troubled lives. But the approaching arrival of delegates from around the world added a touch of excitement. In preparation for them, Andrew wrote a letter explaining his disillusionment with the mission. He planned to hand copies to Nicholas Hamilton-Jones and Ralph Sommers in person.

A month before the event, Andrew found a memo pinned to the bulletin board.

To: Roodepoort Staff
From: Dr. Ralph Sommers, International Office
Date: January 27, 1975
Subject: Change in venue of International Council

The venue of the International Council has been changed from Roodepoort to Union Bible College near Pietermaritzburg in Natal province. Unfortunately, this may preclude many of you from attending. However, we will find lodging for those of you who have been officially asked to make presentations. I trust this does not inconvenience or disappoint many of you. R. S.

Eighteen

As Andrew reread the memo, a sense of despair swept over him. Then he realized someone was standing at his elbow.

"So," said Jack Ferguson, "It looks as if our new IP has little sense of democracy. The people who aren't there cannot challenge the status quo. Well, I didn't want to attend anyway. If they meet in Pietermaritzburg, they might cause less trouble up here."

"I have no desire to attend their sessions," Andrew said. "But I'd hoped to meet some of them."

"They'll fly into and out of Jan Smuts airport, so they'll likely want to visit the work here in Roodepoort. My guess is they'll come here after the council so the visit won't interfere with their ready-made deliberations."

Andrew sighed. "I had greater expectations for Sommers than this suggests. I'd like to meet him face-to-face."

"Write him a note. Give it to Peter, our dear old field director. Sommers might want to see you after the Council."

Andrew squeezed Jack's arm. "Thanks. I had planned to do that anyway."

A few minutes later he sat at Mumsa's desk. "Have you heard the latest? About the move of the council meeting to Pietermaritzburg?"

She waved a piece of paper at him. "Yes, and my husband and I got memos confirming our attendance. They'll find a place for us to stay at the college."

Andrew's spirits rose slightly. "That's one good sign! Now I must go and write a letter to the new boss, to let him know what a bad situation we have here."

When Andrew reached his office, his spirits rose even higher. Two large manila envelopes waited in his in-basket. He opened the first and a pile of gospel tracts spilled out on his desk. About half of them—

printed on newsprint—contained no color or graphics. The rest used better paper, but only a few displayed color, and three or four had simple drawings. Andrew wondered what he had. It looked like a collection of second-rate printing from early in the century. He peered inside the envelope to find a sheet of folded paper stuck to the side.

He pulled out the paper, opened it to see a letterhead. Across the top of the page in black Helvetica characters he read the words, *Gospel Tract Publishing Association, London.*

Before reading the letter, he shook his head and thought, *This looks as antiquated as the tracts.* But as he read, he tensed with excitement.

We have seen the work you did for the mission organization, Medical Help South Africa. It is time to update our publications and feel you are the person to help us. If God's Word Mission can spare you from what must be a busy schedule, please quote a price on preparing four-color graphics for the enclosed 50 gospel tracts. We have a team of writers editing and updating the text for each tract.

In his excitement, Andrew almost forgot the second envelope. When he opened it, he found another commission from Med-Help. He grabbed the phone and dialed his home number.

"Nancy, we may have turned the corner."

"What corner?"

The words tumbled from Andrew's mouth, "The mission corner—the South African corner. Things have suddenly started to get better."

"Andrew, slow down."

"Okay, okay. They have moved the International Council meeting to Natal. That means we won't have to attend, which is good. But they have invited African Church representatives and that's a real breakthrough."

Andrew waited for Nancy's response, which took a few seconds.

"Good, but what about the rest of the problems?"

"I just received a commission, two actually, to do some graphics work for other mission organizations. Work that could keep me going for months. They'll pay our mission very well, and we can put the profit toward our new press building."

"Well, it does sound interesting, but a new building won't change attitudes. Let's talk more tonight."

Andrew noted the skepticism in Nancy's voice as she replied. Her lack of enthusiasm didn't dampen Andrew's excitement. But after writing a letter to Dr. Sommers with copies to Hamilton-Jones, Peter Fowler, and Gordon Muir, outlining his disappointments with the mission, he realized they still had a long way to go.

He spent the rest of the day working on estimates for the commissions. The following day he prepared sketches, printing standards, and color samples to illustrate how he proposed handling the work. He copied everything to Gordon Muir and sent it off by registered mail. They might not hear back for weeks.

The next weeks slipped by without any improvement in Nancy's outlook. Even Andrew lost some of his enthusiasm about what he had seen as a positive turn in events. Sunday services at the African Church and the weekly maids' meeting remained the high points in their lives. On Sunday of the week of the International Council, with Pastor Makunyane and Mumsa away at the meeting, the church elders asked Andrew to preach.

On Tuesday of that week, he found two notes, one from Dr. Sommers, the other from Hamilton-Jones, requesting meetings on Saturday as they traveled through after the council meeting. It seemed they had got Andrew's letter and felt it deserved a personal response.

On Friday Elizabeth bubbled into Andrew's office and handed him a telegram. It contained only two lines:

LIKE YOUR PROPOSAL. STOP. PLEASE PROCEED. STOP.
FULL AUTHORIZATION TO FOLLOW. STOP. GTPA LONDON.

Andrew stared at it, wondering what GTPA meant. "Ah, I get it! The Gospel Tract Publishing Association. And by proposal, they mean they want me to go ahead and create the graphics for their tracts. Great!"

He immediately wanted to share the news, but Gordon and Mumsa were at the council meeting. He called home.

"It sounds good," Nancy said, "but I'm more interested in what happens tomorrow when the VIPs come to see us."

Saturday dawned dull and overcast.

"It's an omen," Nancy declared at the breakfast table.

"Since when have you become superstitious?" Andrew asked.

"Who's being superstitious? God is able to send messages through the weather. He may have a message—a warning for us."

"You guys expecting bad news?" Edward piped up.

"Not any worse than most days," Nancy fired back. "You and John get a wiggle on. We have mission guests arriving at 10 o'clock and we want you out of here before they arrive."

"Oh yeah, this is the day we go to the Carlton Center in Jo'burg," John said.

Andrew dropped some money on the table. "Here's ten Rand each to add to what you already have. Buy some African curios so that you'll have something to remind you of South Africa when we go home."

"Wow, we're going home?" John practically glowed with excitement.

"Sometime, but not today," Nancy said. "Now get moving. And here's some change for train fare."

With the boys gone, Andrew helped Nancy tidy up the house and do the dishes. They put on a pot of coffee and settled down to await the visitors. At five minutes after ten, Sommers and Hamilton-Jones pulled up in front of the house in a borrowed car. Andrew met them at the door and seated them in the living room.

Sommers was a tall slim man with an austere-looking face, clearly one who was not used to anyone disagreeing with him. Andrew's hope began to dwindle just at the sight of him.

Nancy entered from the kitchen and asked cheerily, "Can I get you coffee?"

"No thank you," they answered, almost in unison.

"We have only a few minutes," Dr. Sommers explained. "We have to visit with four other missionary families."

Andrew felt his heart sink within him. *They're not going to listen to what we have to say.*

Dr. Sommers leaned forward, obviously signaling his intention to control the conversation. Hamilton-Jones sat back, apparently willing to let him.

Sommers spoke. "Nicholas and I have discussed your situation and the...er...problems you have identified. We would like to make some strong suggestions. First you have mentioned the lack of concern the mission seems to have for the African Church—"

"And for the African mission workers," Nancy cut in.

He gave her a withering look. "You must understand that as leaders of God's Word Mission, our responsibility relates only to the missionaries under our care. We cannot get involved with relationships between the mission and the African church. The African Church leaders will have to look after their own affairs."

Nancy jumped in again. "But our whole reason for existence is to work with African people—"

"Mrs. Heath, please don't interrupt. Let me finish."

Arrogant b—! Andrew's conscience pricked him for thinking those words.

"You two have run into some major adjustment problems—not at all uncommon for missionaries on their first term. You're older than most first-termers. Maybe that has something to do with it."

Andrew and Nancy kept their mouths shut, but nothing would silence Andrew's mind. *Right. That makes it harder to brainwash us and turn us into racists.*

Dr. Sommers continued, "Nicholas and I agree that you should take your furlough sooner than next year when, according to policy, it would normally occur. Say just before the December break—that will let the boys finish up their South African school year. You will also have a few months to complete any projects you may have. Going home will help you to reevaluate—to look at things from a distance."

Sommers leaned back and Hamilton-Jones took over. "Andrew,

you could use the time in Canada raising money for the new press building. I have no doubt you could raise all we need in a year at home. Then on your return you could resume these assignments you seem to be getting from other mission organizations. We in the Canadian council will help with the travel costs. I checked with the books before leaving Canada, and discovered your travel account could use some help."

Andrew again held back his thoughts. He hadn't joined the mission to raise money. He joined to work with African people, to help develop reading and study materials that would assist the churches to train their members.

Sommers leaned forward again. "Providing you can get through the next few months without another blow-up, I think your time away will help you and the others recover from the debacle over the African girls being pulled out of the missionary homes. I'm not sure you or the field council did the right things."

The words rushed through Andrew's mind, but he stopped them short of his mouth. *They want to blame us for their racist attitudes.*

Nancy seemed more in control. "Should we begin telling the folks at home about our return....I mean, about our early furlough?"

"Certainly," Hamilton-Jones said. "It will help your supporters to understand the reasons for your early furlough—to raise money for the press building."

Andrew fumed inside. So we lie to our supporters. *He's giving us a good story to hide the real reasons.*

After a moment, he found his voice. "What about the assignments I just accepted for graphics work? I may not be able to get them all finished by December. They involve a lot of money."

The two mission executives looked at each other. Hamilton-Jones turned to Andrew. "Maybe Nancy could go home ahead of you and begin the fund-raising while you spend whatever time you need to complete the assignments."

Neither Andrew nor Nancy responded; they simply stared at each other.

"Why don't we leave the details of the decision with you? Let the FD, Peter Fowler, know your decision as soon as you can," Sommers suggested.

"I could drink a cup of that coffee before we move on," Hamilton-Jones said.

Nancy rose immediately and disappeared into the kitchen. She returned seconds later, shaking her head. "I'm sorry. I forgot to leave it on the stove. It's cold."

The two visitors left. Andrew and Nancy retreated to the kitchen. Nancy poured two cups of steaming coffee and set one in front of Andrew.

"What's this?" he demanded.

Nancy smiled for the first time since the visitors had arrived. "I lied."

"What will we do now? I'm more upset and confused than ever."

"Andrew, I don't know what you're going to do. But by the end of next week, the boys and I will be on a plane heading home. You stay a while and work on your precious graphics assignments for a month or two if that's what you want!"

"You and the boys would never raise any money. Why not wait and we'll go together?"

Nancy shook her head. Her eyes flashed.

"Andrew, you don't get it. I'm going home to stay. They might call themselves God's Word Mission, but they are the most ungodly bunch of hypocrites I have ever had anything to do with."

Andrew just stared at his wife. He knew she meant business, and he knew she was right.

They talked and planned for the rest of the day. By the time the boys returned home from the Carlton Center, they had worked out the details. Nancy and the boys would get a plane to Toronto well before the year's end. She would go to Kitchener and find a place to live and register the boys in school. He would stay in Roodepoort to pack their things. They still had the steel drums from the trip out. What he couldn't pack or sell, he would give to African friends. They would let the mission believe they had accepted the plan to take an early furlough until Andrew got home. Then they would officially resign.

As for the graphics work, Andrew would try to complete it or find a local commercial artist to take over the assignments, or simply beg off.

"If we do things any other way, if we tell them now that we're quitting, they'll hassle us over the plane fare. We don't need that kind of a fight," Nancy said.

As Andrew listened to his wife, he thought, *She has become the stronger of us. I've been acting like a spineless wimp.*

Gathering up what little courage he had left, he said, "We came here for a fight, Nancy, to fight against the forces of Evil. But look who we ended up fighting!"

Andrew's own words echoed back at him. He sounded like a frustrated evangelical preacher—but maybe he had become just that.

Andrew sighed and collapsed back on the sofa. He spoke aloud, not sure if addressing Nancy, himself, or God. "I don't think we are alone. Steve seems to have got into a similar mess in India."

Book Five

Nineteen

George Atkinson seemed a quick learner. But then Steve was used to training foreign missionaries or nationals straight after a one-year internship. Unlike them, George had already completed training as a surgeon. After just five months he would soon be good enough to fill in while Steve took the short vacation Rajalingam had told him he needed to relieve his stress. But the source of that stress was Rajalingam.

Perhaps he's the one who should go away for a while, not me, Steve thought.

George was also fun to have around. He was witty and positive in his approach. Their discussions stimulated Steve academically, something he'd really missed. He was quickly becoming fond of George. On weekends, they would often spend time together in the hospital library, reading journals and discussing what they read.

"By cracky it's hot in here," George said. "But look at you. Steve, you look cool as a cucumber."

"I don't feel the heat as much as you 'cause I've been here longer. But I know my heat regulation system is working hard when I wipe salt crystals off my forehead. The weather is dry now, but wait till it gets hot and humid. Then sweat drips on whatever you try to read. That's when I do my thinking in the pool, or relax on the balcony with the fan going full blast—and a gin and tonic in my hand."

"It's good to prevent malaria they say."

"What? Gin?"

"No, Steve, tonic water."

"Of course. It's the quinine in the tonic water. That reminds me of a little red book the Mission gave me on my way to India. It was called *How to Keep Healthy in the Tropics*. Apparently it was prepared for the British troops, about a hundred years ago by the sound of it. My favorite line is this one. 'Contrary to public belief, it is not necessary to drink large quantities of alcohol in order to remain healthy in the tropics.' Now isn't that a hoot?"

George gave a low chuckle. "Ah yes, I can just see the old British Raj in the Officer's Mess drinking gin and tonic to prevent malaria, and giving the credit to gin."

"Speaking of the heat, George, why don't we go visit the Madras Medical School Library? It's air-conditioned and I'm allowed to use it. I don't have a car to get there, but you do."

"Great idea. Let's also visit Madras Fort. I hear they have a huge icehouse there. Seems that in the days before refrigeration, they used to drag icebergs there from the Bering Strait behind a ship, and cut them up to make ice cubes."

"Aha. Then they could keep the gin and tonic cold. It is amazing how far people will go to preserve their health."

They both had a good laugh over that one.

Trips by car to the library in Madras soon became their weekend getaway. Yolanda came along and went shopping.

"How'd you come by this car?" Steve asked him as they drove there one day.

"My uncle won a lottery and felt guilty when the family accused him of gambling. The only way out was to buy a car for a missionary. That's how I got lucky. But tell me, my good chap, how do you tolerate the poverty that we see all around us? It almost breaks my heart, but I can do so little about it. All these beggars. I can't give money to all of them. Now this makes *me* feel guilty. We in the West have so much, and these beggars have nothing."

"I see two approaches, George. You could say it's their problem, their own fault for being Hindus. If they'd kill a lot of rats instead of respecting them as ancestors, I've heard there could be enough food to feed every one of them. While this may be true, I prefer the second approach."

"What's that?"

"I concentrate on the fact that I'm doing the best I can to make a better world for those within my reach. You could say I just bury my head in my work. But I'm doing all I can to help the lowest of the low,

186

those with leprosy. No one should expect more than that. So I don't feel one bit guilty. If everyone would do as we are doing, there might not be any poverty at all."

"Now, Steve, what about the heat? You don't seem to mind that either. You told me it gets much hotter next month and by May it's unbearable. How do you manage?"

"By the time you've been here a year... how long will you be here, George?"

Steve was desperate to learn his own fate and knew it must have something to do with George's presence in Janglepit.

"We haven't been told what the plans are. Seems Rajalingam hasn't decided, or if he has he's not telling. But we've signed on with the Mission for five years. If we like it here we'll come back for a second term. A lot depends on how Yolanda feels, and that's a bit dodgey right now."

"Well, to answer your question, George, a year from now, two at the most, you should be sufficiently used to the heat to not mind it much. But in May the sun is directly overhead. It's over Calcutta in June and returns here in July. In July we have the first of the rains. This makes it sticky but a little cooler. By that time you know the weather can only get better. So what we do is head for the hills for the whole month of May."

"You don't mean those little cone-shaped things we can see just east of us, do you?"

Steve chuckled. "Oh no. They're just a thousand feet high, remnants of an old mountain range, the Eastern Ghats. They're fun to climb in December, but don't even think of it in this heat. Further south there are much larger hills, 5000 to 6000 feet high. There it's quite cool in summer. One good place to go is the Niligiris, Tamil for blue hills. Further yet is Kodaikanal. That's where they have a fabulous golf course surrounded by pine trees. Conoor in the Niligris has a golf course too, but no pine trees."

"What's so special about pine trees?"

"Give yourself another six months here, George, and I'll bet you'll have forgotten what they even smell like. When I smell pine trees it restores my spirit, reminds me who I am."

"Ah yes, but that's because you're from Minnesota. For me it takes a pint of British ale."

"You can get that here now, order it from Singapore. But don't let Rajalingam find out. He read the riot act to me for giving beer to some visiting Americans."

"Speaking of Rajalingam, Steve, what say we ask him to put an air-conditioner in the hospital library? It's beastly hot in there. I'd like to study in there in the evenings. We have some dashed-good journals I'd like to get into."

"Great idea, George. You talk to him. I'm kinda busy right now."

The last thing Steve wanted was another confrontation with the one they called the "Raj." But George insisted he should be the one to ask. After all, he was 'The Chief."

Steve put the encounter off as long as he could, but in late April it had to happen. That year, 1974, April was declared to be the hottest in Madras since the British had started keeping records. Rajalingam had finished his morning work, cut short by the intense heat, and was leaving for his air-conditioned rooms at home when Steve and George caught up with him in the corridor of the administration building.

"Sir," Steve called out, "can we have a quick word with you please?"

"Be very quick then, Steve. It's much too hot to stand around here."

"Good point, sir. And it's also too hot to study in the library. The brain can't think in this heat."

"You people have nothing to complain about. Spend your time operating in that air-conditioned operating room. That's what you're paid to do."

"At seven dollars a day," Steve said, "I wouldn't mention the pay if I were you. We need to keep current with the journals if our work is to be of the caliber that brings honor to the Lord, and to this institution I might add."

"But be sensible, man. If the library was air-conditioned, the nurses could go in there and be air-conditioned. That wouldn't be right now, would it?"

Steve glanced at George, who stood with his mouth open. He

looked like he wanted to speak, but said nothing, until Rajalingam asked him if the screens had been installed on the drains from the sinks in his house.

"That was done some time ago," George said.

Rajalingam smiled. "We want you to be happy here. I have great plans for you. We wouldn't want any snakes crawling into your house through those pipes and frightening your wife. Now if you'll give us a few minutes alone, I want to have a few words with Steve."

Here it comes, Steve thought as they both watched George walk away toward the main hospital building.

Steve followed Rajalingam into the superintendent's office. With the flick of a switch the overhead fan began whirling and wobbling noisily. Steve fantasized that one day it might shake itself loose and fall on Rajalingam's head.

"George is doing well, I hear," Rajalingam said. "He should be able to take over from you now."

Steve felt his eyes bulging. "What about the research?"

"I've obtained permission from the Indian Council of Medical Research for him to be appointed as your assistant. Although he's a foreigner, he's not an American and just an assistant. We do things by degrees. So you can leave the station for awhile. I've arranged for you to spend three months in the Niligiris, at the Missionary Hostel in Conoor. There's a golf course nearby. It will be a pleasant change for you, and I'm sure George can manage without you for three months."

And if three months, why not longer? Steve was certain this was another thing Rajalingam was "doing by degrees."

After an overnight trip by train to the base of the hills, Steve boarded the little blue steam-powered locomotive that would slowly climb upward on a narrow gauge track to his destination. This train consisted of the engine, the coal car, and three coaches that could each hold eight passengers. It was almost an exact replica of the one he'd taken to Darjeeling nearly three years earlier, the one Kipling wrote about.

How, with a crew of six, he wondered, *can they ever make money on this six-hour run?* On the steeper slopes, a cogwheel under the engine engaged a series of teeth between the tracks so the wheels would not slip. Whether going uphill or down, the engine was always on the downhill end of the train to prevent losing any coaches if a coupling broke.

He'd made this trip once before, but the sights were so refreshing that he was beginning to enjoy it as a new experience. The temperature grew pleasantly cooler as they passed from a tropical climate to a semi-tropical one. The trees they passed told the story, as palm and banana trees gave way to more northern species such as beech, aspen and pine. Monkeys swung from the branches and chattered unafraid as the smoke-belching monster chugged slowly up the hillside. Once in a while, a purple-flowered jacaranda tree in full bloom came into view. At a road crossing Steve saw monkeys frolicking in a jackfruit tree.

As the train passed round a bend to the right the whole landscape changed. Tea plants covered the hillside, interspersed with tall thin trees that shed their bark. Steve took a deep breath and filled his lungs with the sweet smell of eucalyptus. When the train reached a level area for the first time, it slowly reduced its speed. They had arrived at Conoor.

He knew he had only a few seconds to get off before the shrill whistle would announce the train was leaving for its final destination, Ootacamond. A 12-year old boy insisted on carrying his suitcase and, with amazing agility, hoisted it onto his head.

Over the next few weeks the pressure in the back of Steve's head gradually eased. He spent many evenings sitting on the hostel's large veranda overlooking a small hill entirely covered in rose bushes.

He enjoyed playing golf five days a week, even though the course had few pine trees around it. Each morning and night he read his Bible, something he'd tended to neglect during his busy life at Janglepit. He became content once more to take a back seat, to let God take control.

He resolved to be less pushy, to step back and see what might happen. He would follow God's plan for his life, wherever it might lead. His battle with Rajalingam was, in his own mind, a battle between good and evil. He always thought he was on God's side. But had he unwittingly scored some points for the enemy? He wondered about this and decided a less aggressive approach might be the better one to take.

Twenty

Steve returned to Janglepit from his forced leave of absence a new man. He smiled and sometimes whistled. He was convinced he would soon be going home to America and had happily resigned himself to the situation. He accepted that he could not achieve all he had expected to do in India, but felt satisfied he had helped many people there. Also, he had made many contributions to the advancement of medical science. It was a pity he could not stay on and do more, but the decision to leave was not his. His role now would be just to keep out of trouble.

A few months after Steve's return, the November rains brought cooler weather. At about five o'clock every day, a torrential downpour made stepping outside feel like having a shower fully-clothed. Anyone not at home when it started waited half-an-hour until the rain ended.

Steve usually worked in the office until the weather cleared. He had no reason to go home early, no one to go home to, only Sakundra his maid. She always had supper ready at six o'clock precisely. By then the rain had stopped.

For George it was quite different. His beautiful wife, Yolanda, was waiting for him with open arms at the end of each day. George always headed up the path promptly at half past four when the hospital day officially ended.

On one occasion in late November, George was detained in the O.R. He was about to leave when the rain began and stepped back into the hospital. As Steve entered his office, he noticed George's face twitching.

"Are you okay, George?"

"We had a problem yesterday, Steve, almost a disaster."

Steve's eyes widened. "What happened?"

"Yolanda asked to have the drains cleaned. One of them was

blocked. After cleaning them, someone must have left one of the covers off. When I got home, I found her standing on the kitchen table while a four-foot long snake circled the room, flicking his tongue at her. She'd been standing on that table all day long."

"A snake? What kind? I hope it wasn't a spitting cobra!"

"I screamed till the gardener came and chased it away. He said it was a baby python. Some baby!"

"She must have been scared out of her wits."

"So scared she doesn't want me to leave her alone. She'll worry because I'm late. She never liked India and—I didn't want to tell you this, Steve—now she wants to return to England."

Yolanda began having diarrhea. Nothing seemed to help. A dysentery specialist in Madras eventually made the diagnosis—stress-induced ulcerative colitis.

On the first day of April, Steve had another stormy meeting with Rajalingam. It was getting to be an annual event. Steve wondered if it had something to do with the heat. Rajalingam had once told him that, because he had not completed his probationary time satisfactorily, when he went home at the end of his five-year term, it would be as a "failed missionary" and he could not return. So now there was no point in even staying five years. He was glad he had George to take over.

The Madras specialist had other plans. George and Yolanda must leave India for good. For their good, not Steve's. With the Atkinsons' impending departure, the whole situation had changed. Now the mission wanted him to stay, to carry on the essential role he had played from the beginning.

And to take more abuse.

He felt like a prisoner who'd been granted parole—and then had it taken away. Now they wanted to even extend his term until a replacement could be found. If to be used of God meant to be abused by Satan, he knew he had to accept. He would carry the cross he'd been given.

After George and Yolanda left, Steve grew more lonely and despondent day by day. He'd had few other friends. Yasmina was his only confidant. She'd come to be a kindred spirit, in spite of all the taboos that engulfed them.

He longed for companionship, fellowship with his peers. He wrote often to Andrew in South Africa, but had no response for many months.

Just before leaving for his vacation in early May, he finally got a letter. But it didn't make him one bit happier. It sickened him to hear about apartheid and its negative effect on Christian missionary activity.

On the last Friday of June, while still in his thin cotton scrub suit, Steve left the O.R. to dictate an operation note to Yasmina. He cared very deeply about her, even though he knew his feelings were exactly what Doraiswami had called "an emotional entanglement that must be avoided."

He pushed open the door to her office and jumped in surprise. She was sitting behind the typewriter with her elbows on the desk, her head bowed and covered with the free end of her red sari—sobbing.

"Yasmina. What's wrong?"

He came around to stand in front of her. She looked up at him with swollen eyes, holding the end of her sari in her left hand. As he had long suspected, she didn't always wear a bra. The front of her thin blouse, drenched with tears, was almost transparent. Steve struggled with his lower nature, won the battle, and shifted his gaze to her glistening eyes. Through them he felt he could see her soul. *Poor dear thing.*

"Oh, Dr. Manley, my father says I must leave my job. In a month I am to be married. What can I do?"

"No, Yasmina. You mustn't leave. I need you here. You're my only friend."

"I must do as my father says. He has arranged for me to marry a man they tell me is old and ugly. He is very rich and very ugly. B-but you, y-you are..."

"Go on."

"You are not ugly."

"Well, thank you very much."

"I mean... I'm so happy here working for you. I don't want to leave you. And his mother is such an awful, evil woman. My sister tells me she has an evil spirit living inside her body. The bride and groom must live in his parents' house where, until his mother dies, I shall be her servant."

Spiritual matters were not foremost in Steve's mind at that moment. He drew up a chair and sat down where the typewriter would come between them.

"Tell me about this evil spirit."

Yasmina wiped her eyes and blew her nose before she continued.

Ah, those lovely eyes. Those long black eyelashes.

"Everyone knows that when she becomes enraged with anger she turns into—how do you say it in English—a female dog.

"Oh, you mean she becomes a b—" The word wasn't fit for the ears of this innocent young woman. "Yes, I know what you mean. But she doesn't really become an animal," he explained. "It's just an English expression that means she acts like one."

"Oh, how I wish I could fly away to the mountains—the Himalayas, change my name, and hide where no one can find me."

Steve stood up and gestured with open arms. "You could fly to America and change your name to Mrs. Manley. No one would find you then."

"Oh, Steve!" She rushed into his arms and flung her own around his neck. "I've wanted to love you since the first moment I saw you. But I couldn't let it happen. I had to hold back my heart with both hands, till I heard you say 'Mrs. Manley.' Now I will joyfully go against every taboo. I will love and serve you forever to be worthy of that name."

As he held her close, he felt the pressure of her breasts against his body. His free hand began to slide cautiously...but wisdom conquered passion.

"Yasmina, I too have struggled against society. So often I wanted to hold you like this, against all the rules. But I always tried to do the right thing, tried to get along. Now I know they don't appreciate my work here. I can just walk away and not really be missed. And I'm going to take you with me. All I need is 48-hours' notice to make all the arrangements. We'll take the early morning flight eastward from Madras to Kuala Lumpur."

Steve marveled at how well he could think in such a situation. His surgical training had well-equipped him to make snap decisions, unhampered by emotion.

"We'll make further plans on arrival. No one will suspect we would leave by that route. If anyone tries to stop us, they'll think we're leaving through Delhi to London. Just let me know when you can be ready."

He lowered his lips to her waiting half-open mouth and tasted the sweetness of her kiss. Gently he ran the tip of his tongue around the edge of her teeth till he felt her grow heavy in his arms.

She fainted at the very moment Steve heard, "What is going on here?"

He looked around to see Doraiswami standing in the doorway.

It was over. They immediately dismissed Yasmina—they said it was for her own protection.

Steve received only one week's notice. Not fair, when his five-year contract still had three months to run. But since his first encounter with leprosy, he had known that life could be unfair—and now he had no prospect of happiness in India.

He wondered if he would ever see Yasmina again. He could buy her a ticket, but he had no idea where she lived. And there was no one he could trust to contact her discretely. *Aha, perhaps Brother Yesudasan.*

Yesudasan had just finished mopping the O.R. floor when Steve burst in. As soon as he heard the story he said, "She lives in my village just down the main road. Give me a note and I'll take it to her. No one else shall hear of it. Of that you can be quite certain."

Steve's heart felt lighter as he went home to pack his personal belongings and unreported research data. He knew he had sufficient information there for at least four really first-class papers in international journals. No point in submitting to the Indian journals. He'd often done this in the past to help educate those who lacked the foreign currency to buy international journals. He'd done so much for India already, and for leprosy patients throughout the world.

He knew he could do so much more but they didn't seem to want that. The Mission to the Outcast was casting him away. It was time now to think of his own future, to establish his reputation in America.

Steve had one last official chore. This Sunday, as on many previous occasions, he was scheduled to give the chapel sermon. It was one last chance to witness for his Lord in India. It would be his farewell speech. But it must not be too personal. It had to be something that would help the people here, those he would never see again.

Inside his house, his maidservant met him. "Two letters for you, Doctor."

He thanked her and looked at the return addresses.

"Aha, a letter from Andrew. Good news from Africa is just what I need. What's this? One from Jennifer? I haven't heard from her since... since that day in Toronto...that day she rejected me."

Hastily he tore open Jennifer's letter.

1307 Royal York Road
The Kingsway
Toronto, Ontario

June 17, 1975

Dear Steven,
I almost began with "my dear Steve," as in the old days. But you are no longer mine and I only have my own weakness to blame for

that. But you are still dear to me, very dear, and always will be. I wonder if you can forgive the foolishness of a weak, selfish young woman. I am much stronger now. There is no point in going into details by letter. If you are willing to see me, I shall fly to you on the next available jet.

I look forward to a reply, even if it is "No." At least that will end the agony of waiting.

Yours always,
Jennifer

"Why now, Jennifer?" Steve cried out in anguish. "Why not a year ago? Last month? Yesterday? Who knows what might have been? But it's too late. It's over."

Sakundra, who had waited quietly in the room, looked at him with eyes wide in surprise. He walked past her into his bedroom, slammed the door, and got down on his knees at the edge of the bed and began to pray.

"Lord what is your will for my life? Did you send me here to work forever as a medical missionary, and then I failed you? Or did you send me here to do a short-term job when I was happy to stay for life? Have I done your will or disappointed you? Did you send me here to lift Yasmina out of bondage? Or will she suffer more at the hands of racial bigots in America? Oh, Lord Jesus Christ, speak to my heart! Show me your way and grant me the strength to walk in it."

Seeking some solace from his friend in Africa, he got up, dried his tears, sat down in a chair, and opened Andrew's letter. What he read made his whole body quiver.

Roodepoort, South Africa

June 13, 1975

Dear Steve,
I've finally got hold of myself and am writing this as I wait for the plane. I don't think you're going to like what I must tell you. It's a story that starts with tears, and ends with weeping and wailing.

Anyway, as I told you in the previous letter we decided to return to Canada. Nancy and the boys went home before me...

Twenty-one

A ndrew watched the Boeing 747 taxi toward the runway at Jan Smuts Airport. He, Nancy, and the boys, had done this often during their four years in South Africa. They had watched departures and arrivals as mission personnel came and went. Even more often, they had stood here on the observation deck watching aircraft for the sheer joy of it. The airport, with its visitors from around the world, became a joyful touchstone that symbolically connected them with their friends and relatives at home.

Today, however, the airport spoke of separation, for the big plane carried Nancy and the boys on a flight that would take them to Amsterdam and on to Toronto. He watched the line of windows, and mentally created an image of three excited faces and six waving hands. Only in his mind could he see them—even a pair of powerful field glasses could not have picked out individuals looking out windows at that distance.

He watched as the jumbo jet turned off the taxi strip and accelerated down the runway. Too soon it leaped into the sky and faded from sight.

Andrew brushed tears from his eyes and headed for the lower floor and the car park. He felt as if his heart had turned to stone and settled into his stomach.

"Get over it," he said aloud. "You have a lot of work to do before you can join them."

"*Sa'bona, Baba* Andrew."

He looked in the direction of the voice to see a great crowd of black people moving away from the arrivals area. A tall slender African woman broke clear of the others and strode toward him. He blinked his eyes to clear the remnant of tears, and felt his heart race as he recognized her.

"*Sa'bona*, Lucy, what are you doing here?"

Her black eyes sparkled with excitement. "I came to meet Gatsha Buthelezi, the Paramount Chief of the Zulus. He arrived back today from visiting Europe, so I took the day off to be here."

"It looks like quite a few others did the same," said Andrew, glancing toward the receding crowd.

"He's our leader, our chief. He's a great man."

"Did you get to speak to him?"

"Not this time, but I have talked to him often."

Andrew's eyes moved from her face down her body, sheathed in a tan suede coat. She swayed slightly, like a willow tree in a gentle breeze. He looked back into her eyes and tried to stifle the fire that began burning deep within him.

"How are you getting back to Roodepoort?" he asked.

"In a taxi with eight or ten other people."

"Don't do that—I have my car. I'll give you a ride."

They wove toward the car park through typical airport crowds. Lucy, being discrete, walked a half-step behind. He wished she would walk just ahead, then gave himself a mental kick, accusing himself of having the hormones of a teenager.

At the car, he motioned her to the front seat. He knew his fellow missionaries wouldn't like it. But what they didn't see wouldn't hurt them.

He steered the car free of airport traffic and headed for the country road that Jack had shown them on the day they arrived.

"What were you doing at the airport, Baba?" she asked.

He hadn't planned to tell anyone else. Only Mumsa and her husband knew they had no intention of returning to South Africa, but Lucy's presence crushed his resolve and overpowered his inhibitions. He told her the whole story, begging her to tell no one.

"They will find out we aren't returning after I get home. I want to get all my graphics work finished and will quietly sell or dispose of our things and pack up what's left. If I can get everything done, that should take about eight weeks."

Lucy stared at the passing scene before speaking. "You will need help packing. Let Elizabeth and me come and help you in evenings or on the weekends. She would never talk."

"She did the last time! She blabbed and caused all kinds of trouble."

"*Xa!*" The emphatic Zulu *no* with its loud click sounded like a pistol shot in the enclosed car. "We caused the trouble. And we didn't think to ask her to keep quiet."

Andrew melted again. "Okay then, if you can convince her to say absolutely nothing."

"You'll need other help—a man with a Kombi to move the furniture you give away or sell. Jack is your friend, so ask him. He would keep quiet."

For the last few days, Nancy had done his thinking for him. Now Lucy had stepped right in and taken over.

"I really hadn't thought of the heavy stuff. I'll ask Jack."

They drove on in silence, the Austin rushing effortlessly through the Transvaal countryside. He thought about the car, the most wonderful car he'd ever owned. He hoped he could get one like it in Canada.

He didn't consciously think of the woman beside him, but on the very edge of his awareness, he knew her presence filled a part of the gaping hole left in his heart by the departure of Nancy and the kids.

They rolled through Allen's Nek, into suburban Roodepoort, and towards downtown.

"I'll drop you off around the block. You can walk to the office, finish the day's work, and catch the Kombi back to the hostel."

She nodded, obviously understanding the implications.

He pulled up in front of a row of Indian shops, their iron-barred windows making him think of a row of jail cells. The thought of jail cells reminded him that people in South Africa go to prison for miscegenation, their name for interracial sex.

Automatically he squeezed her hand as she prepared to open the car door, just as he used to do to Nancy. Lucy leaned toward him, kissed him gently on the cheek, then left without a word.

That kiss hadn't been at all African! He sat in the car for 15 minutes, confusion and guilt flooding his brain. Maybe he should stop this now. But he needed someone around him. Someone who understood him. Someone he...he loved.

The next seven weeks raced by in a whirl of busyness for Andrew. Each day he reported to work as usual. His fellow workers knew Nancy and the kids had left the country and assumed they had begun their furlough. Andrew simply explained that he would join them soon. He worked on the graphics projects assigned by outside organizations and informed them that he could not accept further commissions. He planned to contact them from Canada—maybe he could do their work when he got settled.

In the evenings, he sorted and packed. Jack and Lila came two nights a week and on Saturdays, with Lucy and Elizabeth joining them on Saturdays. Between the Fergusons and the two African women, they quietly found buyers for the furniture and appliances. Andrew decided to give everything that remained to Pastor Makunyane and Mumsa. They could give any unsold items to needy people.

He wrote Nancy every three or four days, telling her about the great help he was getting from the Fergusons. He didn't mention Lucy.

In the second week, he received a letter from Nancy. It said in part, "I'm staying with my sister, but will have an apartment by the time you get here. I've had no contact with the Canadian office—I believe Hamilton-Jones doesn't know I'm here."

By the seventh Saturday, the house was virtually empty. Andrew had held back a bed and linens, a table and chairs, and a few kitchen utensils. He booked his flight home for the Monday following the eighth weekend. Jack offered to sell the Austin and forward the money.

"Lila and I are off to Kruger Park for the week," Jack told him. "We'll come back to get you to the airport a week Monday."

On the following Monday, one week before his planned departure, he sat in his office, tidying up paperwork. Things he didn't want to deal with he pushed into a large envelope.

He grinned as he realized Gordon could deal with them later—when he knew they were not coming back. Maybe he would tell him the day he left.

"*Baba!*"

"Lucy, you startled me. You came in so quietly."

Andrew's eyes followed the curvature of her body as she slid onto the edge of his desk and gracefully crossed her legs. Even when sitting, she reflected such animal energy that a man would think she might spring at any moment. He hoped no one would see her there. But he didn't want her to leave.

"I guess you don't need Elizabeth and me next Saturday," she said.

"No, everything is done, thanks to you, Elizabeth, and the Fergusons."

"You will need to mop the floors and dust a bit. I'll come Saturday and help you. I can get there by five in the afternoon—and I'll bring some food so you don't have to cook anything."

Before he could answer, she wiggled off the desk and slipped away.

Within the hour, Elizabeth appeared at his office door.

"*Sa'bona, Baba.* I just came with a question."

"Yes, Elizabeth."

She looked about as though assuring no one could hear. "Now that you are not coming back, what are you going to do with that?"

She pointed a black shiny finger at the graphics camera.

"My goodness, I forgot all about it! Thanks, I'll give it some thought."

She gave a jaunty wave and bounced out the door.

Andrew stared at the camera and groaned. How could he have forgotten his most-prized possession? His memory took him back to Canada, the day he had found it at a trade show.

"It's a Gevaert, 20 by 24 inch," the salesman had said. "It'll do a great job with line work or half-tones—last you a lifetime."

Andrew had gone into debt for it, but soon afterward stored it to go to college. He identified with it—it spoke of his career, of his very life.

He considered many possibilities. He grinned as he pictured himself struggling onto the plane with it. They allowed cameras on board, but not a graphics camera the size of a kitchen stove. He could leave it for whoever replaced him, but it would likely sit unused for years. Maybe Jack would pack it for shipment back to Canada. With that thought, he settled into a blue funk that lasted the rest of the week.

Each day for breakfast he had *Weetbix* cereal, the South African version of Weetabix, or *mealie pap,* along with a cup of coffee. At noon he bought *boerewors* on a roll; he knew he would miss these tasty sausages in Canada. He took home fish and chips for the evening meal and spent the night in his lonely, empty house.

During each day in that last week he fussed around in his office, but did very little real work. He stewed about his camera. How could he have forgotten it? With Jack away, he couldn't even discuss it with him.

On Friday afternoon, he stuck his head into Gordon's office.

"Got a minute?"

"Come in, Andrew, I haven't seen much of you; I guess you've been getting ready for furlough. I should have talked to you sooner, but while you're away, we would like to put a new couple in your house. You'll have to store away any things you don't want them to use."

"I have already done that."

Gordon looked surprised. "Oh, now when are you going? Is it three weeks hence?"

Andrew shook his head. "Would you believe three days?"

Gordon's mouth dropped open. "How...how did I not know that?"

Andrew felt a pang of guilt. He really didn't want to hurt Gordon.

"Because I deliberately didn't tell you. Nancy and I will not be returning to the field. We will tender our resignation the day I get home. I'm sorry, Gordon."

Gordon collapsed into a rumpled heap. He gestured, but no words came.

"Gordon, I'm still trying to figure out what to do with my camera. We can talk about it on Monday before I head for the airport."

Gordon said nothing, just sat in his chair and stared at the ceiling.

Andrew rose silently and left, feeling now more guilty than ever. He drove home and parked the Austin in the driveway. He would miss that car. He looked at the house. He'd never lived in a better one. He walked through the front door, thinking, *Three more lonely nights here.* Then he remembered Lucy was coming tomorrow. He began to sing as he carried his fish and chips to the kitchen.

∽

Andrew woke early to a brilliant South African day. He slid from the bed and walked naked to the bathroom. He enjoyed the rush of air over his bare body, so he often looked for an excuse to avoid dressing.

Now finished in the bathroom, he reluctantly dressed for breakfast. When he reached the kitchen he put two Weetbix in a bowl and made a pot of coffee. He'd warm it up when he wanted more during the day.

At about 10 o'clock he walked downtown, intending to kill his day visiting his favorite shops—he needed film for the trip home. He ate at a fish and chip shop, arrived home at three, and immediately turned on a burner under the coffeepot.

Now what? he asked himself, two hours before Lucy was due to arrive. He knew he shouldn't have agreed to her coming, but he also realized he couldn't say no.

"Ah, Andrew," he said aloud, "you should do some laundry so you'll be clean for the trip home."

He gathered up his dirty clothes, tossed them into the bathtub, and covered them with hot water. He would play washing machine, tramping on them the way he had done for his mother as a little kid when the washer didn't work. He pulled off his shoes and socks, then decided to do a thorough job, and stripped off all his clothes, tossing everything in the tub—whites and colors together.

By four o'clock he had hand rung the laundry and carried it to the back door. He actually started to open the door when he realized he couldn't go to the clothesline in his still-naked state. He laughed at himself and said aloud, "Andrew, do you want to get arrested two days before you leave the country? Get some clothes on."

He turned to head for the bedroom, but stopped when he saw the coffee. He filled his cup and leaned against the counter.

"*Sa'bona Baba*," said Lucy as she burst through the unlocked back door carrying a picnic basket. "Sorry I'm early, but I got an unexpected ride."

Hot coffee spilled from the cup and splashed on Andrew's thigh, but he never felt it with the shock of coming face-to-face with Lucy.

She put down the basket, grabbed the towel that had covered it, and wiped the coffee off his body.

"Don't worry about having no clothes. I've seen lots of bare male bodies. African teenagers swim in the nude—boys and girls together."

"We're not exactly teenagers," Andrew answered, grabbing for the towel to cover himself, but she flipped it into the sink.

Lucy wore a snug silk dress. He could see every curve of her body. She might as well be naked herself!

The following minutes passed in a storm of passion. Andrew realized they had moved to the bed only after he had emerged from the grip of lust and emotion. For more than an hour they lay with arms and legs entwined.

They interrupted their love-making to eat the food Lucy had brought and spend a little time sleeping. At nine the next morning, they showered and dressed.

Andrew tried to make sense out of what they had done. "I'm sorry, Lucy. I didn't mean to—"

"Don't blame yourself. No man should go unsatisfied for two months. Anyway, I planned it as a going-away gift. You made it easier by being ready. Just remember, when you have your clothes off, you never know who might happen along."

By mid-morning, Lucy slipped away, carrying her basket. Andrew did not accompany her to the door. He knew he'd be in deep trouble if anyone saw her leaving. It would be far worse if he were at the door when she left. The law and the mission board would see missionary miscegenation as the worst kind of moral and social sin, a social disgrace.

He waited two hours before pulling on clothes and hanging yesterday's wash on the line. What would the neighbors think of a missionary doing his laundry on a Sunday? But that didn't matter. Nothing mattered anymore.

Andrew sat in a straight-backed chair at the table and buried his face in his hands. He suddenly realized he had missed the service at the African church. He should have been there to say good-bye. He could never face Mumsa. In some mysterious way she would know what had happened.

He smashed his fist against the table and cried, "Dear God, what have I done?"

He wept as he thought of his missionary career in shambles and his life completely messed up. His wife had gone away for two months, and he had been too weak to remain faithful. If she found out, it would destroy everything. He got up from the chair to pace around the room.

His thoughts marched back and forth with equal vigor. He knew he couldn't face anyone at work the next day...not Mumsa...not Gordon...and he certainly mustn't run into Lucy again.

After a few minutes, the tension subsided enough that he could think. He would slip into the mission building and collect any personal items still there. He could call Jack to take him to the airport in the morning.

Within minutes he was in the car and on his way to the mission building.

He entered by the front door, listening carefully to assure himself no one else was making a Sunday visit. He tiptoed through the quiet building, feeling like a thief. In his office he checked the desk drawers for any forgotten items.

Nothing. He might as well not have bothered.

When he looked at his precious graphics camera, unexpected fury sprang up within him. The camera represented his profession, his past, and even his identity. He had left his career to train as a missionary and joined the mission, only to come here to this forsaken place. He had sacrificed greatly, but lost even more because of a group of hypocritical missionaries and his own fleshly weakness.

In an instant, rage overcame all rationality. He grabbed a two-by-four intended to hold open a window, and swung it at the camera. The first blow demolished the bellows and knocked the camera askew, throwing it out of alignment. The second bent the light support arms and shattered the quartz-iodine bulbs. The third smashed the control handles. When sanity returned and he realized the extent of his fury, he broke into great heaving sobs. He must have sat at his desk for half-an-hour sobbing like a baby, before the worst of his rage settled. He picked up his car keys and rose to leave.

Before he could, Gordon Muir appeared at the doorway. In his own distraught condition, Andrew barely noticed Gordon's agitated state.

"Andrew, what's wrong? You didn't show up at the African Church this morning. They had a presentation ready for you."

Andrew said nothing.

"They called me, so I went to see if you were ill. When I arrived at your place, I saw Lucy leaving with a basket—the same basket I saw her carrying from the station on Saturday afternoon."

Words choked in Andrew's throat.

"I hesitated to go to your door, afraid of what I would find. I went home, but I couldn't get you out of my mind. Then I returned to your house and saw your car had gone, so I came here."

After a moment's hesitation Gordon continued, "Andrew, did Lucy stay at your place overnight?"

A moan shook Andrew's body. He stumbled backward toward his desk.

"Dear God," Gordon said. "What did you do? You have really messed up your life—and disgraced the mission."

The remaining rage and all his energy drained from Andrew's body. He collapsed into his chair. Mentally, he couldn't even bring up a picture of Nancy and the kids. His past, his career, his reputation—everything seemed like blank pages in a photo album. Only a picture of a beautiful, sensuous African woman filled his inner vision.

"I'm afraid I've destroyed much more than that."

Steve, I know you'll find this hard to understand. I could blame it on the tension, the frustration—

Steve could read no more. He fell back in the chair and stared at the wall, seeing nothing. His body began to shake uncontrollably. The letter dropped from his trembling hands, skillful hands that soon fell motionless at his sides.

Twenty-two

Steve awoke and shivered. He reached down to the floor to retrieve all the pages of Andrew's letter. Methodically he folded each one, tore it twice, and made a pile of the pieces on the small rug in front of him.

A coal oil lantern sat on a nearby table with a package of matches. Steve took one of the matches and set fire to the paper. He sat back and smiled as he watched the letter burn. Only when he smelled the odor of burning wool did he come to his senses, flip over the rug, and begin tramping on it.

As smoke drifted up from the edges, he stamped until he had completely extinguished the fire. He heard a knock at the door and looked up to see the night watchman staring at him in disbelief.

"Smell smoke. Is problem?"

Without replying, Steve ran up the stairs, threw himself fully clothed on the bed, and wept until morning.

The voice of Sakundra awakened him. "I bring breakfast, Doctor." She gently set the tray on his bedside table. "You sad to leave India?"

"Yes, that too."

After nibbling at his breakfast, he phoned for the carpenter to crate the few small pieces of furniture he'd managed to buy. Perhaps he could also find some oil drums to put the less valuable items in. He was surprised no one answered the phone—until he realized it was Saturday.

While packing clothes in his suitcases, he thought about next day's chapel message. If he used it to say good-bye to everyone he had known and worked with, he wouldn't have to go around and say farewell today. This thought appealed to him. He was not in the mood to face anyone.

At 6 o'clock sharp next morning, the sun shone through Steve's window and directly into his eyes. Long ago he'd arranged his bed so that this would happen. He always liked to get an early start on the day. But not today. He felt tired and wanted more time to sleep.

Sakundra came in with his breakfast tray. After she left he got up, put the toast on his balcony for the crows, and carried a cup of coffee into the bathroom to have a shower.

Time passed so quickly that he neglected his morning devotions. He only remembered to pray when he passed through his front yard and walked down the path toward the chapel.

"Please give me the right words to say, Lord," he prayed, "help me touch hearts in a way that will bring glory to your name and make the world a better place. And please forgive me for ignoring you this morning...in my confusion."

Crowds filled the chapel well before the time scheduled for the service to start. At the back of the single open room, there was one stone bench built against the wall, reserved for foreigners and visiting dignitaries. Everyone else sat cross-legged on the cool marble floor. The patients, easily distinguished by their shabby clothing, always sat in front of the staff. But today there was not enough room. Many others stood outside, some leaning on crutches, and looked in through the large open windows.

Yesudasan told Steve, "I think all patients not bed-bound are here to wish you well, Dr. Manley. They hold you very dear in their hearts. Nurses and physios do also."

"Tell me about Yasmina," Steve whispered anxiously. "Did you give her the message?"

"With deepest regret I must say they have taken her away somewhere, they tell me...to prepare for marriage. I was unable to locate her, but I shall continue my search."

Steve let out a low groan and walked over to take a seat behind the podium. Tears slid down his cheeks and onto the floor between his feet. The congregation sang several hymns, someone read the chosen Bible passage and prayed. He just sat there as if in a daze until he heard, "Dr. Manley will now bring us the message God has laid on his heart."

His legs had never felt so weak as he rose unsteadily to his feet. He opened his Bible, looking frantically for his notes, but could not find them. *This one will have to be from my heart.*

A young man in white trousers and a white shirt open at the neck approached him. "I shall translate for you, sir."

"No need. I'll speak in Tamil."

The youth raised his eyebrows as if in surprise, looked around, and seeing Steve's chair empty, sat down in it.

Steve began by thanking all the staff for their unwavering support during his time there. "We are all part of a team. No one works alone. If I have done any good among you, it is because you have helped me."

Rajalingam, sitting next to Doraiswami on the bench at the back, said quietly, "How well he speaks Tamil."

Doraiswami began to blush but said nothing at first. On regaining his composure, he said, "Dr. Manley is a resourceful person, you must know."

"Yes, with our resources."

Steve told of his sadness about leaving India. A half-hour into his sermon a short-statured man came in through the entrance to his right, turned his head to glare at Steve, then sat down with the patients in the front row, pushing aside a crippled old man to make room. Steve paused to stare at the intruder. He had a shiny head, completely bald, and shaped like a top. His thin handlebar mustache did nothing to improve the sour look on his face.

Steve completely lost his train of thought, cleared his throat, and began to say something he had never intended. "Jesus was a man of compassion. He was concerned about the poor and defenseless, the sick and the suffering. All the women in his day were powerless to defend themselves. So there was a special place in his heart for women. Things are not so much different in India today. You people give your daughters as slaves to men they do not love. They are powerless to help themselves, and many may end their lives in misery. Oh yes, you are following Indian tradition, you say. But instead, you should be following Jesus."

He lifted his Bible from the pulpit and waved it at the audience. "Some of you trust in that false prophet Mohammed and the rubbish he has written—"

"Blasphemer!" screamed the little man in the front row. He jumped to his feet, shook his fist at Steve, and shouted, "You will burn in hell." Looking around at the others present, he added, "You are all infidels." He spat on the chapel floor. "I curse this place."

An old man with one leg in a cast, leaning on a pair of crutches, struck the troublemaker across the top of the head with one of his crutches. The little man grabbed it, twisted it out of the old man's grasp, and shoved him to the floor. Then the rude little man jumped over the fallen body and quickly left.

The crowd, stunned into silence, heard each of his footsteps as he walked away along the sandy path. Then everyone began talking at once.

"Who was that?" Steve asked Yesudasan.

"Salim Ali Khan, Yasmina's father."

"Let us close the service," the chaplain said, "by singing number 274, 'My Heart is Resting, O My God.'"

Rajalingam left during the first verse and went to his office. He had important business to take care of. Two days earlier a letter that looked like a job offer had come for Steve from the Mayo Clinic.

Without understanding why, he had delayed passing it on. Now he was curious about its contents. With his gold-handled miniature Gurkha knife he carefully opened the envelope and gently unfolded the letter.

It was an offer of a clinical teaching appointment at the Mayo Clinic. Today's performance convinced Rajalingam that Steve was too much of a troublemaker, even for America. He felt honor-bound to write and tell them so.

First, he would tell Steve, but not immediately. He still didn't have a replacement for him. This and other urgent matters would keep Rajalingam busy till dinnertime. Then he would confront Steve at home. The thought sent a tingle up his spine. There would be no job for Steve at the Mayo when they found out what a scoundrel he was. The look in Steve's eyes when he learned this would be worth the wait.

Three garlands around his neck were not enough to raise Steve's spirits as he plodded up the dirt road that led home.

Home, he thought, *I'm going home...Where is my home?...I don't have a home.*

By nightfall he had begun to think of Jennifer but realized how little he now cared about her. It was Yasmina he wanted—and she was out of reach. There was just one thing to do. He would talk to the Lord. God would tell him what to do.

Steve went into the ground-floor bedroom next to the living room. He had intended to use this place for nerve-growth research before the cobra killed all his rabbits. When Rajalingam destroyed his plan to spend his whole life in India, this long-term project also died. Since then it had served as a prayer room. He liked to go there in the evenings and, in a darkened room lit only by a small lamp, read God's Word as he knelt by the side of the bed.

A record player sat beside this single bed, against the wall opposite a large window. He lifted the lid, turned on the machine, and placed on the turntable his favorite record: *Beneath the Cross of Jesus.*

This hymn always brought peace to his soul whenever life's road was rough. He sat on the bed and listened as a melodious soprano voice sang:

"Beneath the cross of Jesus I long to take my stand;
The shadow of a mighty rock within a weary land,

A home within a wilderness, a rest upon the way,
From the burning of the noontide heat and burdens of the day."

Ah, yes, Steve thought, *that is India—the burning heat and the burdens. But it's not my home. Never was. I only thought it was. Heaven is my true home.*

He walked over to the dresser beside the window to get his Bible, laid it open on the bed, and knelt down at the edge of the bed as the song continued:

"Upon the cross of Jesus, my eye at times can see
The very dying form of one who suffered there for me.
And from my contrite heart with tears two wonders I confess:
The wonders of his glorious love and my unworthiness."

Partway through this verse Steve began to pray, "Lord, forgive me for my often harsh words, my quick temper, and my impatience. I've tried to help, but in trying so hard I've sometimes hurt others. Help me to look beyond the present and see your plan for my future."

The next verse expressed his feelings so exactly he had to sing along:

"I take, O cross, your shadow for my abiding place;
I ask no other sunshine than the sunshine of his face,
Content to let the world go by, to know no gain nor loss,
My sinful self my only shame, my glory all the cross."

Though his eyes were closed, he could see light all around. At first golden, it paled and brightened into a dazzling white. He closed his eyes even tighter and heard the roar of a rushing wind that shrieked ever louder until it almost deafened him, then faded away. Yet he felt no wind on his body—rather a sense of being held, almost enclosed. His spirit was at peace.

A knock at the door disturbed his reverie. Without waiting to be asked, Rajalingam entered, waving a letter in his hand.

"Scoundrel! Behind my back, you wrote off to the Mayo Clinic for a job. The fools say they want you. Who would want you when they know what you are really like? And I'm going to tell them. As I live and breathe, you'll not work there, perhaps not anywhere."

Steve felt the blood drain from his face. "Why? Why would you do that?"

"Who's out there in the bushes?" Rajalingam said as he went over to investigate the rustling of bushes. Looking out the window into the darkness he said, "Someone's out there."

They both saw a man with a rifle and another trying to take it from him.

Steve jumped backward when he heard the thud of a high-powered rifle. Blood spurted from Rajalingam's chest. Steve rushed forward to catch him. The bullet had entered the right side of his chest, just below the nipple.

The sucking sound Steve heard told him Rajalingam's right lung was collapsing. Reflexively he pulled a clean, folded handkerchief from a nearby drawer and held it firmly to the chest wound to prevent any further air going into the chest cavity.

"Take slow deep breaths, sir. You're going to be alright, in a little while."

Yesudasan rushed into the room with Yasmina following.

Steve's eyes widened, and a smile swept over his pale face. "Yesudasan, get the O.R. ready. Do we have a chest tube?"

"We have never done any chest surgery here, Doctor."

"Well, I have. Get a hose about a quarter-inch diameter, firm wall. When he's in stable condition we'll get him off to Madras University Hospital. His lung may be punctured, and in any case, it would be wise to have the chest surgeons take that bullet out. Have an ambulance standing by."

"Yes, sir, I mean, Dr. Manley." Yesudasan left running.

By this time, Rajalingam's lips had turned a dusky shade of blue, and he was once more breathing quickly.

"Will he be alright?" Yasmina asked.

"In time, but I think his lung has been punctured. The air coming in through the hole in the lung is now building pressure in the chest to collapse his good lung. The sooner we get that chest tube in the better."

Two men came in and loaded Rajalingam on a stretcher. Steve and Yasmina followed them to the operating room.

Next morning Steve visited Rajalingam on the chest surgery ward of the university hospital. "How are you to-day, sir?"

"Alive, thanks to you. That's what they tell me. But why, Steve, why would you save the life of someone who wants to block your appointment to the Mayo Clinic? I thought I understood you, but I don't really know you at all."

"God is not willing that any should perish."

"That's in the Bible, isn't it? How does it go?"

"Peter's second epistle says, 'The Lord... is not willing that any should perish, but that all should come to repentance.'"

"Steve, I have come to that point. I'm really sorry I wanted to block your path. I now see you have qualities I never appreciated."

Steve's eyes glistened. "And I have been rude and arrogant with you...I guess with many people."

"Why don't you stay on a bit? We need someone with your ability here."

Steve closed his eyes for a moment before replying. "I shall certainly stay till you are on your feet again. Also, the police have blocked my exit until they decide what to do with Yasmina's father, Ali Khan."

"What's that all about?"

"I guess you were pretty much out of it, after the gun went off. Ali Khan tried to kill me, but thanks to Yesudasan's interference, he shot you instead of me. I'm going to see if I can have the charges dropped. He was only trying to do what he thought was best for his family—that is, if you don't mind. After all, you were the one injured, not me."

"Exactly, and that's why the charges should not be dropped. He nearly killed me. If it weren't for you, I would be dead."

"But he didn't mean to kill you. So there is no motive. If he goes to court, he'll get off. So why should we go to all that aggravation?"

"Steve. Possibly for the very first time, I'm beginning to agree with you. This experience has changed my life for the better. I know that sounds bizarre. But I've had a near-death experience, and I'm grateful to be alive."

Epilogue

Toronto
August 1990

Heads turned as the middle-aged black woman swept along the sidewalk. She was wearing a full-length gown printed with large angular patterns in rich earth tones. The hem of her gown floated evenly just clear of the sidewalk, offering only the occasional glimpse of sandaled feet. Black, curly hair with sparse hints of gray put the finishing touch on a picture that must certainly trigger one word in the minds of those who watched—Africa. She entered the lobby of the Scotia Center and studied the directory until her eyes found the company name: Canada Wide Publishers.

"*Yebo*," she said aloud and turned toward the elevator.

A security guard looked up from his desk but otherwise ignored her—all of the world's costumes and characters pass daily through Toronto. The lady from Africa paused again on the 14th floor and studied the large glass doors to the publishing office. With a determined, but liquid stride, she propelled herself into the office and stopped before a vacant desk bearing the sign: *Reception, Joan Clayton.*

"I'll be right with you," a female voice called from a side office.

As she waited, her black eyes swept the luxury suite, then focused on a partially closed door bearing the sign: *Vice-President, Art Department.* The incumbent's name, appearing beneath in gold leaf, triggered a smile that revealed a set of perfect teeth. After looking about for the missing receptionist, she shrugged and headed for the door.

As she pushed wide the door to the vice-presidential office, the receptionist finally appeared and called, "Wait! You can't just walk in there."

The short, slightly overweight, bald man behind the desk gaped, then regaining his composure, spoke to the one who had followed the black woman into the room. "It's okay, Joan. This is an old friend. One of the best friends I have ever had."

Joan backed out of the room and closed the door.

"Mumsa, is it really you?"

"Yebo, Baba Andrew, it really is me."

"What are you doing here, in Canada?"

"My son and daughter-in-law have moved to Toronto to study at Ontario Theological Seminary. Friends in South Africa raised the money for me to make a visit."

Andrew walked around the desk and directed Mumsa to sit with him at a small conference table. "How are you?" he asked.

"I'm fine. We are all fine. The real question is, how are you?' You never wrote. After your...your fall, you just disappeared."

"Mumsa, I'm so ashamed. I let all of you down. I sinned against my wife and against God. I...I never expected to see you again."

Mumsa leaned toward him. "So how are you now? Are you still too embarrassed to see me?"

"I still feel shame, but I shouldn't. Nancy chose to forgive me and God has forgiven me. I spent days, no weeks, weeping on my knees, begging God to forgive me. It took time to get our lives back together, and we had to give up plans for further ministry. A public failure like mine stands out like an open sore on a person's life."

"Was your sin greater than that of the racist mission leaders you worked with? God can forgive and heal them, you, and me. He's always put me back on the right path."

Although Andrew couldn't picture Mumsa ever getting off the straight and narrow, he didn't challenge her. "But it takes time for some people. I had a friend once, another missionary, a medical doctor who had a difficult time, much as Nancy and I did. He was a good friend, one I loved regardless of his dogmatic and often arrogant attitude."

"I remember. You read me his letters from India."

"He fell in love with his secretary, a beautiful Indian woman, Yasmina. Her father tried to kill him and when he successfully argued in the courts that all charges should be dropped, her father gave permission for them to marry—in America. He didn't want to be involved and was happy he didn't have to pay a dowry."

Andrew sat motionless as his mind raced back and forth over the decades. "Steve works at the Mayo Clinic, and has even agreed with the request of his old archenemy, Rajalingam, to go back to South India from time to time and help in the training of young surgeons. So he managed to survive, forgive, and rebuild relationships. I didn't do that. Instead, I ended up sinning and running."

Mumsa sat quietly for a few moments, then spoke. "Nobody 'ends up' anywhere this side of heaven or hell. Always remember, God will one day write the final chapter in all of our lives."

About the Authors

 **DON RANNEY** has a B.A. (Anthropology) and M.D. from Toronto. He obtained his surgical qualification (FRCS) in England. While there, he served briefly as a medical officer with the British Special Air Service. After a year of Bible college back in Toronto, he went to India as an orthopedic surgeon to perform leprosy reconstructive surgery. During 4 ½ years he trained five surgeons, wrote two medical books, and published 14 scientific papers. He had gone there for life but his mission board considered him "unsuitable" and sent him back to Canada, a disappointed and discouraged man whose marriage and faith in God teetered on the brink of collapse. During the last few months in India he searched his soul and discovered the problem to be a mismatch between his own view of God and the policies of the mission board. At that time, he sketched out the Indian side of this story based on his experiences there.

After arrival back in Canada he became Associate Professor of Kinesiology at the University of Waterloo, Ontario, Canada, where he established the School of Anatomy and worked for the next 30 years. His publications now include four non-fiction books, 112 scientific papers, six short stories (one of which won an award), and two poems. He has produced one educational video. *When Cobras Laugh* is his first novel. He is a member of twelve professional organizations from writers of fiction to hand surgery and chronic pain. He is fond of downhill skiing, canoeing, and roller-blading. He remains active in medical practice and pain research with eight papers in progress as well as a sequel to this novel. Readers may email him at Ranney@hsfx.ca.

For more information about Don Ranney:
www.ahs.uwaterloo.ca/~ranney

RAY WISEMAN's early memory—being pushed up a rope ladder and over the side of a tramp steamer at age two—set the tone for his eclectic lifestyle, work experience, and training. He has spent much time traveling, and most of his life looking from the hilltop of one adventure to the beginning of the next. Born in England, Ray has lived in Canada and South Africa. He has made extended visits to Africa and Asia.

Ray counts writing as his fourth career. He began his working life as an electronics technician, then returned to school to study for the Christian ministry, spending two years in the pastorate and nearly five years in South Africa with a missionary society. Returning home, shaken and disillusioned but not defeated, he worked as a video systems engineer and technical writer/publisher before retiring to pursue a career as a writer and speaker. For many years he edited *Partners* magazine, has written nearly 1,000 newspaper columns and features, and authored eight books, including best-selling *Disciples of Joy*, and award-winning *Exploring God's Route 66*.

Ray graduated from RCC Schools (electronics), has a B.A. (general program) from the University of Waterloo, a B.G.B.S. (Biblical Studies) from Briercrest Schools, and studied linguistics, cultural anthropology, and communications theory at the graduate level in Toronto and Nairobi. He is active as a professional member in two writing organizations, teaches writing seminars, and critiques and coaches new authors.

For more information about Ray Wiseman:
www.ray.wiseman.ca

CAPSTONE
FICTION

The place for inspirational fiction . . .
a place to call home.

We're all about respecting an author's hard work
and creating a new market for inspirational fiction.

For more information

Visit **www.capstonefiction.com**

or write:

CAPSTONE PUBLISHING GROUP LLC

P.O. Box 8, Waterford, VA 20197

Printed in the United States
116527LV00006B/55/P

9 781602 901438